"A well-researched and skillfully-woven blend of historical fact, fiction and engrossing storytelling. Helms's impressive writing and use of dialogue bring to life the characters and story in this fast-paced novel."

—L.D. Hill, Civil War collector, researcher and genealogist
Decorated Fleet Marine Force Corpsman, Vietnam

"Helms recounts the fascinating tale of a common Southern family unintentionally divided by the Civil War. His characters' narration makes for fascinating reading. This engrossing story should be eye-opening for anyone seeking to learn more about America's darkest hour."

—Dr. Stephen Leach
Associate Dean, Florida State University,
Panama City Campus
Major, United States Marine Corps Reserve (Ret.)

"Helms does a masterful job allowing us to relive this tragic episode of our country's history from inside a family deeply fractured by The War Between the States. He takes the reader beyond the battlefield in describing the Malburns' personal tragedies, and the inner strength that allowed this Southern family's ultimate survival."

—Norman L. Fowler
Commander, 1st Lt. Thomas H. Gainer Camp #1319
Sons of Confederate Veterans

D0721479

Of Blood and Brothers: Book One
E. Michael Helms

ISBN 9781938467516

Published by

köehlerbooks™
an imprint of Morgan James Publishing

5 Penn Plaza, 23rd floor
c/o Morgan James Publishing
New York, NY 10001
212-574-7939
www.koehlerbooks.com

Publisher
John Köehler

Executive Editor
Joe Coccaro

In an effort to support local communities, raise awareness and
funds, Morgan James Publishing donates a percentage of all
book sales for the life of each book to Habitat for Humanity
Peninsula and Greater Williamsburg.
Get involved today, visit www.MorganJamesBuilds.com

Also by E. Michael Helms

The Proud Bastards

For my grandsons, Liam and Levi;
may you never have to experience
the bitter taste of war.

OF BLOOD

BROTHERS

BOOK ONE

E. MICHAEL
HELMS

NEW YORK

VIRGINIA

We few, we happy few, we band of brothers;

For he today that sheds his blood with me

Shall be my brother;

SHAKESPEARE, HENRY V, ACT IV, SCENE 3

Acknowledgments

No man is an island, or so wrote English poet John Donne in 1624 in his *Meditation XVII*. Certainly no writer is an island, with apologies to the late J.D. Salinger.

Hearty thanks to the members of my former critique group who labored with me through the early first draft of this work: Norris McDowell, Ric Hunter, Bill Woods, Irma Riley, Nadine Collins, the late Jean Graham, and Karen Helms.

I'm also indebted to the numerous authors and diarists (far too many to list here) whose writings provided the historical accuracy and realism to make the Malburn brothers' story come alive. Whether living or dead, your words continue on for those seeking knowledge and inspiration about this tumultuous period in our nation's history.

A pat on the back for my agent, Fred Tribuzzo of The Rudy Agency, for his hard work and tireless effort in finding the right publisher for this novel.

Last, but certainly not least, loving thanks to my wife, Karen, the best friend, partner and critic I could ask for. I'm proud and grateful to be part of "the team."

—E. Michael Helms

Calvin Hogue
Malburn Reunion
May 1927

ONE

I FIRST HEARD OF THE Malburn brothers late one Friday afternoon in the spring of nineteen twenty-seven. I was a year out of college and working as a reporter for the *St. Andrew Pilot,* owned and operated by my uncle, Hawley Wells. It was after five when he summoned me to his office. I walked through the open doorway and stood in front of his desk. The office reeked of stale tobacco. Dust particles swirled in the sunlight streaming through the high windows. A tall floor lamp spilled light across the cluttered desktop and onto the worn hardwood floor.

Uncle Hawley sat hunched over his desk scribbling on a yellow legal pad. As usual, there was a well-chewed Cuban cigar clenched in the corner of his mouth. I bided my time, listening to the scratching of pen against paper and the rhythmic hum of the ceiling fan. I was hesitant to interrupt him. His blustery temper was legendary among the *Pilot's* staff. Finally I gathered my courage and cleared my throat.

"You wanted to see me, sir?"

He didn't answer or look up, just kept writing and mumbling.

"Sir, Mister Dinkins said you wanted to see me?" I glanced at the wall clock behind his desk. There was less than an hour to get home and wash up, pick up my girlfriend and drive to City Hall.

Covering the city commission meeting was a new assignment and I was determined to do an exemplary job. I wanted to prove to my uncle that this cub reporter he'd hired as a favor to his baby sister was capable of handling more than local sports, farm news and garden club socials.

The fact that my girl, Jenny Cotton, worked as a stenographer at the county courthouse didn't hurt matters either. The way I saw it, with Jenny's flawless note-taking combined with my writing talent, the esteemed publisher and editor-in-chief would have no choice but to recognize budding genius when he saw it; nepotism be hanged.

Uncle Hawley wrote a few more lines, then laid the pen down and rocked back in his chair. He stared at me for a moment as if I were a perfect stranger, and then took off the ink-stained visor he habitually wore at the office. He wiped a hand across his brow, brushing back imaginary strands of long-lost hair.

"What is it?" he said, the cigar bobbing up and down.

"Mister Dinkins said you wanted to see me." I was beginning to sound like a stuck Victrola.

"Dinkins, yes." He glanced down at the yellow pad, then looked up, took the cigar from his mouth and pointed it at me.

"You cover the game this afternoon?"

"Yes, sir, ready for print."

"Well who the hell won, boy?"

"We did, four to one," I said, *we* meaning Uncle Hawley's alma mater, Harrison High.

He slapped the desktop. "By damn, that's good news!" Uncle Hawley was a baseball fanatic of some magnitude. He'd once dreamed of playing in the majors, but never made it further than Class D in the now defunct Tri-States League. He grinned and stuck the cigar back in his mouth. "Up by two games in the conference. We beat Holmes County next week, we're going to State."

"Yes, sir," I said, feigning enthusiasm. I found most organized sports boring. Fly fishing was my passion, a pastime largely unheard of here in the warm waters of the Deep South. "If the Hurricanes play like they did today, they're a cinch." Uncle Hawley just sat there grinning, so I made a show of pulling my watch from my pocket and examining it. "I need to be at City

Hall in a half-hour, sir. You wanted to see me?"

His grin receded into a familiar scowl as he dug through one of the stacks on his desk. "Ah." He pulled a wrinkled sheet of paper from the pile, stared at it a moment and then looked up. "Got a job for you tomorrow. I was going to put Dinkins on it, but his missus is a week past due already."

"Tomorrow? But tomorrow is Saturday, sir. I've already—"

"Listen up, boy," he said, waving the paper like a semaphore. "The news waits for no man. Now, you want to be a journalist or were you just wasting your time and your daddy's hard-earned money at that fancy university?"

My ears burned as I reached for the note. Tomorrow's matinee at the Ritz was out of the question now, most likely the beach bonfire too. Good thing my girlfriend was the understanding sort. I glanced at the note scrawled in Uncle Hawley's heavy hand: *Malburn brothers, North and South, Econfina, Saturday noon May 28.*

I read it again, trying to decipher my assignment. I dreaded asking for more information. When it came to conducting business, Hawley Wells was a man of few words. He expected the hired help to read his mind and carry out his will explicitly.

"Well get going, boy," Uncle Hawley said. "The commissioners'll be done with business and halfway to the speakeasy before you even get there. And see Dinkins on your way out," he called as I hurried through the doorway. "He'll fill you in."

———•———

It was well past noon Saturday by the time I reached Bennet, a shabby little settlement some twenty miles north of Harrison. The map Harold Dinkins had drawn was easy enough to follow, but I hadn't counted on being delayed by a road construction gang and a ferry captain who refused to cross Bear Creek until some farmer friend showed up with a truckload of new potatoes.

I drove past weathered buildings and scattered farmhouses until I came to a large rickety barn with a rusting Barbasol sign nailed to the gable. I stopped and checked the directions again, then turned my prized 'twenty-five Model T roadster—a graduation gift from my parents—onto a sandy rut that intersected Bennet Road. The car lurched and bounced along the twisting downhill trail through dense stands of scrub oak and longleaf pine toward Econfina Creek. The chassis bottomed out a few times, but that didn't concern me nearly as much as the branches on either side that clawed the length of my freshly polished pride and joy. I cursed myself for ever taking this blasted job and Uncle Hawley for giving it to me. I swore at the splattered lovebugs smeared across the windshield, the dust and heat and general discomfort of the Florida Panhandle countryside. I vowed I'd move back home to the amiable hills of southern Pennsylvania—with or without Jenny—before the oppressive swelter of another Gulf Coast summer set in.

A mile or so later the road mercifully leveled out and the sandy ruts gave way to washboard clay. Just ahead was Porter's Bridge, a rickety looking affair fashioned from railroad ties and rough-hewn planking. I stopped the car and got out for a closer inspection. The structure obviously predated Henry Ford, and I wondered if it was safe even for light wagon or buggy traffic. While contemplating whether or not to risk a crossing, I noticed several vehicles parked in a clearing on the far bank. Well, if that many cars and trucks made it safely across, I reasoned, I suppose I could too.

I got back in the roadster, pedaled into first gear and aligned the front tires with the weathered boards. Offering a silent prayer, I eased forward. The bridge vibrated a little but seemed stable enough. Halfway across, a troubling thought occurred to me that maybe those other vehicles had come from *that* side of the creek.

I felt like Moses at the Red Sea when I finally reached the far bank. I hadn't dared risk so much as a sidelong glance during the perilous crossing, so I stopped for a minute to view the countryside. Despite my recent outburst directed at West Florida and its multitudinous shortcomings, I had to concede that Mister Dinkins was right—it *was* a beautiful setting for a family reunion. The sun-dappled Econfina flowed clear and swift between fern-blanketed limestone banks. Live oaks shaded the picnic area with sprawling moss-draped branches. Through breaks in the trees I saw people sitting around tables and strolling about the grounds.

According to a reunion handbill Mister Dinkins gave me, the Malburn clan had gathered here yearly during the last weekend in May since eighteen sixty-six:

For it was on the 28th of May, 1866, that Daniel, eldest son of James and Clara Malburn, completed his long and arduous journey home from a Yankee prison camp. Word spread quickly throughout the Econfina Valley about the miraculous return of this son long thought dead. Family and friends gathered posthaste to celebrate Daniel's safe and fortuitous homecoming.

That a family reunion had persevered for sixty years was newsworthy in itself, but what really piqued my curiosity was that Daniel's younger brother, Elijah, had reportedly fought for the North. My own grandfathers had also found themselves on opposite sides during that most agonizing epic in our nation's history.

I was eager to learn how the Malburn brothers had conducted themselves when they faced one another at that initial reunion some six decades past. Had the fraternal bond been irreparably breached? How had this brother-against-brother quandary affected their immediate family? Were the Malburns still a house divided, or had all been long-ago forgiven? What of their friends, neighbors, the generations that followed? What had prompted Elijah Malburn, a son of Florida and the South, to join the Union Army in the first place?

From what scant information Mister Dinkins had gathered, there were conflicting stories about what actually occurred. I had so many questions, and only—or so I then thought—a few precious hours to glean the answers from these venerable gentlemen who, though begot from common loins, had once been mortal enemies.

TWO

A SHORT DRIVE PAST THE bridge, I turned left onto a steep wagon track marked by a sign: MALBURN REUNION. It led downhill through a hardwood thicket to a small meadow where dusty cars and trucks were parked alongside farm wagons and buggies. At the far end of the clearing a number of tethered horses and mules munched the spring grass, ears twitching and tails flicking at insects.

I parked the roadster in some shade a safe distance from the other vehicles. Glancing into the rearview mirror, I straightened my tie and ran a comb through my hair, then grabbed my boater and climbed out. I dusted off my white poplin suit and followed the wagon track through the trees. The trail narrowed and turned downstream. In the distance I heard laughter and the sawing of a fiddle over banjo and guitar. The aroma of roasting meat filled the air.

A few yards farther on, the brushy woods thinned out and I came to a parklike arbor of stately live oaks. Spanish moss swayed in the light breeze. People young and old mingled and wandered about, some decked out in Sunday finery, others wearing faded overalls or everyday gingham dresses. Nearby, couples were tossing horseshoes. Beyond the horseshoe pit, giggling girls played hopscotch and a group of barefooted boys shot marbles inside a circle scratched into the hard dirt.

I headed for a long table that sported a red, white and blue banner proclaiming: WELCOME! PLEASE SIGN IN. Sitting behind the table a pleasant, middle-aged woman wearing an old-fashioned bonnet and dress looked up and smiled. Before her lay a leather-bound spiral register and a quill and inkwell. Dozens of photographs and old tintypes, some loose, others framed, were spread across the tabletop.

"Hey there," she said, never losing the warm smile. She gave her head a half-turn, eyes squinting quizzically. "Which branch did your acorn fall from?"

"My what . . . did what?" I didn't have the slightest idea what she was talking about.

She chuckled and pointed to the register. "The family tree, sugar. Which side of the family you hail from? I'm Alma Hutchins, nee Malburn," she said, offering a plump hand. "Don't believe I've had the pleasure."

"Oh, no, I'm not related," I said, shaking her hand. I reached in my vest pocket for my press card and clipped it to my lapel. "Calvin Hogue. I'm a reporter for the *St. Andrew Pilot*. I'm here to do a feature on your family reunion."

She stared at the card, alternating glances at me with the photograph on the card. "Then you'll be wanting to talk to Ben Gainer. He's our family historian." She shifted in her chair and looked around. "Don't see him right now. He's somewhere hereabouts."

Ben Gainer—the name struck a familiar chord. "Does Mister Gainer practice law in Harrison?" I'd covered a trial a few months earlier—breaking and entering with petty theft if my memory served me. Benjamin Gainer had represented the defendant, a transient veteran of the World War.

"One and the same."

I pulled my memo pad from a coat pocket and jotted down the name, making note of his position as the Malburn family historian. I returned the pad to my pocket. "I was really hoping to talk to Daniel and Elijah Malburn. The Civil War veterans."

Alma threw back her head and laughed. "Well, young man, I

wish you luck. You'd likely get more talk from a plow mule than them two."

That was news I hadn't banked on hearing. Had I wasted my time driving out here? And what would Uncle Hawley have to say Monday if I showed up empty-handed? Would a run-of-the-mill story about the reunion be enough to appease him? After all, the Malburn reunion was one of the oldest continuous family gatherings in the entire country.

"My editor is counting on me to bring their story to our readers," I mumbled, scanning the display of photographs. My eyes fixed on what looked to be a recent portrait of a wizened old soldier in uniform. I picked up the framed photo for closer scrutiny. The thin, slightly stooped man wore a broadbrimmed hat and a fancy double-breasted waistcoat. Elaborate embroidery decorated the collar and sleeves, and a Confederate battle flag was sewn over the left breast. "Would this be Daniel Malburn?"

Alma nodded. "That's my Uncle Dan."

"Would he be here today by any chance?"

"Course he is, sugar. He wouldn't miss the reunion for the world, unless he was on his deathbed." She pointed past me toward the creek. "Most likely find him sitting under that oak yonder, if he ain't already got up to eat. That's his favorite spot."

I glanced and saw the tree, but a number of people obstructed my view. I turned back to Alma. "Do you think he'd be willing to talk with me for a few minutes?"

She cocked her head. "Well now, that all depends."

I waited a moment. "Depends on what?"

"Well, sugar, it depends on whether or not he's feeling up to talking, or what kind of mood he's in, or maybe even the weather. Your guess is as good as any." She adjusted her bonnet and smiled. "Won't hurt none to try. Go on and see. He might bark a little, but he's too old and got too few teeth left to do much biting these days."

"Thank you, Mrs. Hutchins." I tipped my boater and started to leave.

"Hold on there, young man."

I turned back to see her writing in the register.

"I got to put you down on the visitors' page. How you spell that last name of yours?"

"Hogue," I said, "H-o-g-u-e."

"Hogue . . . done." She looked up and grinned. "I wish you luck, Calvin Hogue. And don't you leave here without fixing yourself a big plate of barbeque. You could use some meat on them bones."

I found Daniel Malburn sitting in a rickety bentwood chair in the shade of the broad oak, just as Alma had said. A few feet beyond, the Econfina babbled against limestone banks as it flowed like clear sweet tea on its journey to St. Andrew Bay and the Gulf of Mexico.

At first glance I thought the old gent was dozing, but as I drew nearer his head tilted back and I caught a flicker of eyes beneath the brim of his gold-tasseled hat. Gnarly fingers rested on the handle of a hardwood cane propped between his knees. The other hand lay in his lap, clutching a briarwood pipe. The ornate gray uniform hung loosely on his sparse frame. Try as I might, I failed to envision this innocuous old-timer having ever been caught up in the roaring whirlwind of mortal battle.

"Good day, sir," I said, offering my hand. "My name is Calvin Hogue. Mrs. Alma Hutchins said I might find you here. It's an honor to meet you."

For a moment he ignored me. Then he looked up and stared me full in the face, still disregarding my proffered hand. "Folks been coming here since eighteen and sixty-six, and ever year there's more faces shows up, and ever year there's more I don't recollect," he said, the gravelly voice rolling past a bobbing Adam's apple and out the thin-lipped slit of mouth. He craned his neck and studied me with rheumy, pale-blue eyes, one fogged with a cataract. "And you," he said, lifting his hand from his lap and pointing with the stem of the pipe, "I don't rightly recollect."

I withdrew my shunned hand. Maybe Alma was right, I might as well go back and interview one of the mules grazing in the clearing where I'd parked. I shook off the silly notion and offered my hand again, hoping my first impression was wrong.

"Calvin Hogue, sir. I'm a reporter for the *St. Andrew Pilot*. The Harrison newspaper."

He looked at my hand, then extended his own pipe-filled one.

Noting the pipe, he transferred it to the other hand. "Pardon me for not getting up, Mister Hog," he said, shaking my hand. "But that'd be more fuss than these old bones feel up to just now."

"It's Calvin *Hogue*, sir, with a long oh. H-o-g-u-e."

He frowned. "You talk funny. Where you from, Mister Hog with a long oh?"

I hesitated, not wanting to agitate him further. "Carlisle, Pennsylvania, sir, a few miles north of Gettysburg."

"Humph, Yankee," he muttered under his breath, more grunt than words. "Figured such." Then his eyes grew wide. "You ain't kin, is you?"

"No, sir, I'm here on business. I was hoping to do a story on you and—"

"Thank you, Lord Jesus," he said, eyes rolling heavenward. "One goldamn Yankee in the family is more'n plenty. Caused me more woe than a body ought to carry. My very flesh and blood," he said, voice trailing off.

"That's what I'd like to ask you about," I said. "I understand you and your bro—"

"Now don't go thinking I don't love him," the old Confederate said. He lifted his cane and jabbed it into the hard earth, eyes narrowing to slits. "He *is* my brother. Besides, that old wound scabbed over years ago. Folks don't understand, is all. Hell, let 'em think what they want."

"I'd like to, sir," I said, "understand, that is. If you'd allow me a little of your time, I'd like to learn the true story about you and your brother."

He leaned back in the chair that creaked like arthritic joints. "Now why in tarnation would I tell you a goldamn thing?"

I took off the boater and fanned myself, scrutinizing my thoughts. "Mister Malburn, from what little I know, your brother is a paradox. Some say he was a traitor, others call him a hero. Some accounts say your family accepted things for what they were and all was forgiven. Other sources say the war tore the Malburns apart and the rift hasn't completely healed to this day."

I paused, hat in hand, feeling beads of sweat begin to trickle down my temples. "My own grandfathers fought in the war, sir. Grandpa Hogue for the North, Grandpa Wells for the South. So I feel a certain affinity with your situation. A shared bond, if you'll allow me that."

I waited, hoping I hadn't overstepped my bounds. The day grew hotter, or was it the heat of his stare? In the distance a woodpecker drummed on a hollow trunk and a raucous flock of crows cawed. Finally the old soldier leaned forward and tapped the end of his cane at my feet.

"All them highfalutin words. Just what is it you after . . . Calvin, ain't it?"

Calvin? Well, that was quite a step up from Hog! There seemed to be the faintest gleam in his unclouded eye, and his frown had eased into a poker face. I might yet get my story. "Yes, sir, it's Calvin. And with your cooperation I'd like to tell readers of the *St. Andrew Pilot* the bona fide story of the Malburn brothers. Set the record straight, once and for all."

He looked down at his lap and brushed at a bit of spilled tobacco, then leaned on his cane and struggled to his feet. "You like barbeque?" he asked, straightening to his full five feet seven inches or so.

I smiled and patted my stomach. "My mouth's been watering since I got here."

"Well let's go fix us a plate then. A body ought not jaw on a empty belly."

———◆———

Clouds had begun to gather, so we sat under a pavilion talking over plates piled high with roasted pork, garden fresh vegetables and cornbread. But between eating and a near-steady stream of Daniel's friends and kinfolk greeting him, I was making little headway getting my story.

When I mentioned his flashy uniform, he threw back his head and laughed. It was a far cry from the homespun butternut he and his pards had worn during the war. But "these here fancy trappings" seemed important to the family. It just wouldn't do for him—at eighty-four years of age, the Malburn patriarch and eldest surviving forebear of the late great War for Southern Independence—to be decked out in anything less than the best finery available.

"Time was the young'uns flocked like cubs to a bee tree wanting to hear all about what I done in the War," he said. "Me and Joe Porter spent hours with them young'uns, spinning yarns about the War." He grinned. "Hell, some of 'em was even true. Ol' Joe was my best pard, Lord rest his soul," Daniel said, smile fading. "Been gone six years now, it is."

When I broached the subject of his brother, his brow arched. "Ought to be here shortly. Best you talk to him."

The old man pulled his tobacco pouch from a coat pocket and packed his pipe. He struck a match, held the flame to the bowl. "Best stretch these ol' bones before I take root," he said after a puff or two. "You welcome to come along if you please." He braced with the cane and stood. It seemed to take a full minute for his weary joints and muscles to cooperate.

A sudden flash of lightning laced across the northern skyline, followed by rumbling thunder. The old soldier startled and sat back down, his face pinched. He noticed me staring and offered a halfhearted smile. "Sometimes catches me unawares, heh-heh."

Rain drummed on the canvas. At least I'd had the good sense to keep the top up on the roadster, but with this storm I'd never get the story I was after. How in the world was I going to explain my failure to Uncle Hawley come Monday?

"Sir, I thought I might ask you a few questions about the war until your brother arrives."

Daniel drew on his pipe and glanced my way. "More'n likely he done come and gone."

"But, I thought you said he'd be here in a while?"

"That I did. Didn't say nothing about him staying long."

The words had scarcely left the old vet's mouth when there came a storm such as I'd never experienced in all my twenty-three years. The sky turned black as night, as though a great window shade had been drawn across the heavens. The wind rose and howled like a pack of wolves. Treetops swirled counterclockwise and cold sheets of rain swept through our shelter.

In a dazzling flash of lightning I saw Alma Hutchins throw an oilcloth over Daniel's head and shoulders. "You hold that tight now, Uncle Dan," she shouted above the din of rain and thunder.

Alma turned to me. "You come here by motorcar, sugar?"

I clamped a hand atop my boater to keep it from flying away, and nodded.

"Could you carry him home? He sure don't need to be catching the croup at his age."

"Be glad to," I said, hoping against hope that Daniel lived somewhere on *this* side of the creek.

Alma flashed her big smile. "I thank you kindly, Calvin. It's just a little ways past the other side of the bridge yonder."

She bent over close to the old man's ear and shouted, "Calvin here will ride you home in his motorcar. Them boys of mine'll take care of your wagon and team. Now don't you fret none, sweetie. You can count on it."

THREE

MERCIFULLY, THE STORM EASED SOME by the time I drove back across Porter's Bridge. Not far past the bridge Daniel pointed out a narrow road on the left. I turned and followed the winding lane through sparse woods and open pastureland. A half-mile or so later we came to a homestead at the edge of a field of knee-high corn. I steered the roadster down the trace of a driveway and parked in front of his place. It was a modest old cabin with weathered clapboards and a high-pitched roof covered with cedar shakes. The structure rested on stacked stone piers. A split-rail fence fronted the home.

It was still raining, so I got out and opened my umbrella and handed it to Daniel, then helped him from the roadster. He swung open a wooden gate and I followed him up stone and mortar steps onto the porch, which was littered with wet, windblown pine needles and leaves. Daniel handed me the umbrella, then slipped the oilcloth off his shoulders. He shook it a couple of times and draped it across a nearby rocker. "Don't much cotton to motorcars," he said, "but I'm obliged for the ride home. The umbrella too."

He ignored my "You're welcome" and looked past me into

the twilight as the rain intensified again. "I been feeling a mite poorly the past few days. Don't need to be getting soaked to the bones and catching my death. That'll come soon enough, I reckon, heh-heh."

Daniel scraped his shoes on a woven rope mat in front of the stoop, then opened the unlocked door and stepped inside. "Ain't no telling when this rain'll let up. No sense trying the road to Bennet in this gullywasher." He turned and motioned to me. "Come on in and sit a spell."

I scuffed my shoes over the mat and followed him inside. Daniel leaned his walking cane against the wall next to the doorframe. "Here, let me get shed of that hat and coat for you." He took my dripping coat and boater and hung them on a wooden peg nailed to the door, then did the same with his.

It was the first time I'd seen him bareheaded. My eyes were immediately drawn to an ugly scar above his left temple running like a wide part from his hairline past his ear. I looked away just as he turned and pointed to a straight-backed chair near the wall. "Pull that chair up near the heater here. I banked the fire this morning." He struck a match and lit a kerosene lantern sitting on a small table next to a rocker with worn quilted cushions. "It's right nippy after that storm, ain't it?"

I agreed and moved the chair while Daniel opened the cast iron heater and stirred the coals with a stoker. Sparks darted out the door. He grabbed a couple of dry logs from a small stack on the floor and arranged them over the glowing embers. Soon, the sweet smell of wood smoke drifted through the room. "There. That'll warm things right up. Nothing like a good wood fire." He shuffled over to the rocker and sat. "Forgetting my manners," he said, before he'd settled in the chair. "You hungry?"

"No, sir, I couldn't eat another bite after all that good barbeque."

"Me neither. I'm full as a tick in a hound's ear. Might could tolerate a little nip or two, though. Got some good corn whiskey in the kitchen. One of my nephews makes it. Best in three counties. You warm up your writing hand and I'll go pour us a snort."

Daniel stood and moseyed down the hall and disappeared through a doorway. I heard the clinking of glass, then a match flared and yellow light filtered into the hallway. After a minute or two he ambled back into the room and handed me a tumbler half-filled with clear liquid. "Here you go. Good for what ails you, heh-heh."

I hesitated, sniffing the contents.

Daniel grinned. "Tarnation boy, it ain't snuff. Drink up." He tilted his glass and took a hearty swallow. "Ah, even better'n it was this morning."

I wasn't much of a drinking man at the time. It was the Age of Prohibition, and except for an occasional weekend party during college where I had a mug or two of homemade beer with my fraternity brothers, I abided the law of the land. But I didn't want to appear rude, and seeing it caused the old man no apparent ill effect, I hazarded a sip. Vapors seared my sinuses. My burning throat constricted in protest.

Daniel laughed as I gasped for breath. "Told you it was some good!"

Safe inside his own home and bolstered by the moonshine, the reticent old gent seemed to relax in both body and tongue. I sat quietly and let him ramble on about this and that, now and then letting the slightest drizzle of whiskey trickle down my throat. After a while it *did* tend to grow on you.

"Now, what was we talking about down yonder before the storm chased us?" Daniel said. "You ever see such lightning?" he continued without waiting for an answer. "Them big trees weren't no place to be sitting in such a storm. No, sir." He paused and turned an ear to the now-distant thunder. "As I recall, you was asking about the war. Funny how storms and such makes a feller remember certain things. Sometimes it's a sound, a smell maybe, or how light falls across a field. Might mean nothing one day, next day it conjures up something dark that pains you like a festering wound.

"You recollect I told you how me and Joe Porter used to entertain them young'uns with our soldiering exploits? Well, sir, there's a passel of things I ain't never told nobody. Such things is best left be, best kept deep inside," he said, tapping his chest. "Lord knows I've sweated to keep 'em there, to shed 'em from memory. But ever now and again they spark up like these here aching bones of mine. At the goldamndest times too." Daniel took another swig of liquor. "Ain't that some fine whiskey? Crazy times we living in ain't it, what with Prohibition and all. Goldamn Yankee gov'ment. Drink up boy, there's plenty more.

"Look here," he said after a long draw on his pipe, "was you being straight about wanting to hear my story?"

His question caught me in mid-swallow. I nodded, my eyes squinched and my throat burning.

"Reckon so, being as you tolerated me this long. You seem a right nice young feller, even if you is a Yankee. Cain't hold that agin you though, can I, heh-heh, what with my own brother being one. Even though he weren't natural born to it like you."

Daniel looked away for a minute. He rested the pipe on the table and scratched idly at the scar on his scalp. He seemed to be deep in thought, struggling with something. Finally he spoke, not sadly, but rather matter of fact. "Thing is, I ain't long for this earth, gospel truth. Don't ask and don't doubt it, boy. It's just something a body knows. Come next reunion I'll be resting beside the missus."

I was too dumbfounded to say anything.

"See that picture yonder?" Daniel said, pointing to the mantel above the wood heater.

"This one?" I asked, indicating a dour-faced group photograph from the period when it was still considered unfashionable to smile for the camera.

"No, sir, next one over, in the gilded frame. Yep. That's my missus. Weren't she a sight to behold in that fine dress?"

"Yes, sir, very pretty."

"That dress come special ordered, all the way from Nashville. That picture was took on our wedding day, eighteen and seventy, it was. Feller traveled all the way from St. Andrew to photograph us. I still ain't got used to calling it Harrison. Why is it they go and change a town's name after all them years? Well, it don't make no nevermind to me what they call it. I'll soon be walking them streets of gold up in Heaven, arm in arm with the missus."

I still couldn't bring myself to say anything. What do you say to a man who's bent on announcing his imminent demise? Fortunately, Daniel didn't seem to require or even expect any input from me.

"Death is a sure thing, Calvin. Sure as this here rain will

stop and the sun will rise in the east tomorrow. Ain't nobody ever got out of this world alive, except for that prophet feller in the Old Testament. The very one my brother's named after. Got my doubts about him too, heh-heh. It ain't a bad thing, just nature's way. Oh, you young yet. Probably think your days ain't numbered. I knowed plenty that thought such. Buried a heap of 'em too. One thing I learnt, time don't wait for nobody or nothing. Time's a turning, like it always has, like it always will."

The old man paused long enough to tap the spent embers from his pipe into an ashtray, then repack and light it. He rocked slowly in his chair. "All right then," he said, "reckon I'll tell you my story. Don't know how much we can get through this one night here, but if you willing to sit still and listen, I reckon it's time I talked it out."

Now that was good news indeed. Willing to listen? To tell the truth, the moonshine had me feeling so warm and mellow I hoped the night would drag on forever.

Daniel drew on his pipe and stared at the wood stove for a moment, then turned his eyes to me. "Chickamauga, now *there* was a fight! Never heard tell of it, you say? Not surprising, you being born and raised up north. Bet you growed up believing the whole war rose and set at Gettysburg. Most folks do. Well, sir, there *was* another Confederate army other than General Lee's. Bet you think the war ended at Appomattox Court House in April of 'sixty-five too, but it ain't so. Truth is, the Army of Tennessee fought on nearbout a month after Lee went and surrendered. And there was other troops west of the Mississippi that held out even longer.

"What I'm getting at, boy, is the war was fought all over the South, including right here in the Econfina Valley. Didn't know that either, did you? Well, it's the gospel. Brother Eli can vouch for it. But more about that later.

"You wanting to know about Chickamauga. Well, sir, that battle took its name from a creek that run through the ground we fought over. 'River of Death,' the Cherokees called it. Right fitting name, it was. It was mostly a wilderness of rolling hills and valleys covered with woods thick and tangled as any you ever seen. A few hardy souls had cleared land enough for farms. They was scattered here and yonder along what back then passed for roads. The major road run north from LaFayette, Georgia, on up to Chattanooga. I mention that there particular road because we spent the best part of a afternoon fighting back and forth across it. Yes, sir, that road was nearbout puddled with blood before it was over." Daniel paused and drained his glass.

"Some say Chickamauga was the Army of Tennessee's most glorious hour. Truth is, there weren't much glory to it, not back in 'sixty-three. Funny how time changes how folks look at things, ain't it? Me and Joe Porter and some other ol' pards took us a train trip back up yonder in 'ninety-five when they dedicated it as a National Military Park. Spent two days retracing our brigade's footsteps with some army officers acting as our official guides. Right nice young fellers, they was. They explained all the whys and wherefores and how comes we never knowed about the battle whilst we was fighting it. Walked us all over the Viniard farm where we fought over the LaFayette Road on September nineteenth, then on over to Horseshoe Ridge by the Snodgrass farm where we scrapped late the next day. Stirred up a lot of memories, it did. Good and bad.

"But I reckon you ain't wanting to hear about all this after-the-war reminiscing. You wanting to hear about the war itself," Daniel said, struggling to his feet. He reached for my glass. "Let me go fetch us another snort and I'll get on with it."

Daniel Malburn
September 1863
Chickamauga

FOUR

IN SEPTEMBER OF 'SIXTY-THREE we'd spent the best part of two weeks tramping up and down the dusty red roads of northwest Georgia. *We* meaning Company K of the Sixth Florida Regiment, Trigg's Brigade. All that marching was at the behest of one Braxton Bragg, Commanding General of the Army of Tennessee, Confederate States of America. General Bragg was itching to do battle with a certain Yankee general name of William S. Rosecrans and his Army of the Cumberland, United States of America.

Well, sir, late on the eighteenth of September part of our army stumbled into theirs and commenced skirmishing. That there initial engagement come more by fluke than strategy. Truth be told, most the fighting that went on at Chickamauga was more happenstance than grand design. The land itself seen to that.

Anyhow, when the aforementioned fracas heated up, Colonel Trigg's brigade was a far piece south beating the briars for Yankees. Word soon come down for us to move north straightaway. We set out at quickstep towards the sound of the guns, but nightfall caught us still on the south bank of

Chickamauga Creek.

Most of the roads thereabouts was hard enough to travel in daylight. And since the shooting had mostly petered out by then, Colonel Trigg ordered a halt at a place called Dalton's Ford. We posted our pickets and bivouacked for the night. Weren't no campfires allowed, being as the enemy was within spitting distance. It was a right cold night too. The moon set early, but the sky lit up with no end of stars. Strange how things can seem so peaceful the way God meant for it to be, then a few hours later all Hell comes a'calling.

Next morning before the sun peeked over the hills, we forded the Chickamauga and commenced marching north through a cold fog. A hour or so later we halted on a ridge overlooking a big open field. There we formed a line of battle and laid on arms.

One thing a feller learns to do whilst soldiering is to wait, war being one part fighting and ninety-nine parts waiting. Another thing I learnt early on in my soldiering days was to grab sleep whenever and wherever a body could. And since we was waiting, I figured there weren't no harm in me sawing a few logs whilst doing my soldierly duty. After more'n a year's practice I'd learnt to snatch sleep good as any porch hound, and I commenced to do just that.

I was having the goldamndest dream that morning. Dreamt I was back home, sitting in the kitchen inside the big house, it being winter and cold out. My dear mama was sitting at the other side of the table holding a platter piled high with pan-fried ham. There was grits and red-eye gravy too, eggs fresh from the henhouse, and hot biscuits dripping with sweet cream butter and molasses.

I was warm and content as a suckling pup, pondering how good it felt to be safe at home facing such a grand feast. My belly was just a'growling for that food. Thing is, ever time I tried to eat, somebody commenced pounding on the door. No sooner would I get a forkful up to my mouth, then *boom-boom-boom* went the goldamn door. Right vexing, it was. Mama kept saying, "Don't pay 'em no mind, son, just go on and eat," but soon as I'd lift that fork the pounding would recommence. Well, sir, this went on for some time till finally I'd had a bellyful. Of the pounding, I mean. I ain't eat a bite of that fine food yet. Next time it happened, somebody was in for a proper thrashing.

Well, here it come again, *boom-boom!* I dropped my fork and slid my chair back to stand up, but before I could do so somebody grabbed my shoulder from behind. Mama's eyes went wide like she'd seen ol' Beelzebub hisself, then she let loose a God-awful scream.

And that's when I woke up.

"Dern bluebellies is getting closer," Joe Porter says. "Figured you might want to wake up and enjoy this shelling with the rest of us."

I squinted at the sun climbing above the treetops. Figured I'd been sleeping for a hour or so. "Damn you, Joe Porter," I says, my gut growling. "I ought to save them Yankees the trouble and shoot you myself. I was fixing to have a grand feed and you went and spoilt it."

Joe ducked as another round passed over and exploded in the trees some fifty yards behind us. He looked at me, grimacing like he hadn't shat in a week. Like the rest of us scarecrows, his face was thin and nearbout dark as a nigra from all the wood smoke and dirt. "How long you reckon they expect us to just lay here and take this?"

I didn't see as how Joe's question deserved answering, what with him having ruint my dream. So I rummaged in my haversack and drew out a chunk of greasy cornbread and a piece of rank fatback, the last of three days' rations we was issued the previous morning. That cornbread was some poor. Had so much cob ground up with it you could've called it corn*cob* bread and not been lying. Guaranteed to give a body the ripsnorting gripes. That cold fatback and cornbread sure weren't the feast of my dream, but it would have to make do till we could go foraging.

Another shell come roaring over, closer this time. Joe ducked again, then stared at me and shook his head as I commenced to eat. "If you don't beat all I ever seen. How can you think about that belly of your'n at such a time? Ain't you human like the rest of us, Danny boy?"

I grinned and kept chewing. Truth be told, I was as scared as the next feller, but I'd vowed long ago not to show it. No use in worrying. When your number come up, you was done in. Weren't nothing going to change that. "Got to keep my strength up." I bit off another hunk of gristly fatback. "Somebody's got to chase them goldamn Yanks back to Tennessee."

A few hundred yards to our north, rolling musketry joined the cannonading. "Sounds like them Alabama boys is hot into it," says Yerby Watts, my other good pard. Yerb was laying to my left. A short ways farther on behind a big oak stump was his younger brother, Hamp. We'd seen a Alabama regiment skirt the tree line on our right flank earlier that morning and move on north through the woods on the far side of our field.

"Better them than us, I reckon," says Joe.

Yerb threw his head back and laughed. "Somebody toss old Joe a sugartit so he don't shat his breeches if he sees a Yankee."

"Oh, you mean like you done up at Cumberland Gap?" Joe says, and winks at me. "First sign of a Yank, you'll be skedaddling for the rear."

"Hang you, Joe Porter, you know I done no such a thing." Yerb let fly a stream of tobacco juice in Joe's direction. It sailed over me and splattered just shy of its intended target. "I was carrying a message from Tom to Cap'n McMillian and you damn well know it."

Before Joe could retaliate, another shell come in and exploded far down the left of our regimental line. A big flock of crows rose out of the field, squawking and flapping in circles. Then they flew off west towards a farmhouse at the far edge of the clearing. I watched them crows envious-like, wishing I could rise up and take wing with 'em.

"Lord a'mighty, that'n was right on," Joe says, pointing. "Look a'there, Danny boy, some poor mother's son is done gone to his reward."

Ugly gray smoke hung above a crowd of soldiers that was tending to the casualties. "I think that's Company I, yonder," I says, just as another round come screeching in, closer yet. Close enough so it showered us with dirt and small branches and leaves. Things was heating up. Volley after volley of rifle fire echoed to our front. Sounded like a thousand woodsmen hard at work with axes. Artillery rumbled like thunder now, shell after shell roared in along our line. Most passed overhead and blowed up in the woods back of us, but here and yonder one found its mark.

Now come a shell that shrieked and exploded directly overhead. Airburst! Fragments buzzed through the air like somebody kicked up a nest of yellerjackets. Burnt gunpowder hung thick as swamp fog.

Yerb's face was pressed hard agin the earth, but I could hear him yelling "Goddamn 'em! Goddamn 'em!" over and over.

Joe was hugging ground for all he was worth. "Damn bluebelly sum'bitches," was all I could make out from him.

I don't recollect if I had any choice words to add to our situation or not, because right then something whacked me hard on the left hip. I let out a yelp. Felt like a dozen hornets done stung me in the same spot, it burnt so. I rolled onto my other side, scared to look. Figured my leg was a goner. I eased my hand down my hip and felt around, pleased to find the leg still where it belonged.

Yerby crawled over, wide-eyed as a hoot owl. "Say Joe, help me out here. Danny's been wounded!"

Joe plumb forgot about the incoming shells and scrambled the few feet to my side. "Where you hit, Danny boy?"

"Right here on the hip," I says, fighting to keep calm. "Burns like holy hell."

Young Hamp stared at me, pale as a ghost whilst Joe moved my canteen aside and looked me over. Then he busted out laughing. "Look here, Yerb. Danny's got hisself a sure enough mortal wound."

Yerby eyeballed my wound, then grinned. "Joe's right, pard, you gone up for sure."

Well, sir, what had been fear turned quick to vexation. "Damn you two gophers, how bad is it? No fooling now."

Joe and Yerb looked at each other, all droll-like. "Well," says Joe, "I reckon you'll live to fight another day."

"You will at that," Yerby says. He grabbed the strap of my haversack and lifted it over my head. "But this here haversack is done for." He handed me what was left of it.

Them two peckerwoods seemed a sight more concerned about my accoutrements than my life and limb, so I finally worked up the grit to eyeball my wound. Weren't no blood staining my breeches. I slipped 'em down enough to venture a look. There was a fist-size patch of blistered skin surrounded by a nasty bruise, but it weren't near bad as I'd imagined. Figured then I'd live. Gentle as I could, I greased it with the last bit of fatback.

Whilst the Yankees kept up the shelling I looked over the remains of my haversack. The flap and most of the front section was gone. My tobacco pouch was sound, but my pipe was smashed to bits. My pencil, writing paper and candles was okay, but my housewife with all its sewing goods was ruint beyond use. A raggedy hole had burnt through my towel. I unfolded it and was mighty relieved to find the tintype of my betrothed had survived. Next to it was a jagged dollar-size fragment, still warm to the touch.

Well, sir, that folded towel had saved me. I could lay hold of another haversack soon enough, but a leg weren't so easy to replace. I held up the spent fragment to show my pards. "Boys," I says, "this is getting to be right serious business."

FIVE

FOR THE NEXT HALF-HOUR we laid there and took what the Yanks throwed at us. Weren't much harm done that I recollect. Mostly just riled us. Some of the boys fired back oaths and other niceties at the unseen Federal gunners. A spell later a courier from regimental headquarters come riding up with orders for us to form ranks.

Well, sir, that order was met with no small amount of cheering. We was plumb fed up with laying like groundhogs ducking cannon fire. Figured most anything would be a welcome change. I used my rifle for a crutch and stood up betwixt Joe and Hamp. Favored my wounded hip a minute, then tried putting my full weight on the leg. It was a mite sore but otherwise sound. Figured it would do. I weren't about to leave my pards whilst I could still hoof it.

Shells kept falling here and yonder as we formed rank in columns of four. Our lieutenants strutted up and down the line like banty roosters, crowing out commands. Our squad's lieutenant, Tom Gainer, come prancing up like a peacock. "Come to attention, men," he says, repeating orders we'd already obeyed. "Form ranks, column of fours."

Tom was a boyhood pal of ours and our former messmate

before he went and got voted up to officerdom. Three or four
years older than me, Joe, and Yerby, he'd been our school teacher
for a spell after poor Miz Olgelby caught the ague and went to
meet her Maker. Tom had just got back from a furlough to home.
He was all decked out in a fancy new gray frock coat with gold
embroidery on the collar and sleeves befitting his uppity rank.
Wore a spanking new felt hat with a small gold dove toting a
olive branch in its beak pinned to one side. That hat and brooch
was a wedding gift from his recent bride, who happened to be
my older sister, Sara. Which meant me and Tom was brothers
of a sort, by marriage.

Yerby elbowed me in the ribs. "Whoowee, ain't Tom a dandy
all gussied up in that there new uniform!"

Joe stretched his lanky self back to attention, grinning like
a bear in a bee tree. "Halloo, Gen'ral, sir!" he says, and snaps a
smart salute Tom's way. "Look at them fancy sleeves, boys."

"Hey, Gen'ral, where'd you get them dandy chicken guts?"
says Hamp.

Truth be told, Tom *did* look a whole sight better'n most of us
in our raggedy butternut homespuns and dirty slouch hats. He
stopped and glared our way. "Come on, boys, quiet in the ranks.
Form up now, and mind your dress."

Me and the boys made a show of straightening our file just
as another shell come howling in. Up and down the ranks troops
commenced scattering and hugging earth. But not Tom, heh-
heh. No, sir, he just stood there with his hands on his hips like
he was at some Sunday get-together. Reckon becoming a officer
had give him a dose more courage, or else a mite less horse sense
than us fellers.

"Dammit boys, get up and form ranks," he says. "They're
overshooting us. There's nothing to fear."

We come to our feet but our heart weren't much in it, what
with the air still buzzing like a beehive. "Overshooting my ass!"
Yerby says, as we reformed our ranks. "What's that humming
by my ears?"

"I just as soon keep my head on my shoulders if it's all the
same to you," says Joe, a mite agitated.

"Leave Tom be, boys," says I, "he's just doing his job." Then
under my breath I says, "Besides, cain't y'all see he's plumb

tuckered out from his honeymoon?"

Well, sir, that set the others to snickering as the command to shoulder arms was give. In another minute Company K commenced marching at quickstep with the rest of the Sixth Florida, leaving that incoming artillery behind.

We crossed the field and found a road that passed through the tree line to our front, then moved by the right flank for half a mile or so till ordered to halt and lay down again in line of battle. We was facing west this time, along the crest of a ridge a couple of hundred yards north of a farmstead. A few hundred yards to our front, across a shallow valley, stood yet another tree line. Beyond them trees a right heated battle had commenced. Thick clouds of gray smoke from hundreds of rifles rose up like summer thunderheads. Ever now and again the Yanks fired a shell our way just to let us know they hadn't forgot us.

It was high noon now, and ol' Sol burnt bright in the cloudless sky. The morning chill had give way to the heat of late summer that hung on in them rolling Georgia hills. Seeing as we was in no immediate peril, Joe commenced blowing a lively tune on his mouth harp. Yerb pulled his hat over his eyes and tried to snatch some sleep. Young Hamp, who had only been soldiering with us a short spell, stared bug-eyed across the valley watching out for Yankees.

Laying there under that hot sun I soon got powerful thirsty. I grabbed my canteen, grateful that the shrapnel had spared it. It was a dandy flannel-covered metal canteen I'd got off a Yankee cavalryman we'd captured up near Knoxville a few months back. Me and him made a fair swap of it. I give the Yank two plugs of tobacco and my wooden canteen that leaked a mite for his. He seemed right satisfied with the trade, seeing as how I could've just took it from him anyways.

We'd filled our canteens whilst fording the Chickamauga that morning. I uncorked the stopper and took a swig. Swished it around a bit, then swallowed a little at a time, letting it trickle down my craw. It was tolerable. Wet, anyways. When you're soldiering, water is gooder'n gold, even if it is a mite muddy and leaves grit in your mouth, gospel truth. Anybody that's really been thirsty will swear it. But right then I couldn't help thinking of the sweet water I'd growed up drinking from the clear springs that feeds the Econfina. Felt a mite homesick. Started reminiscing about home and loved ones till the sounds of the battle all but disappeared.

I rolled onto my back and reached inside my shirt and drew out the towel where I'd stuck it since my haversack got ruint. I unfolded it and took out the tintype that was wrapped in a handkerchief embroidered with my initials. I run my fingers across them letters and nearbout felt like crying. My Annie had stitched them with her own loving fingers. She'd give me the kerchief and tintype as a token of her undying affection on my nineteenth birthday, the very morning me and the other boys from Bennet rode off to Quincy to join up with Captain Angus McMillian's company of volunteers. That was March of 'sixty-two, and now, a year and a half later, I missed Annabelle Gainer more than words or heart could tell.

I gazed at Annie's sweet likeness, traced a finger over her high cheekbones and beautiful doe eyes—compliments of her and Tom's full-blooded Cherokee grandma. Annie's hair was pinned up in back with chestnut ringlets dangling across her shoulders. Below her delicate throat hung the cameo locket I'd give her Christmas of 'sixty-one. Her eyes and lips carried just the hint of a smile, like she knowed something nobody else did and weren't telling.

A voice went and ruint the spell. "She sure is purty, ain't she?"

I looked and seen Hamp Watts crawling back up the slope. He stopped next to me and finished buttoning up his breeches. "Had to piss like a plow mule. Dang near wet myself." A shell whistled over. Hamp ducked, then looked up at me and grinned. "Ain't got used to it yet, I reckon."

"Well, sir," I says, "when you do, you be sure to tell me how you done it."

Hamp joined up with Company K when he come back with Tom from Tom's furlough to marry Sara. Except for a little skirmish whilst on picket duty a couple weeks back, he hadn't yet tasted battle. Hamp was fair of skin, had eyes blue as a clear autumn sky, hair yeller as a haystack. The boy looked downright angelic, truth be told, like one of them cherubs in picture Bibles. Only thing lacking was a halo, but Hamp always did have a streak of the Devil in him, heh-heh.

Us Malburns and Watts had close ties from years back. In eighteen and forty our daddies traveled together from North Carolina to West Florida to homestead along Econfina Creek. Our farms laid a stone's throw from each other across the creek. The families was forever swapping goods and work. Me and Yerb growed up good friends, and soldiering together had brung us even closer. But Hamp, well, I looked on him like my own younger brother. Him and Eli was goobers from the same pod. They was born within a month of each other and been best pals since pups. Even shared the same wet nurse for a spell when Hamp's ma took ill.

Hamp took the tintype from me and stared at Annie. "Reckon you know I was sweet on her. Me and Eli both."

My Annie was sixteen at that time, just a few months older than Hamp and Eli. Them three had been pals when they was young'uns. Then a couple of summers back, Annie up and sprouted from a gangly tomboy into a fetching young belle. She commenced pursuing more womanly matters, whilst Hamp and Eli still favored fishing and swimming or running barefoot through the woods, playing wild Injuns.

It was long about then that Annie caught my eye. Almost overnight that skinny little schoolgirl had molted like a butterfly into a right charming woman. She took a shine to me too, and we courted for the best part of a year. Then Mister Lincoln and the Union states commenced to make a ruckus over the newly declared Confederacy. Well, sir, me and the boys didn't cotton to having Yankees invading our sacred soil, so we up and joined the army to defend hearth and home. Not wanting to chance losing Annie to some cad that stayed home, I went and asked her daddy for her hand, and she consented to become my betrothed.

I took the tintype back from Hamp. "Yep, I know you was sweet on her, but she outgrowed you two peckerwoods long ago." I wrapped the tintype and stuffed it back inside my shirt just as a rousing cheer rose up from the far right of our line. A long column of Confederates was kicking up dust as they marched along a road and disappeared into a stand of trees. I squinted through the dust, trying to make out who they was from their flags, but it was too thick.

"Them's Gen'ral Hood's Texas boys!" yells Joe.

I rubbed my sore hip. Wouldn't be long now, I figured, and set about checking my cartridge box and caps and getting my other accoutrements in order.

Well, sir, all that dust must've caught the Yanks' attention, because their gunners commenced a walking barrage towards the road. Sent the last of them Texans scurrying for the trees. Us Sixth Florida boys could smell the coming fight now. It was in the air, ever bit as real as the dust and smoke. There weren't no stopping it.

SIX

A FEW MINUTES LATER, THE command to attention was give by Tom and the other lieutenants. Rifles and accoutrements clattered as Company K got to its feet, formed up and made ready to march. Now the talking amongst the boys commenced, the way it always done before a big scrap. Funny how a body behaves whilst facing surefire danger and likely death. It ain't a easy thing, knowing you might've seen your last sunrise that very morning. Gospel truth.

Ever soul had their own way of gritting up. Some of the old hands commenced swapping jokes, laughing at the prospect of soon departing this earthly life. Gallows humor, they call it. A few of the newer boys that hadn't yet seen a real fight was spouting oaths of bravery and glory. Others offered up prayers or read their Testaments. Not a few swore off drinking or gambling or whoring. Some just kept mum. Pards swore to look out for each other during the fight. Promises was swapped betwixt squad members to search after the battle should somebody turn up missing.

Somewheres down the line some fool shouts, "Hope them Texas boys leaves some bluebellies for us."

Joe shouts back, "Reckon there'll be a barnyard full of Yanks to go around 'fore long."

Yerb took a swig from his canteen and spit. "Damn, this stuff ain't fit for a mule to drink. Tastes like a chamber pot."

"Well, Yerb," I says, "I ain't never tipped up a chamber pot myself, but you right. That mud cain't touch the spring water back home."

Hamp took off his hat and fanned hisself. Sweat dripped down his fuzzy cheeks, his straw hair was matted dark in a circle. "Say, does anybody know what day this is?"

I thought about it a minute. Might've been Thursday, maybe Friday. Seemed like the days all just run together somehow. "Thursday," says Yerby.

"No it ain't," Joe says, scratching his armpit. "It's Saturday. You and Danny and Hamp was on picket Tuesday when we last got mail. You didn't get your'n till next morning, remember? You sure bellyached about it enough." He counted on his fingers. "That was three days ago, so that makes it Saturday."

Yerby pressed a finger agin the side of his nose and blowed out a glob of snot. "Don't make no nevermind what day it is. Ain't saying you right though, so don't take it such."

The command to shoulder arms was give. Hamp slapped his hat back on and pushed the brim up out of his eyes. He looked around and grinned as he hefted the heavy Enfield to his shoulder. That rifle was nearbout long as he was tall. "Well, boys," he says, "if this here is Saturday, then tomorrow's my birthday."

Two horsemen come riding along Company K's front from the direction of regimental headquarters. One was our company commander, Captain Angus McMillian, mounted on his big bay gelding. The other'n was his aide, some lieutenant whose name I cain't recollect, riding a spirited gray stallion. Now, most captains of infantry was afoot like their men, but Captain McMillian had raised up and equipped Company K with his own money and he weren't about to give up his fine mount. The captain's coattails was flapping like wings, the brim of his black felt hat was swept upwards like it was pinned thataway. He slowed, pulled hard on the reins and wheeled that big steed about to face us. Sat there a minute, stroking his long brown beard and eyeballing our formation up and down. Then he yanks his hat off, whirls it high overhead and shouts, "To victory, boys!"

We cut loose a chorus of shouts and cheers and commenced waving our own hats. Then Captain McMillian took off galloping down the line in a swirl of hoofbeats and dust.

Young Hamp shouts, "Whoowee, we going see the elephant today, ain't we Danny!" He was grinning like he was fixing to march in a Independence Day parade instead of into battle.

"Looks that way for a fact," I says. Then something come over me I cain't explain. Something just weren't right. Hamp didn't belong there with the rest of us. I grabbed his shoulder and shook hard. "Look here, this ain't no picnic we going on. You stick close to me and Yerb and Joe. Don't go getting yourself lost, you hear?"

Hamp looked at my hand on his shoulder, then back at me. "I will," he says, all sullen-like. Don't reckon I'll ever forget the look on that boy's face, like I'd went and ruint his Christmas morning. Them eyes of his looked like a whipped pup's. To this very day I regret speaking such harsh words, but I cain't take 'em back now.

A few minutes later we commenced marching north off that ridge at quickstep. We crossed the valley and struck the road the Texans had took. Once we gained the road, most the jawing halted, being it was a struggle just to breathe amongst all the swarming dust we kicked up. Them that had 'em handy covered their nose and mouth with handkerchiefs. Me and others used our hats best we could. Tramping feet and hacking coughs played accompaniment to the steady roar of musketry and cannon fire that growed louder as we drawed nearer the trees.

I looked west towards the sound of the growing battle, knowing we'd soon strike the enemy. My gut went cold. Seems it's the way of a soldier to doubt his own grit before a big fight, and I commenced to do so now. I'd done my duty in previous scraps up in Kentucky and Tennessee, and figured I'd do so in this one. But from the sound of them guns, this fight promised to be a sight worse than anything I'd seen so far.

We followed the road into the trees. Burnt powder drifted like fog through the thicket and mixed with the red dust, coating everthing it touched. My throat was parched. I sorely wanted a drink of water, but figured I'd best save what I had for later. My eyes was raw from gunpowder and sweat, making it nearbout impossible to see. Things was heating up quick. Artillery thundered and muskets barked like a thousand axes chopping wood.

We passed through the trees and turned northwest onto a wider lane that cut a red swath across a fallow pasture a few hundred yards wide. Stray minie balls commenced to snap and whine. My canteen strap was rubbing my neck raw. I tucked the edge of my blanket roll under it and that helped a mite.

Up ahead, ghostly soldiers appeared out of the veil of dust and smoke. Their faces was stained pewter, their uniforms blanketed with dust. They plodded like broke-down mules along the roadside, giving way to our column. Bloody bandages bound heads and arms and legs. Others seemed unhurt, but their eyes had a look of despair or defeat, like lost souls. Some was without weapons, and I swore not to throw down my rifle no matter how hot the fight got.

Another hundred yards fell by. Soon we come upon the dead. Some was whole and looked to be sleeping. Others was blasted into pieces. Most was clad in Federal blue, but a goodly number wore Confederate gray or butternut. One poor soul was sprawled in the middle of the road. Some of the boys stepped over the body, but I give him a wide berth. I chanced a peek and shuddered. It was a Southern boy, looked to be no older than Hamp or my brother Eli. A jagged hole big as a man's fist was punched through his chest. He laid flat on his back, staring up like he was relaxing on a lazy summer afternoon, conjuring shapes out of the passing clouds. His eyes weren't yet glazed over, his face untroubled, peaceful even, like the thought of dying had never pestered him.

Of a sudden a shell shrieked and exploded ahead, then more come raining down. Our column commenced scattering along both sides of the road. I plumb forgot my sore hip and parched throat and double-quicked for a dry creek bed that paralleled the road some thirty yards away. A spooked artillery horse raced by, wild-eyed and lathered, broken harness and trace chains of a wrecked limber trailing behind. I stumbled and nearbout fell, but somehow kept my feet and jumped into the ditch alongside

Joe Porter and Tom Gainer.

Joe was on his knees, blowing like a winded horse. "Lord a'mighty," he says, pointing over Tom's shoulder, "look a'there!"

I looked up the creek bed. Yonder stood a leg clad in light-blue Yankee breeches. It was caught in a tangle of briars that growed over the streambed, standing straight up like it was at attention and waiting on orders to march off somewheres. The foot wore a scuffed black brogan. There was a bloodstain where it had once joined a hip. Otherwise, the limb appeared unscathed. Only thing missing was the body it lately belonged to. Goldamndest thing I ever seen.

"Lord, lord a'mighty!" Joe says, turning pale.

I stared at that leg, thinking it a most amazing thing. I wondered if its owner was yet amongst the living, or one of the fresh corpses I'd seen. I finally forced my attention from the dismembered limb and scrambled over to Tom, who was crouched agin the bank, peeking over the top. His fancy new uniform was a mess now, stained dark with sweat and the powder of red Georgia clay.

"You see where Hamp or Yerb went?" I says.

Tom shook his head and kept squinting through the dust hovering in layers above the field. "They're overshooting again. Either firing for luck or else their spotters are half-blind."

"I seen 'em up ahead a ways," Joe says, crawling over to join us. He hawked up a wad, spit and wiped his mouth on a dirty sleeve. "Think they made the ditch okay."

A few minutes later, the shelling petered out, but the battle still raged beyond the tree line ahead. If the sound was any measure, it was some fierce scrap. Tom stood up and looked around. "I'm going to find out what the situation is. You two stay put and keep your eyes peeled." He pointed at Joe. "Dammit, Joe, clean out that barrel before it blows up in your face." Then he scrambled out of the ditch and trotted off.

Joe lifted his Enfield and stared at it. "Well damn it to hell," he says, then pulled out his jackknife and commenced digging at the mud plugging the muzzle.

I leaned back agin the bank and reached for my canteen. What the hell, I figured, might not be alive to enjoy a drink later. The sun was burning white hot and the air was stifling. In the shade of a nearby cedar, a wren was fussing up a racket. Reckon our little war had went and disrupted its daily routine.

I uncorked my canteen and took a swig. High overhead a flock of buzzards circled. I felt the gooseflesh crawl and tried not to think about the horrible feast that awaited them.

SEVEN

WE HOOFED ANOTHER HALF-MILE or so through more woods and farmland, getting ever closer to the fight. Bitter gun smoke hung like thick fog, choking the air. The order come to halt and rest on arms again. From the faint glow of the sun, I figured it was near midafternoon.

We faced west in a long line of battle behind a split-rail fence at the edge of thick woods. To our front was a rolling cornfield stretching nearbout far as the eye could see. Several hundred yards to the left-front stood a farmstead in a grove of trees a short piece across the LaFayette-Chattanooga Road, which run roughly north to south through the center of the field. This was the Viniard farm, though I didn't learn the name till years later.

On a ridge just this side of the road, a line of Federal batteries stretched across the cornfield. Ever now and then they fired towards our position, but the shells passed overhead. We was plumb tired of waiting and antsy to get on with the fight. To pass time I half-cocked my Enfield and double-checked that the nipple had a fresh cap. Opened my cartridge box and counted the forty-some cartridges for the second or third time. Joe commenced whittling at the maple pipe bowl he'd been working on the past two-three days. The Watts boys was rereading letters from back home.

The First Florida Regiment had been deployed as skirmishers in heavy woods to our right-front. For the past half-hour they'd been in a hot scrap with the enemy. The Yanks had turned their right flank and commenced a galling fire into their ranks. Now the First was falling back. Whilst the First Florida boys made good their retreat, the Yanks' artillery ceased fire. Well, sir, that ain't always a good sign, as we was fixing to learn. I squinted through the smoke. Way out in the cornfield, lines of Yankees appeared. They rose up from gun pits and trenches like specters from a graveyard. Others come pouring out of the far woods in a great blue wave.

Hold steady, I told myself. Keep your head, don't forget to aim low. One cartridge at a time whilst reloading, don't want to blow up the barrel by ramming one load atop another'n. That cold fist grabbed ahold of my gut and squeezed tight. My breathing growed quicker, my palms commenced sweating. Seemed there weren't no end to them bluecoats. It was a heap more Yankees than I'd ever seen in one place, gospel.

From the center of our line, bugles sounded and the drumming of the long roll called us to arms. We dropped our blanket rolls and other accoutrements that might slow us down. Mounted officers come galloping up and down our front, shouting orders and encouraging the troops. Our ranks come alive, moving like a great serpent stretching out to sun itself. Regimental flags unfurled, waving and snapping in the wind. The order come to fix bayonets, and a great rattling like clashing sabers rung out. Some of the boys commenced offering last minute prayers.

Captain McMillian rode up on the big bay, waving his sword. "The eyes of our people are upon us," he shouts, cutting circles in the air above his head. "Let's make 'em proud, boys. Remember, keep your ranks and move forward, ever forward!" His horse reared and danced back a couple of steps. "And aim low, boys. It's Yankees we're hunting, not squirrels!"

Drums beat in time to the blood pounding my temples. I don't recall hearing the order to advance, or even climbing the fence, but there we was all the same marching out into the cornfield, one long rank followed close behind by the second. One foot tramping after the other, and with ever step a little of myself slipping away to hide somewheres inside my mind. I cain't explain it, but at such times something else come forward to take control, otherwise I might've skedaddled.

Tom and the other lieutenants was spread out along Company K's front a few yards forward of our lead rank. Now and again Tom turned and back-stepped towards the enemy, holding his Colt's revolver in his right hand. "Keep your dress boys, guide center, guide center!"

I glanced to my right and seen Joe beside me in his usual place in line. That give me a measure of comfort. Joe might've been high-strung at times, but he could be counted on when things got hot, and this fight promised to be such.

Then the fear left me and I was caught up in the excitement of it all. I punched Joe in the shoulder. "Whoowee, Joe Porter, we fixing to be in one helluva barn dance!"

Joe looked at me, eyes wide and brow furrowed with the worry that always rode him before a fight. He fished in his breeches pocket for a plug of tobacco, bit off a sizeable chaw and tongued it into his cheek. "You one crazy sum'bitch, Danny boy," he says, shaking his head. "Yessireebob, one crazy sum'bitch."

A cottontail bolted from the blasted cornstalks, then a covey of bobwhites exploded underfoot, wings a'whirring as they circled low and flew south. A few yards farther on we come upon a bloated mule swarming with blowflies. I nearbout gagged, it stunk so. I covered my mouth and nose as our line parted around it, me on one end, Joe on the other'n. "Whoowee, fresh meat, boys!" I says, which set 'em to laughing and cussing me.

"Keep your dress!" some lieutenant down the ranks shouts. "Don't let the line bulge thataway."

Joe let fly a stream of brown juice. "Hang the line. I ain't stepping in no mule muck!"

"Everbody with chicken guts thinks they's a goddamn gen'ral!" Yerb shouts.

Behind us a cannon boomed. A hollow whistle cut the air. Gray-black smoke puffed over the advancing bluebellies, then come the sharp *ba-boom!* of a aerial blast. Some three hundred yards to our front, smoke and fire belched from a Yank cannon.

Wind blowed the smoke away from the barrel before I heard the report. A solid shot hit short of our lines, bounced a couple of times, then changed directions and plowed through the cornfield towards me and the boys. It sizzled and smoked and sickled through the dry cornstalks as our ranks parted like the Red Sea to let the ball pass through without harm.

My eyes watered. I glanced left and seen Hamp was betwixt me and Yerb like he'd been told. He was keeping up, stepping along like a veteran. His hat was cocked back on his head and them yellow locks hung down in his eyes. Reminded me of Mister Enfinger's old sheepdog back home. I kept thinking he's just a boy and ought not to be here, he ought to be back home with Eli looking out for the folks and the farms.

Hamp seemed to feel my eyes. He looked at me, grinning like a suckling shoat. "I'm seeing the elephant now, ain't I!"

I grinned back. "Might just see a whole herd of 'em before this scrap is over."

EIGHT

THEM WORDS NO SOONER LEFT my mouth when the front rank of bluebellies dropped to a knee and fired a volley. Hundreds of balls whistled by, along with the awful *thwack* of lead striking flesh like ripe watermelons busting open. Several poor souls dropped. A quick look around told me my pards was safe.

We kept up the attack. A riderless horse come busting through the rear of our ranks. Poor critter was spooked and bad hurt. Its nostrils flared, ears laid back tight agin its head. The saddle had slipped loose and hung along its flank, stirrups flapping like wings. Blood gushed from the withers. I watched the pitiful thing gallop towards the Yankees till the smoke swallowed it up.

Now our artillery commenced barking and theirs answered till it was one great steady roar. The sky was hailing lead. Explosions was turning up that field deeper than any spring plowing. Showers of cornstalks and dirt rained down on us. Seemed like all of creation was being swept up in mortal confusion. I'd just stepped over a dead Yank when a shell howled in and exploded. The blast knocked me to my knees. I looked up and seen a body spinning skyward. Poor feller seemed to hang in midair for a spell, then fell back into the smoking crater.

A short piece farther we halted and dressed our ranks, then on command cut loose a volley into the advancing Yankees. Bits of cartridge paper flitted in the air like fiery gnats. I grabbed a fresh cartridge from my box and bit open the paper, the gunpowder bitter on my tongue as I poured the powder down the barrel. A fixed bayonet makes reloading a chancy task, so I took extra care to press the ball into the bore before using my ramrod to seat the charge. Then I thumbed the hammer to half-cock and replaced the spent percussion cap. By ranks we fired a second and then a third volley into the Yankees with deadly results. The bluebelly line faltered, then commenced falling back.

Captain McMillian come riding through our ranks, trotting his horse along Company K's front. Blood dripped from where a ball or fragment had raked his cheek. "Forward, men, forward!" He wheeled the big gelding around, stood up in the stirrups and pointed his sword towards the retreating Yankees, then spurred his horse and galloped ahead.

Up and down our lines the command to advance was echoed: "Forward at the double-quick, boys!"

"After 'em men, give 'em the steel!"

We took off across the blasted field at double-quick, stopping once or twice to fire a volley and reloading on the move best we could. Weren't long before we reached the forward works the Yanks had deserted. Another halt was called to reform our ranks and reload. There was a heap of dead bluebellies laying nearby, and a few too badly wounded to skedaddle. I looked around at the dead. They wore fine new uniforms, and their accoutrements was topnotch. Our boys commenced collecting souvenirs. I pulled a tarred haversack off a dead Yank that was laying facedown. I didn't much cotton to pilfering from the dead, but that haversack weren't of no more use to him. Besides, the bluebellies owed me one, way I seen it.

In a minute or two the order come to take up the advance. There weren't time to aid the wounded, so we moved on and left them to litter bearers and God. The sight of them skedaddling bluecoats fed our fury till we could nearbout taste victory. Somewheres down the line the Rebel Yell commenced. Others took it up till it rose from a thousand throats. Back and forth through the ranks it sounded, raising such a howl it drowned out everthing. The enemy cut loose another volley but we was so caught up in the charge we scarce noticed. Seemed there weren't nothing could stop us.

We pressed on through the smoke and lead, shooting and reloading as we went. It weren't easy to keep our dress in such a battle. Our line give way here and bulged forward yonder like a big side-winding snake. There was so much smoke the very air seemed burnt. My throat and lungs ached and my teeth was coated with grit. I squinted and seen I was still betwixt Joe and Hamp, but beyond them I couldn't see nothing.

Yet another halt was called to regroup when we reached the bottom of the low ridge atop which stood the enemy's big guns. I was nearbout played out. I dropped to my hands and knees and gulped clear air near the ground like a man dying of thirst. Then a gusting wind thinned the smoke to reveal a fearful sight. Along the crest only a hundred yards away the Yanks had stopped behind rough breastworks to make a stand. Weren't able to see them works before now. They was just in front of the line of batteries that stretched across the field.

The order was give for us to lay down, and for the next half-hour we swapped fire with the bluebellies. It was a standoff, neither side doing the other much harm. They couldn't see us whilst we was laying flat and we couldn't see them hunkered down in their trenches. Our artillery bombarded the ridge to keep the Yankee cannoneers from manning their guns and turning 'em downhill on us. But we knowed once the attack recommenced, our big guns would have to cease fire because we'd be too near the enemy for such close support.

Now a whole passel of riders come galloping along our front. Right off I recognized Captain McMillian on his big bay. The others was Colonel Finley, the regimental commander, and Colonel Trigg, our brigade commander, along with their orderlies.

Well, sir, I figured this couldn't be a good sign. Never before had we been honored with so many highfalutin officers parading along our ranks during a actual fight. Reckon they was trying to steel us for the coming rush up that slope. Their horses was prancing and tossing heads and snorting like they was anxious to get on with the charge.

Colonel Trigg cut a right smart figure in his fancy plumed hat and gray tunic, though he was dusty as any of us scarecrows. I didn't see no sword—I thought that queer for a commanding officer—but a brace of revolvers was stuffed under his wide black belt. Colonel Trigg's eyes was ablaze like a cur prowling a chicken coop. He pulled his big roan to a halt, then turned in the saddle and pointed up the slope. "For God and country," he shouts, paying no mind to the swarm of balls cutting the air. "Let us drive the enemy and take those works!"

Well, sir, we jumped to our feet and let loose as rousing a cheer as ear ever heard. The Colonel swept that fancy hat off of his head and waved it round and around in salute. Then he rode off down the line towards the next company's front, Colonel Finley and the orderlies close behind.

Captain McMillian and his orderly held fast whilst the others rode away. They sat their horses steady despite the balls whizzing by. The captain looked up and down the company ranks, then commenced shouting orders to our lieutenants. The banties saluted and scurried to pass the orders on to their squads. We come to attention and shouldered arms. Dressed our ranks and brung our rifles to right-shoulder-shift. All the while lead whistled and snapped by our ears. How none of us weren't hit is a mystery to me. It ain't a easy thing to stand there waiting whilst hornets that can strike a man dead at any second is buzzing all around. Gospel truth. It's all a feller can do to keep from dropping and hugging earth.

Seemed like forever before we heard bugles signaling for the attack up the hill to commence. Captain McMillian spurred the big bay forward a ways, then stopped and wheeled around. His face was near black with smoke and dried blood, and the whites of his eyes shined like full moons. "You heard the Colonel, boys," he shouts. "Let's give 'em the steel and take those guns!"

On order we come to arms-port, then lit up that hill at double-quick. The Yanks rose up behind their works and cut loose a volley. Looked like a thousand lightning bolts cutting through heavy fog. Balls whipped by my ears. Some poor soul behind me cried out.

"Keep moving! Keep moving and mind your dress," one of the lieutenants shouts. "Come on boys, dress up and guide center!"

"Heck, I cain't even see no center!" says Hamp.

"Thinks he's a goddamn gen'ral," Yerb shouts.

On we pushed till the Yanks greeted us with yet another volley. This time their aim was better and that awful *thwack!* told me a passel of balls had found their mark. Up and down the line men dropped and cried out as the attack faltered. Most of the boys was still on the move, but here and yonder some fell back to look after their stricken pards.

Captain McMillian come riding out of the smoke waving that sword like he was cutting at a flock of blackbirds raiding his corn patch. "Forward men, forward," he shouts. "We're almost upon 'em now. Charge!"

Well, sir, we done just that. A yell went up like the bowels of Hell had busted open and ten thousand screaming demons was set loose. We took off after the captain on the run, leaning into that hurricane of lead.

NINE

THE WIND BLOWED HARD AND parted the smoke. The enemy's breastworks of logs and red earth was only seventy or so yards away. Yanks popped up from rifle pits like groundhogs, fired, then dropped out of sight to reload. From a battery on our left flank, a Yankee cannon opened up. The smoke ring spiraled from the barrel, but the shell passed over harmless. To our front, gun crews scurried around their cannons like rats in a feed bin. Finally there was visible targets to shoot at.

I took aim at a bluebelly ramming a charge down the barrel of a Napoleon twelve-pounder, squeezed the trigger and my rifle bucked. The poor soul sprawled in front of the cannon. A couple of his pards drug him behind the gun whilst another finished ramming the charge. Quick as I could I reloaded and ran forward. The smoke closed betwixt us and the enemy like a heavy curtain drawed shut. I stumbled over something and fell to my knees. Looked up and seen a great blast of flame and yellow smoke bellow from the enemy cannon.

And for a minute time just stopped.

I'd seen it before, up in Kentucky. Cain't say whether I

actually hollered *"Canister!"* or just thought it before I went belly to the ground. Somehow I managed to shove young Hamp down as that terrible blizzard of steel chopped through our ranks.

Well, sir, like I said, time just stopped. At ground level the smoke slowly cleared enough so I could see a fair piece, but it was some terrible sight to behold. Flesh and bone was tore asunder in a horrific deadly swath. It was a nightmare come alive, like being in the very pits of Hell. Three feet above my head the air was a choking shroud of stinking sulphur.

For a spell it was unearthly quiet except for the hollow ringing in my ears. Then, in ever direction voices cried out. A heap of wounded was writhing in pain. Some called out to God or their mothers. Others just laid where they fell, their eyes dull. The dead was sprawled in all sorts of ghastly poses, some whole, others blasted to pieces. Arms and legs and hunks of flesh littered the field with grisly chaff. One feller crawled around in circles, most of his face shot away. He was strangling in his own blood, with ever breath blowing red bubbles where his nose ought've been. Another poor soul sat upright inside a shell hole, his head gone. Blood boiled from the neck stump till he bled out like a slaughtered hog.

A quick look told me Hamp was safe. On my right, Joe laid facedown muttering to hisself. He was pale and shaking but seemed unharmed. He looked over at me and pointed ahead and shouted something, but it was lost in the noise of battle.

Out of the smoke, Captain McMillian's riderless bay come stumbling towards us. One front leg was sheared away at the fetlock, and his bowels drug behind like thick bloody rope. The poor critter whinnied pitiful, eyes wild with pain and fright, blood frothing out its nostrils and mouth. It staggered another few feet, then swayed and fell onto its side. It breathed hard for a few seconds, then rolled onto its belly and tried to get up.

Well, sir, I never could tolerate seeing a animal suffer so. I got to my knees, cocked my rifle and took aim at the poor critter's head. Before I could squeeze off the shot, Captain McMillian appeared like a ghost out of the thick haze. His uniform was spattered with blood and gore, but other than the gashed cheek he got earlier he seemed unhurt. He'd lost his hat, and his great shock of black hair stood out wildly.

I lowered my rifle as the captain cocked his revolver and shot the horse through the head. The horse shuddered, kicked once or twice, then laid still. The captain knelt and stroked the dead bay's forehead, then stood and hurried down our line. That horse had been his mount the whole war. He'd lost a good and faithful friend.

Before we could recover, our reserve company passed through our ranks. A few yards farther on they halted in two files. On command they fired a volley into the Yankees that had rushed from their breastworks to counter our attack. The volley stopped the bluebellies and bought precious time for us and the rest of the Sixth Florida to regroup.

What was left of us Company K boys hurried forward to take our place in the line. For several minutes us and the bluebellies stood our ground at deadly close range, blasting away at each other. There weren't nothing betwixt us but a few yards of shattered cornfield and a wall of burnt powder. Balls swarmed like angry bees.

I never seen nothing like it. Remembering to shoot low, I took aim and fired, reloaded, fired again, over and over till the barrel of my Enfield growed hot to the touch. It was a desperate contest, but I was lost deep inside myself and had no fear. It was like another feller stood there in my place, performing my soldierly duty.

To my right Joe worked a chaw of tobacco whilst he calmly fired and reloaded like he was at a turkey shoot back home. On my left I watched Hamp raise his rifle and get off a hasty shot.

I spit out the end of a cartridge. "Aim low, pard! Shoot 'em in the belt buckle!"

Well, sir, just when it seemed like it wouldn't never cease, the Yanks finally began to give ground. Here and yonder pockets of bluebellies started falling back. We made it right hot for 'em, keeping up a steady fire and dropping a passel as they turned tail. A few stopped to make a stand behind the breastworks near their batteries, but most skedaddled on past the guns and across the LaFayette-Chattanooga Road in full retreat.

We kept up our fire till Captain McMillian come galloping up on another mount. The horse was terrified and lathered with sweat and the captain had a real tussle keeping it from bolting. I recognized the horse as belonging to his orderly, the lieutenant whose name I cain't recollect. I wondered if he was dead or wounded, or only dismounted.

"After 'em, boys!" the captain shouts, his eyes all afire. "Let's drive 'em and take them damn guns!"

We raised a cheer as Captain McMillian waved his sword and spurred the gray to a trot. The Rebel Yell went up as we rushed the Yank battery in a all-out charge.

TEN

I'D JUST GONE A SHORT piece when I seen a patch of Yankee blue through the smoke, so I stopped long enough to get off a quick shot. It was a trick reloading on the move, what with the fixed bayonet and my burning eyes watering so, but I managed. I wiped a hand across my eyes and seen Joe and Hamp was keeping up. Didn't see Yerb. Hoped he weren't kilt or bad wounded.

The smoke thinned again. Yonder stood the enemy batteries and breastworks, only fifty yards away. It was our good fortune that betwixt us and them cannons a passel of bluebellies was surrendering. That kept the Yank gunners from firing on us right away, else they would've kilt their own men trying to get us. But I figured they wouldn't hold their fire much longer.

Hamp slowed down of a sudden, looking this way and that. I shoved him on ahead and shouted for him to keep going. He kept up for a few steps then stopped again and dropped to a knee. "Where's Yerb?" he says, almost in a fit. "Where's my brother?"

There weren't no holding back now. I yanked Hamp up by the collar and pulled him along. "Come on, we cain't stop now. We almost on 'em!"

Our boys was yelling like devils and pushing hard to strike the guns. A passel of bluecoat infantry hightailed it out of their works like flushed rabbits, but the cannoneers held steady, tending their pieces despite the hot fire we was throwing their way. Well, sir, it seemed almost a shame to kill such brave men, but it weren't *Union* soil being fought over and stained with all this blood. Finally the Yank gunners' patience played out. Cannons belched flame and smoke all along the ridge. The air screamed with deadly shot. Bones cracked and flesh tore apart as canister did its awful work.

When that storm of lead passed, we give 'em a final volley, then charged, yelling for all we was worth. There was just a few yards betwixt us and them guns now. I seen Hamp straggling again, so I cuffed him upside the head. "Hurry, goldamnit. We got to get them guns before they reload!"

We was so close there weren't no time to reload, so I charged towards the cannon in front of me, bayonet at the ready. That Napoleon's muzzle looked wide as a bellowing bull gator's mouth. A gunner stepped away from the cannon, lanyard in hand, then a Yank officer behind the gun hollers, "Fire at will!"

I was nearbout on top of 'em when that gunner commenced to jerk the lanyard. I dropped and rolled underneath the barrel betwixt the carriage wheels. Looked back and seen Hamp still charging. I hollered just as the cannon rocked and canned hellfire blowed from the barrel.

Well, sir, what I seen next has haunted me all these long years. Time ain't healed that wound a bit, no sir. Not a bit. Telling it don't help none, but it's part of my story so I reckon it ought to be told. From the waist up, poor Hamp disappeared in a ghastly cloud of sawdust packing and gun smoke stained red with his blood. I watched horrified as his legs kept running a couple of steps, then the knees buckled and they pitched over not two foot in front of the cannon. For a God-awful second they shook like they was cold, then mercifully quit twitching. I seen it, but I couldn't hardly believe it.

The concussion had whopped me in the head like a rifle butt. I was woozy and numb all over. The earth commenced spinning and I fell back. My ears ached. I was nearbout deaf. What little I could hear sounded all hollow and muffled. My face was wet.

I felt around, found my head still in one piece, but blood was oozing out my nose and both ears.

After a spell the world settled down a mite. I sat up, grabbed my rifle and crawled out from under the cannon, trying hard not to look at what was left of poor Hamp. I crawled around back of the gun and seen the Yank that pulled the lanyard was dead. I was still on my knees trying to clear my head when the bluebelly lieutenant come running towards me, pistol cocked and aimed at my head. I lifted my rifle, then remembered it weren't loaded. Well, sir, I thought, if this ain't just jim-dandy. Looks like I'm gone up for sure. Ain't nothing to do but make peace with the Almighty and await my fate. Somehow I accepted it, and found I weren't afraid. Truth be told, I almost welcomed it.

The lieutenant halted a pace away. Time seemed to stop with him. Strange what runs through a body's mind in such predicaments. Underneath all that dust he was a right handsome feller with fine features. Looked to be not much older than me. Wore a trimmed moustache and chin whiskers, but his ruddy cheeks was clean shaved. His fancy red kepi sat atop a shock of dark curls. But them blue eyes was cold as winter when he shoved the barrel of that revolver in my face. I reckon he begrudged me personal, him being so far from home and finding hisself in such a fix.

That barrel was only inches away. For some reason I found this whole kettle of fish fascinating. I stared into his eyes, then at the revolver—a fine Colt's it was, like Tom's. His finger took forever to pull the trigger.

Well, sir, I don't rightly know which of us was the most surprised when that pistol misfired. The Yank lifted the revolver and stared at it all bewildered, like it had disobeyed a direct order. And there I was, on my knees, eyeballing him whilst he eyeballed the pistol. Then it come to me that I was still amongst the living.

Reckon I come to my senses a mite quicker than the Yank did his, seeing as my bayonet had found its way betwixt his ribs before he could draw back the hammer for another try at me. My upwards thrust had stuck him through the vitals. He groaned and commenced gurgling blood, which slobbered all down his front. He dropped the Colt's and grabbed the barrel of my rifle with both hands. Stood there for a second or two, tottering like he couldn't figure out which way he ought to fall. His eyes turned upwards like he was beseeching Heaven. Then he keeled over backwards. Took my Enfield with him when he went.

Whilst the fight went on around me, I rested on my knees and kept staring at the dead Yank. The bayonet was deep in his chest, and my rifle swayed back and forth across his body like a upside-down pendulum. It slowed . . . finally stopped. That poor soul's clock had done ticked its last upon this earth. A misfire had spared me and sent him into eternity. I weren't sure if him or me was the lucky one.

After a spell I caught my wind, figured it was time get back in the scrap. But just as I commenced to stand up, the earth rocked and the whole goldamn world went black again. Don't know how long I was out, but when I come to, I was laying across the dead lieutenant's legs and atop my rifle. The hammer was digging in my ribs. I rolled off him, laid on my back and stared up into the stinking smoke and dust shrouding that field of death. I lifted my hands, moved 'em over my body. All my parts was still with me, and I weren't bleeding nowheres new. I laid there a spell. Balls kept whizzing and snapping, but most was well overhead and harmless. It took a few minutes before it come to me that I was all alone amongst the dead and wounded. The fight had moved on. Our boys must've been getting the best of it because the ruckus sounded a fair piece ahead, across the Chattanooga Road.

I was glad to be alive, though I couldn't figure how I'd managed to stay so. Death had nearbout pocketed me more'n once during this fracas. After a few minutes I figured I'd skulked enough, so I stood and tried my legs. I touched the sore hip that had been bruised by a fragment that very morning. It seemed like days had passed since me and the boys forded the Chickamauga.

Of a sudden I remembered. My belly heaved and my raw throat burned bitter with bile. Hamp. I seen it all again . . . his hat pushed back, them blond locks hanging in his eyes, then nothing but red.

I forced myself to turn around and look, hoping it weren't so. But I knowed it was. Even when I seen the wrecked cannon, the barrel laying upside down and mostly covered with dirt, I still knowed in my gut it was true. What was left of poor Hamp's body had disappeared with the destroyed gun carriage. I took a quick look around but there weren't a trace of him anywheres to be found. I told myself it was better this way. Young Hamp's remains had been committed to the earth from which they come, thus sayeth the Lord God who giveth and taketh away. He shall rise again at the last trumpet call. Amen.

The Yank lieutenant proved stubborn in death. He'd laid claim to my bayonet and didn't give it up easy. I tugged hard, but it was stuck fast betwixt his ribs and wouldn't budge. Finally, I put my foot on his chest and pulled with what strength I had left. Bones cracked, and he belched blood when it come free.

The blade was a mite bent. For a minute I considered swapping it for another. There was a passel laying around that weren't of no use to their former owners. But this bayonet had done its job and saved my life. It had proved faithful as any pard, and I weren't about to give it up. Figured I could heat it later over a fire and straighten it with all the care I'd give a wounded comrade.

I stuck the bloody blade into the ground, then wiped it clean with stalk rubble. Took one more look to make sure there weren't nothing I could do for Hamp. Knowing there weren't, I picked up the Colt's revolver and stuck it under my belt. I'd goldamn sure earned that souvenir. Then I reloaded my rifle and headed towards the fight.

Calvin Hogue
May 1927

ELEVEN

DANIEL TILTED HIS GLASS AND drained the last of the whiskey. He stared at the empty glass, then set it on the lamp table and slumped deeper in his rocker. "I'm plumb tuckered, Calvin. Cain't fight no more war tonight. You probably tired of listening to me ramble on anyways."

I set the notebook and pencil down and gave my own empty glass a longing look as I prodded my numb lips with my tongue. So much for being a teetotaler. I fumbled for my watch and pulled it from my pocket. "I didn't realize it was so late," I said, surprised to see that it was almost midnight. "I'd better be going."

Subdued light briefly backlit the drawn curtains. Distant thunder rumbled as rain continued to pelt the roof. Daniel struck a match. The flare illuminated his tired face as he lit his pipe. He blew out the match with a puff of smoke and slowly rocked back and forth. "Lord, listen to that rain. Them roads won't be fit for nothing but ducks in a gullywasher like this, heh-heh. You best plan on staying the night."

I accepted Daniel's invitation. The rain wasn't the only reason that swayed my decision. After several doses of his magic elixir, I was in no condition to drive, weather be hanged. But that didn't stop me from joining my host for a nightcap before stretching out on the sofa.

Long into the night I lay awake thinking about the old Rebel's experiences at Chickamauga. War had always seemed such a distant, unreal concept to me, something you read about in a few paragraphs or pages in history class. But Daniel had made it come alive. He'd told it so vividly I almost felt I'd been there with him and his pards during the charge across the bloody Viniard cornfield. How could anyone experience such horror and not be forever changed? It gave me a deeper appreciation for those who had actually tasted battle. My grandfathers came to mind, even gruff old Uncle Hawley following Teddy Roosevelt up San Juan Hill.

Uncle Hawley... what was I going to tell him come Monday? I didn't have a cut and dried "brother against brother" story to report. The Malburns' saga seemed much too broad to fit inside a few narrow columns of newsprint.

Suddenly it came to me. Monday I would deliver a generic story about the Malburn Reunion, its genesis and long history. Then, I'd convince Uncle Hawley to let me write a weekly serial about the brothers, their war experiences, their lives and relationship since. If this one evening with Daniel was any indication, there was a wealth of material to draw from. And if Elijah Malburn proved to be half as willing as his brother to reminisce . . .

I awoke to the aroma of sausage sizzling on the cookstove. I sat up, surprised and grateful to find that I was hungry and not the least hung over. After washing up in the tiny bathroom down the hall, I joined Daniel in the kitchen. Since I was already here, I hoped he would continue his story over breakfast. But he balked when I mentioned it.

"Cain't go wasting a fine day like this'n on talk, boy." He paused to fill our coffee cups. "Besides, I got church and a garden to tend to. All that rain'll make weeding a mite easier this evening." By now I knew better than to press the issue. Daniel Malburn would talk when *he* felt like talking, and on his terms.

"Next Saturday evening be good for you, say around six?" he finally offered.

I said that Saturday would be just fine.

"All right, then. I'll feed you supper. Then we can open us another jug to loosen up my tongue a mite, heh-heh."

So, after a hearty breakfast of flapjacks and sausage, we said our goodbyes. I cranked the roadster and was letting the engine warm up when the old man shuffled out the front doorway. He held up a paper sack and motioned for me to come up on the porch.

"Got a little something to tide you over," he said, handing me the sack. Inside was a quart Mason jar filled with homemade whiskey.

Daniel grinned and winked. "Good for what ails you, heh-heh. Gospel truth."

TWELVE

———————•———————

DAWN WAS PAINTING THE HORIZON Monday before I put the final polish on the Malburn Reunion article. At seven I arrived at work with less than two hours of restless sleep and a headache drumming behind my bloodshot eyes. I grabbed a cup of coffee and rehearsed the pitch for my proposed serial a final time as I walked down the hall to the boss's office. I was as ready as I'd ever be to face Uncle Hawley. Still, when I stepped into his office for the usual beginning-of-the-week meeting, I couldn't help feeling apprehensive.

To my immense relief and surprise, Uncle Hawley welcomed my proposal. "About time you put some of your daddy's money to good use," he said, his crotchety way of giving me the go ahead.

Now I had to somehow get in touch with Elijah Malburn and find out if he would be receptive to an interview. If he wasn't, the project, and possibly my job, was sunk. I decided to call on Benjamin Gainer, the Malburn family historian Alma Hutchins had mentioned at the reunion. I reasoned my chances for success would be better if a trusted relative arranged the initial meeting.

When I visited Mister Gainer at his law office and explained what I hoped to accomplish, he was delighted with the idea and eager to help. "To my knowledge no one's ever been able to get those ornery old coots to talk much about the war and what all went on between them after," he said. "Could be the time is right. If you can persuade them to tell their story, well I'm all for it. It would certainly help fill in a part of our family's history."

Wednesday afternoon at the office I received a phone call from Benjamin Gainer. "Uncle Eli says he's willing to meet with you Saturday morning, on one condition."

"What would that be, sir?" I said, not sure I wanted to hear it.

"Well, you have to promise not to take sides."

"Hmm. What does that mean, exactly?"

Mister Gainer laughed. "Beats me, Mister Hogue. With Uncle Eli you never know. He's always talking in ambiguities. Might be he feels unfairly outnumbered, him having fought for the Union and all."

I brought up the fact that I was born and reared in Pennsylvania and had grandfathers who'd also fought on opposite sides of the conflict.

"Well, that's certainly worth mentioning. It might make a difference with how he looks at things. A word of warning, though. Don't go patronizing the old boy. That's one thing he won't tolerate."

The rest of the work week flew by. Early Saturday morning I turned the roadster north and retraced my route to the Econfina Valley. It was a beautiful warm early June morning with clear skies. The roadside was lush green and dotted with colorful wildflowers. There were no obstinate ferry captains or road construction delays to contend with. The lovebugs were all but gone. And Jenny, well, she was being the cat's meow about the whole matter.

Yes, life was good. I just hoped the interview with Elijah Malburn would go as smoothly.

THIRTEEN

I DROVE PAST DANIEL'S CABIN and followed Malburn Road to its end, then turned onto a winding drive bordered by limestone pillars and split-rail fencing. Elijah Malburn lived in the "big house"—the original family home. Daniel had briefly mentioned the house while recalling his experiences at the Battle of Chickamauga. I hadn't given much thought as to why his younger brother had inherited the property and not he.

I parked in the shade of a huge magnolia that dominated one side of the front yard. I shut off the engine and gazed at the house. It was somewhat disappointing to find it didn't measure up to my imagined antebellum plantation. There were no stately columns, no striking facade or impressive portico with ornate railing. What I saw was a rather large but ordinary two-story structure in need of a good scraping and repainting. A porch ran the length of the front and wrapped around one wing of the house. A covered dogtrot led to another smaller building, probably the summer kitchen. A stout weathered barn stood behind the summer kitchen, along with a few smaller outbuildings. While the big house was far from my notion of a Southern mansion, it was certainly a step up from the modest cabin Daniel called home.

I grabbed my notebook and followed a stone footpath to the front porch. Sparse grass struggled to survive in the shaded sandy soil, but in the sunny portion of the lawn fragrant gardenia blossoms blanketed a large healthy bush. High in the branches of a wisteria-choked pine, a mockingbird serenaded the spring morning.

I climbed the steps and walked across the porch. The screen door squawked in protest when I opened it to rap on the front door. Getting no answer, I was about to try again when I heard footsteps inside. I stepped back and closed the screen door just as the knob turned and the front door creaked open. An elderly man wearing faded overalls stared through the screen.

"You wasting your time and mine, sonny," he said, and started to shut the door. "Whatever it is you peddling, I ain't buying."

"No, I'm not selling anything, sir," I blurted before he could close the door. "I'm Calvin Hogue, from the *Pilot*. Mister Benjamin Gainer said you'd meet with me this morning."

He opened the door a bit wider and squinted through wire-rimmed spectacles. "That so? Well if Mister Benjamin Gainer said it, it must be so. Don't stand there and take root, sonny, come on in." With that he turned and vanished down the dark hallway.

Well, things had certainly gotten off to a grand start. Elijah Malburn promised to be every bit as difficult as his older brother. I stepped inside and closed the door. By the time my eyes adjusted to the feeble light, he was nowhere to be seen. "Mister Malburn?" I said, just as a big yellow cat came caterwauling down the hallway.

"Let General Sherman out, would you, sonny? His bladder ain't what it used to be."

"Yes, sir." General Sherman clawed at the screen as I pushed it open. With a parting "meow" he scampered off the porch into the yard. I shut the door and walked down the hall, my footsteps echoing off the hardwood floor. A few framed photos hung on either wall. At the far end came the rhythmic ticking of a grandfather clock. Sunlight streamed through an open doorway farther down the hall. Elijah was inside the room, seated in an overstuffed antique armchair beside a dormant fireplace.

For the first time I got a good look at the younger Malburn brother. There was a family resemblance, though not striking. Elijah was a bit taller and heavier than his older brother. His thin hair had a trace of pepper still noticeable amid the salt, as did his moustache. With his ruddy complexion he appeared more robust than Daniel.

"Sit yourself down," he said, pointing to a similar chair at the opposite side of the hearth. A big white cat lay sleeping on the chair. I glanced at Elijah. "That there is General Grant. Just shoo him off. Go on, he won't mind. Be back asleep before he hits the floor. Laziest cat I ever did see."

"Yes, sir." I carefully placed a hand on the cat's back. General Grant opened one eye, then lifted his head and yawned so wide it looked like he could swallow a baseball. Sure enough, he slid off the chair and immediately curled up on the floor barely a foot away.

"You like cats . . . Calvin, is it?"

"Yes, sir, Calvin Hogue. My girlfriend has a cat. I—"

"Never had much use for cats myself," Elijah said. "Always been more of a dog person. Keep the generals around the house to catch mice and such. They about got too old to be much fit at it." He chuckled. "But they earn their keep by galling my brother." He leaned forward and slapped his knees, laughing himself into a fit of coughing. When he recovered, he said, "Reckon I've had two dozen cats over the years, sonny. Named ever one of 'em after Yankee generals. Dogs too. Ol' General McDowell died last summer. Got to get me another hound around here soon. Even had a team of plow mules years ago I called Burnside and Hooker. You ought to see how it rubs Daniel. Why, if he weren't such a Christian man . . .

"Speak of the devil," he continued, before I could gather my thoughts for a response, "I hear tell you been palavering with my brother."

"I have. Yes, sir." I was getting a hint of what Benjamin Gainer meant when he said this old coot talked in circles. "I spoke with him at the reunion last week. I was hoping to meet—"

"Oh, I seen you two jabbering under that big oak, all right. Filling your head full of his hogwash and other whatnot, was he?"

Things were getting shakier by the moment. How was I supposed to answer the old codger without ruining my chances of winning him over? The Malburns were a trying sort, there was no denying that. It made me wonder how any of their relatives could put up with either one of them. But Daniel had finally come around. Maybe Elijah would too, if my patience could hold out long enough. That might prove to be a mighty big *if.* I took a deep breath to relax.

"Mister Malburn, you and your brother were eyewitnesses to the most momentous period in America's history," I said, choosing my words carefully. "A nation divided, a house divided. Your story deserves to be told, sir. I want to write it, both sides fairly and equally."

"That so?" He pushed back the spectacles that had slipped farther down his nose.

"Yes, sir. Think what a waste it would be if such an important legacy were to pass on with you and Daniel." Suddenly I remembered Benjamin Gainer's warning about patronizing. Well, it was too late to take back the words. I hoped I wasn't digging myself in deeper, but there was no choice but to go ahead with my pitch. "I want to record the Malburn brothers' experiences for history before it's too late."

"Do tell?" He leaned back in the chair and pulled a bag of Mail Pouch chewing tobacco from his overalls. "How come you went to my brother first?" he said, offering me a chew.

I politely declined the tobacco. "I just happened to meet him first. I'd hoped to interview both of you at the reunion. I wasn't aware there were . . . ill feelings between you two."

"Now who went and put such tomfoolery in your noggin, sonny?" he asked, stuffing a wad of tobacco into his cheek. "Ill feelings, *pshaw*! We got our differences, mind you. Most everbody does. But he's family and I love him. Tolerate him, anyhow."

I could almost taste shoe leather. "I'm sorry, sir, I didn't mean to imply anything," I mumbled. Then I remembered what I hoped would be my trump card. "One reason your story fascinates me so is that my own grandfathers also fought on opposite sides during the war."

Elijah's eyebrows arched. He leaned forward a bit. "Do tell?"

"Yes, sir." My hopes brightened a little. "Grandpa Hogue served with the Army of the Potomac, and my Grandpa Wells fought with General Lee's Army of Northern Virginia. I'm not sure what all battles they participated in, but I know for a fact they were both at Gettysburg. I grew up just north of there, in Carlisle."

"That so?" Elijah reached down and picked up a tin can sitting on the floor beside his chair. "So, you a Yankee boy."

"Well, sir, I like to think of myself as an American first." Neutrality seemed the prudent path to trod, given the circumstances. "But yes, I'm Northern born and reared."

He spat a stream of juice into the can and set it back on the floor. "You care for a glass of sweet tea, sonny? I got ice."

"Yes, sir, a glass of tea would hit the spot."

"All right then," Elijah said, pushing himself out of the chair. "I'll go pour us some. Then we can jaw a spell."

Elijah Malburn
1863
A Union Man

FOURTEEN

SO, HOW DID I COME to be a Union man? Well, sonny, I'll tell you. But it ain't a cut-and-dried affair. Best keep that pencil sharp because this might take a spell.

It was a mighty sad day around these parts that morning in October of 'sixty-three when word arrived about the death of young Hampton Watts. I was home at the time, having took a few days off from my duties at the saltworks to check on things at the farm. Making salt was my patriotic contribution to the Confederacy. Might've gone right on doing so for the rest of the war had unfortunate circumstances not got in the way. But more about that later.

My older sister, Sara, received the sad news about Hamp in a letter from her husband, Lieutenant Tom Gainer. Tom was in Company K with my brother Daniel and most of the boys from around these parts. He wrote how they'd soundly whipped the Yankees at Chickamauga two weeks earlier. Sent 'em skedaddling back into Tennessee and had 'em penned up at Chattanooga. It was a great and much needed victory for the South, coming on the heels of the Confederate defeats at Gettysburg and Vicksburg that very summer. But the cost had been heavy for both sides.

And Hamp was part of it.

According to Tom's account, Hamp died a hero while boldly charging the enemy, and did not suffer. Brother Daniel was at his side when it happened. We could all take comfort that Hamp died bravely with honor while performing his patriotic duty, or some such foolishness.

Know what I think, sonny? I'll tell you. I think Hamp wasted his life with all the others that died in that war, all for a pack of blowhard politicians spouting their hot air nonsense till it tore this country apart. Me and Hamp was best friends our whole lives. All fifteen years of it. Fact is, Hamp was kilt the day before his birthday, so he never lived to see sixteen. Now here I am, a old man, while Hamp's been moldering in his grave sixty-some years. Where's the justice in that? I'll tell you. There ain't none.

We was practically raised together. "Goobers from the same pod," my brother used to say. Once shared the same tit when Hamp's ma fell ill and my family took him in till she regained her health. Seemed one of us was always sleeping over at the other's house. We was more brothers than friends.

For many a year I blamed Tom Gainer for Hamp's death. It was a grudge that caused my family some pain, specially sister Sara, I'm sorry to say. But what's done is done and there ain't no taking it back.

How come I blamed Tom? I'll tell you. You see, in late May of 'sixty-three, Tom come home on furlough to marry Sara. Spent the days before the wedding strutting about in his fancy new officer's uniform recruiting for the "glorious and righteous Cause," as he was fond of saying. The day Sara and Tom got hitched, Hamp tried his derndest to talk me into joining the Confederate Army with him. Tom had filled his head with all sorts of nonsense about duty and the glory of soldiering and other whatnot.

I still recollect Hamp's very words: "Eli," he said, them blue eyes of his flashing, "we just got to get into it 'fore the war is over. Why, them Yanks is liable to up and quit anytime now."

This took place soon after word come down about the great victory General Lee and Stonewall Jackson had won at Chancellorsville, mind you. Seemed like Lee and his army was invincible, for sure. The South could almost smell victory in the air that spring of 'sixty-three. Who could know then what a few short months would bring?

Now Hamp always was a eager sort, and he went and signed right up. But I weren't having none of it. Fact is, I didn't much believe in the war or the Cause. Never could understand why folks would stoop to killing each other over ideals or politics or other such tomfoolery. Never did like killing, not even squirrels and such. Just couldn't square it with myself how I could ever come to shoot at another human being.

Hamp, on the other hand, always had a fondness for guns. That boy was a crack shot almost by the time he could walk. His brother Yerby taught him well. We used to tag along with our brothers while they hunted the creek bottoms. They let us carry whatever game they shot, which was great fun for me. Hamp, though, was always pestering them to let him shoot. Later on when we was older we'd go hunting by ourselfs. Oh, I shot a few squirrels and rabbits and such, but my heart weren't never in it. So after a while I give it up for the most part.

Anyhow, a few days after the wedding Private Hamp Watts left with Lieutenant Tom Gainer and a handful of other recruits, bound for Chattahoochee. From there they would take a steamer up to Columbus, Georgia, then ride the rails north to somewheres up in Kentucky or Tennessee where General Bragg's Army of Tennessee was guarding mountain passes and such.

It never occurred to me as I watched them go that it would be the last time I ever laid eyes on my friend.

FIFTEEN

CALL IT GUILT OR SHAME or whatnot, but with my brother and Hamp and other friends off fighting I felt like I ought to be doing something for the Cause other than working the family farm. So, a few days after Hamp and Tom left for the war I decided to take a trip to the coast and check out the saltworks. Back then there weren't no refrigeration like nowadays, mind you. Salt was the only means to cure meat to feed the army.

Now, in 'sixty-two the Confederate government had passed the Conscript Act. Any able-body man between the age of eighteen and thirty-five was considered fair game for the army. But salt was good as gold for the Confederacy in them days, so anybody that could produce twenty bushels or more a day was exempt from serving. I was just fifteen, mind you, but I had always been big for my age and looked a mite older. And it weren't unknown for some overzealous recruiter to "volunteer" a person into the army before his time. So, making salt seemed like a wise undertaking for me at the time. Salt could keep me out of the war, might even prove to be profitable.

St. Andrew Bay had miles and miles of secluded coastline in them days. Still does, in fact. Finest sour mash you ever tasted is made all along the bay nowadays. Revenuers cain't touch what they cain't find, sonny. But during the war it was salt, not 'shine, that was in such demand. Saltworks was popping up in every nook and cranny. I reckoned it would be easy enough to hire on at one of the bigger operations. Might even buy my own kettles and such and set up my own enterprise if the work proved agreeable.

Things was going good at the farm. Corn and cotton fields was thriving. Had a hundred head of cattle or so free-ranging along the creek. Hogs was rolling fat. So, I decided to leave Uncle Nate in charge of things and take Jefferson with me. My brother tell you about them? Well, I will.

Uncle Nate and Jefferson was two of our slaves. Reckon Daniel didn't talk about us owning nigras. Fact is, our family was considered somewhat prosperous as things was measured in them parts. We owned a dozen or so slaves through the years. Shames me to say it, but the truth is the truth. Ain't no sense denying it. When my daddy died we was forced to sell off most of the nigras. Only Uncle Nate and Aunt Nettie and Jefferson stayed on.

Jefferson was their youngest child, and the only one to live past childhood. He was near my age, maybe a year older. Aunt Nettie was our house servant. She also was the wet nurse I mentioned to you earlier. Uncle Nate was my daddy's trusted friend and overseer. Daddy and Nate was close in age. They'd growed up together, like me and Jefferson. When my daddy decided to leave North Carolina and settle here in eighteen and forty, his daddy give him Nate and Nettie and a couple of other slaves as a going away gift.

Now, Uncle Nate and Aunt Nettie was like family. And Jefferson was a brother to me in ever way but color and blood. My daddy built 'em a fine cabin and give 'em twenty acres to do with as they pleased once their regular chores was done. Cabin stood right down the road yonder. You passed it when you come in. It's gone now, burnt down. Nothing left but the chimney. But that's another story.

When Daddy fell off the barn roof and broke his neck in the winter of 'fifty-nine, it was Uncle Nate kept things going till me and Daniel could learn what we needed to know to run a big farm proper. So I knowed Mama and my twin sisters, Ruth and Naomi, would be in good hands while I was off doing my duty and seeking my fortune.

———•———

After outfitting us a wagon with food and camping equipment and such other supplies we thought might prove useful, me and Jefferson said our goodbyes to the family and struck out for the coast. I ought to mention that it took some talking to convince Aunt Nettie to let Jefferson come with me. Scarlet fever had nearly took him as a child, and it left him a touch simple. Jefferson was some big, mind you, and strong as a ox, but he weren't the sharpest tack you ever sat on. Aunt Nettie tended to dote on him, but Uncle Nate was forever telling her that the boy needed to learn to make his own way in the world. Took some coaxing, but we finally talked her into letting Jefferson come along.

Jefferson had never been this far from home his entire life. He stared with wonder at dern near everthing we seen along the way. "When we goan see the ocean, Eli?" he asked before we'd made ten miles. "Mama say the ocean bigger even than Porter Lake. Say it salty as cured ham too."

"Ain't the ocean, it's the Gulf of Mexico," I told him.

Jefferson propped his chin on a meaty fist and stared at me. "But Mama say it the ocean."

"Well, it's like the ocean, only they call it the gulf," I said, wishing I'd just let it be.

"Mama say it the ocean."

"We'll see the ocean in a couple of days, Jeff."

Took the best part of two days to reach the bay. Roads back then weren't near what they are nowadays. Midafternoon the second day we reached Anderson, a little hamlet on North Bay whose namesake owned a fleet of fishing boats and a fish house. Word was, Mister John Anderson also ran one of the biggest and most profitable salt operations in all of West Florida.

I halted the team in front of the fish house. Looked like any old warehouse to me, just a weatherbeaten airy old clapboard building. Seemed like the next good squall might bring it toppling down on itself. *J. Anderson & Sons* was painted in big black letters above the wide double doors that stood open.

I left Jefferson to watch the team and wagon and walked through the doorway. Inside, the light was poor and took some getting used to. But the smell of fish was strong. Must have been fifty or more workers inside, standing behind rows of long workbenches. Most was nigras, but there was several older white men and a few boys scattered here and there amongst 'em. Bushel baskets full of salt and fish, mullet I took it to be, was stacked alongside each bench. Some of the workers was scaling and splitting the fish, their sharp knives flashing in what light poured through several high ventilation windows. Others was busy salting and packing the fish in brine barrels fast as any good fieldhand ever filled a cotton sack. Regular assembly line they had going.

"Can I he'p you, boy?"

I looked to my right towards the voice. Old man was sitting in the shadows, his chair tipped back and resting agin the wall. "Yes, sir. I'm looking for Mister Anderson. Heard he might could use some help at the saltworks."

Well, with that the old man sat upright, then walked over to me. He was short and wiry, come up about to my shoulders. Had on a pair of old coveralls and wore rubber boots that come halfway up his knees. In the better light I seen a face that was tanned near black and wrinkled as a dried apple. His gray beard was stained brown around his mouth and chin. He looked me up and down with his squinty eyes. "John Anderson don't deal in salt making," he said. He waved a hand towards the barrels. "This here salt you see all come from Cuba."

"Do tell?" I said. "Well, that ain't what I heard."

"And just what is it you heard, boy?"

I grinned at him, took my time looking around the big room. "Well, mister, I heard if a man had a mind to do so, he could take a little trip west of here, say, up along Alligator Bayou?"

I waited a minute, letting that sink in, then folded my arms. "Yes, sir. And if he was to look hard enough, why, he just might find a right big saltworks around them parts. Leastways, that's what I heard, mind you."

Still tickles me to this day, the look he give me. Turned three shades of red he was so riled, like a dog with the hydrophobie. "Look here you rat snapper," he said, just a'fuming. "Why should I go telling you any damn thing? Don't know you from Adam. They's spies thick as sand gnats 'round this here bay. How I know you ain't here spying for them damn Yankee blockaders?"

Well, sonny, I couldn't argue his point. Fact is, back then there *was* a goodly number of spies and deserters holed up along the bay. "I'm Elijah Malburn," I said, "from up Econfina way. My father was James Malburn. Our farm grows food that we sell to feed the Confederate Army, my own brother and many friends amongst 'em. So it ain't likely I'd bring harm to my own people by spying for the Yankees."

"Malburn, eh?" he said. "Do believe I've heard the name." He stroked his beard for a minute, kept muttering, "Hmm, umhmm," or some such.

Know what he done then, sonny? I'll tell you. Gets up on his toes and shakes a finger in my face. Said, "You breathe a word of this to a soul, I'll track you down and cut off your nuts for crab bait, or my name ain't J.J. Jonas."

Then he drawed me a map to Anderson's saltworks.

SIXTEEN

GOOD THING ME AND JEFFERSON picked us a strong team and a stout wagon for our trip, because getting to the saltworks weren't no easy business. It was June and it was some hot. Rained on and off the rest of the afternoon. That cooled things off a touch, but made our travel all the more rougher. The pig trail we followed through the piney woods and marshes was near impassable in places. Twice the wagon bogged down up to the axles. Had to unload most of our supplies to lighten it. With Jefferson pushing and me goading the Morgans, we managed to pull the wagon free and continue on. Second time the wagon got stuck I dern near got bit by a cottonmouth thick as my arm. If Jefferson hadn't spotted it and shouted a warning it would've struck me for sure. Fetched the ax to kill it, but it crawled under the wagon and got away. Jefferson come out of that mudhole like he was walking on water.

By sundown we was used up. Found a high spot of ground under some big pines and made camp. Jefferson pitched the tent while I unhitched and tethered the Morgans. Then I went hunting for firewood. There was plenty of dead scrub oak laying around, so I gathered up a goodly pile for the night. Also found some chunks of fat lighter for a smudge fire to keep the skeeters away. Smudge helped some, but them dern bloodsuckers still liked to've toted us off that night.

We ate fried ham with potatoes and cornbread for supper, then turned in. Soon Jefferson was snoring along with the chorus of crickets and frogs and whatnot singing their night songs. Never knowed him to have any trouble getting to sleep. Me now, that's another story. Sleep always did come hard for me. Still does.

Anyways, I laid awake for I don't know how long listening to the bugs and owls and such. Fact is, I was a mite wary. Rumor had it there was bands of deserters and conscript shirkers hiding out in them parts. Felt better knowing my shotgun was there beside me. Ever now and again I reached out the tent flap and stirred the smudge to keep it smoking good. The night was warm and the skeeters pestered me to no end, but finally I drifted off.

Woke up next morning at first light. Whippoorwills was calling, and it had cooled off considerable. Jefferson was still asleep. He had worked hard freeing the wagon yesterday, so I let him sleep and slipped out of the tent to start a fire and put the coffee on. While the coffee was boiling I fed and watered the Morgans. I had fatback in the frying pan and was fixing to put it on the fire when the horses lifted their heads and whinnied. Then a hard voice called from the trees.

"Who are you, and what is your business here?"

Almost dropped the dern pan, it startled me so. Looked up and seen a rider walking his horse out of the shadows towards the fire. He was backlit by the sunrise that hadn't yet burned off the morning haze. Before I could get a good look at him, several other riders joined him in a half-circle about our camp. I set down the pan and held my hand up to greet the lead rider who I now seen was a Confederate officer. Leastways he wore the fanciest uniform amongst them, with braided sleeves that reminded me of Tom Gainer's jacket. The others was a ragtag bunch from what I could see in the poor light. What I did see plenty clear was all them pistols stuffed inside their belts. Weren't a man amongst 'em that didn't have at least two, some more.

"You deaf, boy?" the officer asked, coming a little closer. "I asked, who are you and what are you doing in these parts?"

Found my tongue quick when I seen his hand wrap around one of them big pistols he toted. "Name's Malburn, sir. Elijah Malburn. Of the Econfina Malburns." Couple of riders turned their horses and walked them towards the backside of the tent. Goosebumps pricked my neck when they passed from sight. Could almost feel them pistols aimed at my back. I heard Jefferson rustling inside the tent and hoped he wouldn't come busting out of there with the shotgun.

The officer shifted in the saddle, crossed his right leg over the pommel. He leaned forward and looked hard at me with cold, dark eyes. "And what is your business here, Mister Malburn? A hunting expedition, I suppose?"

Well, sonny, that set the others to laughing. Didn't see the humor in it myself, not at all.

"Oh he's hunting all right, yes sir, Captain," the man to the officer's right said. "Bet I know what it is he's hunting too." They went to laughing even harder while my heart went to pounding. Had me by the short hairs, that's a fact.

"No, sir," I said. "I'm here looking for—"

"Halloo, they's another one in the tent, Captain!" a rider behind me called out. With that, ever man sitting a horse drawed forth a pistol. Hammers went to clicking as they cocked 'em and my knees went to knocking.

"You there, inside the tent. Come out here where we can see you," the captain ordered.

The tent flap pushed open and Jefferson come crawling out on all fours. Kept crawling all the way over to where I was beside the fire before he slowly stood up. Started shaking when he seen all them revolvers pointed our way. "Is they goan shoot us, Eli?" he whispered through his chattering teeth.

"Looks that way," I said without thinking. Realized that scared him even more, so I added, "You keep quiet now, let me handle this."

"Why, it's a nigger," somebody said. "That your nigger, Malburn?"

"It's a runaway I bet. You a runaway, nigger?" another said.

"The Lawd is my shepherd, I shan't want . . .," Jefferson said, shaking like he had the palsy.

I put a hand on his shoulder to calm him, said, "His name is Jefferson. He belongs to my family."

"... make me to lie down in green pastures ..."

"Hush up, Jeff," I said, "that ain't helping none."

"It he'pin *me*, Eli!"

The captain swung down off his horse and strode towards us, still carrying the cocked pistol. He was a tall, lean man. Looked to be in his mid-twenties or thereabouts. Wore a beard like the others, only his was better kept. He stopped across the fire from us and waved his revolver in our direction. Jefferson flinched. I gripped his shoulder hard to make him be still. If he took off running it might all be over for both of us. "Who did you say your people are?" the captain asked.

"James Malburn was my father, sir. He settled up along the Econfina twenty-some years ago."

"Malburn. Yes, I believe I know the name." He uncocked the revolver and slipped it under his belt. "Good people, I hear. Your father has passed, then?"

The captain's voice had lost some of its bite. I felt a mite relieved. "Yes, sir, four years now. Accident took him."

"I am sorry to hear it. Our Cause could use such good men."

I waited, not sure how to answer that. Then I thought about Daniel. "My brother is off fighting with the Sixth Florida. Captain McMillian's company."

His eyes widened. "Angus McMillian? I know Captain McMillian. A brave and patriotic man." With that he looked over his shoulder and waved a arm. The clicking of metal was music to my ears as his men uncocked and put away their weapons.

Jefferson quit shaking some, but fear had done washed the color right out of him. He was near pale as a mulatto. The captain turned back and eyed us real close. "Duty dictates that I know your business here, Mister Malburn," he said, the edge coming back to his voice.

"I'm hoping to find work at Mister John Anderson's saltworks."

The captain's eyes locked on mine. Felt like he would burn a hole right through me, he stared so. "John Anderson is my father. I am Captain William Anderson of the Gulf Mounted Rifles. These men are under my command."

Sonny, you could have pushed me over with your pinkie
when I heard that. Riding guard for his daddy's business, was
he? Didn't know if that was good news or bad. Thought it over
for a second, then smiled real friendly like. "That so? Glad to
make your acquaintance, Captain. It's a comfort knowing you
and your men are hereabouts protecting us."

"Why are you not serving with your brother?" Captain
Anderson said. Made me right nervous how them cold eyes of
his held so steady without blinking. Wondered if he was born
that way, or if maybe soldiering had give him that stare.

"I'm only fifteen," I said. "Wanted to join up, but my brother
told me it was my duty to stay home and work the farm for our
poor widowed mother and young sisters." It weren't all a lie,
what I told him.

"Fifteen . . . I took you for older." His eyes narrowed like a
coiled rattler's. "Then why are you here and not back at your
farm doing your duty?"

Had to think that one through a minute. "Farm's doing
good. Crops is all planted and such. Uncle Nate—that's Jefferson
here's daddy—is taking real good care of things. Thought I might
be more useful making salt than staying home idle. What wages
I earn will help my family."

The captain nodded. "Salt *is* important to our Cause. But
why should I believe your story? There are spies all around this
bay."

Then I remembered the map and reached into my breeches
pocket. Hands grabbed for pistols and I froze.

SEVENTEEN

"WHOA, I AIN'T ARMED," I said, easing my empty hand out of my pocket. Seeing all them pistols pointed our way, Jefferson went to shaking and mumbling Scripture again. "I got a map. Mister Jonas drawed it for me back at the fish house. Got his mark on it."

Captain Anderson held his pistol on me, said, "If that's so, let's see it."

I reached in my pocket real slow and pulled out the folded map. Handed it to the captain, never taking my eyes off that muzzle staring me down.

The captain put away his pistol and unfolded the map. Looked it over a minute. "That's Jonas's mark, all right," he said, then turned to face his men. "Old Jonas sent us some more, boys," he said, and they all near busted a gut laughing.

Didn't have the foggiest what was so funny but I found out soon enough. Know what that dern scoundrel Jonas had done? I'll tell you. Turns out that map didn't lead to the saltworks at all. Led us right to Captain Anderson's camp instead. Leastways it would have if his lookouts—videttes, they called 'em—hadn't smelt our fire first.

When they'd had their fun with us, Captain Anderson walked over and slapped me on the back, said, "Can't be too careful these days, Mister Malburn. Anyone comes snooping around for information about the saltworks, Jonas sends them to me. His mark tells me you are probably to be trusted."

"We come here to make salt, like I told you," I said, a mite irritated. Wondered if I was fixing to be recruited into the Confederate Army instead.

Captain Anderson ignored my words. Looked past me and called to one of the riders. "Sergeant Ellis, check out the wagon."

A lanky man wearing a slouch hat pulled low over his eyes, dismounted and walked over to our wagon. Drew back the tarp and spent a minute or two rummaging through our supplies. "Mostly provisions, Captain," he said. "Cornmeal, flour, coffee, sugar, salt pork. They's some powder and shot too."

The captain locked them steely eyes on me again. "You said you weren't armed, did you not?"

Well, sonny, here was another fine fix I'd jawed myself into. "I got a shotgun," I said, "for hunting and such. Kept it in the tent last night, lest a bear or panther or whatnot come along." I pointed towards the tent. "It's there yet."

Captain Anderson ordered another man to fetch my shotgun. He stepped inside the tent and come out holding the old double-barrel my daddy had give me on my tenth birthday. Brung it over and handed it to the captain. "This your only weapon?" he said, after looking it over.

The wind had picked up and smoke from the campfire was tearing my eyes. Hoped the captain and his men wouldn't take it for crying. "Yes, sir, that's it," I said, trying to sound brave. "Oh, I got a jackknife in my pocket. Jefferson here does too."

The captain smiled at that, then handed me the shotgun. "My men and I would be obliged if you'd invite us to breakfast. Then we will escort you to the saltworks."

"Yes, sir," I said, grinning with relief. "Be proud to share what we got." I pointed to the coffeepot. "Coffee's ready, what there is. Help yourself."

I turned to Jefferson, said, "Finish up your praying and go fetch the cornmeal and another slab of fatback from the wagon. We got guests to feed."

Captain Anderson was a man of his word. After a breakfast of fatback and mush, we struck camp and set out for the saltworks. Half his men rode well ahead of our wagon, the others trailed behind. In a few minutes we come upon videttes strung out along both sides of the trail. They saluted the captain as he rode by. Couple hundred yards or so farther on we come to their company bivouac. Men was sitting about in front of their tents, some cooking, some cleaning weapons or such. Now and again one looked up and swapped "halloos" or other whatnots with our escorts.

We passed on through and headed west down a trail that run between a big cypress swamp and a marshy field for a mile or more. Flocks of green parakeets was feasting on cockleburs and thistles growing in the field and alongside the road. They tolerated us till we was almost on 'em, then off they'd fly, just a'squawking. Soon the road left the cypress swamp and cut through a big pine forest. It was a mite cooler in the shade of the pines. Here and there I heard the cooing of doves or woodpeckers drumming in the distance. Once, a big whitetail buck bolted across the trail, flag a'waving as it bounded into a titi thicket.

Near midmorning we come to a fork in the trail. Captain Anderson called a halt. He rode up to the wagon and dismounted. "This is where we part, Mister Malburn. My men and I have business on west of here." He pointed to the trail that turned south. "Follow this road and you'll find the works an hour or so away." Then he reached in his coat pocket and pulled out a folded paper. "When you arrive, show this note to my father or his foreman, Boss Miller. It explains who you are and states your business."

I mentioned before that Captain Anderson was a man of his word, didn't I? Well, he also took me at *my* word. I had told him I'd be proud to share what we had with him and his men—meaning breakfast. But now his boys went to lightening our load till the wagon bed was dern near empty. Well, sonny, that stuck in my craw. Never could tolerate a dern thief. Still cain't.

Sergeant Ellis must've read the look on my face. Walked over and grinned, said, "You won't be needing all this at the salt camp. They feed you right smart there."

Captain Anderson did leave me the shotgun and loads. Said

it might come in handy if the Yankees come raiding. Then he tipped his hat and bid me goodbye.

Felt like giving them thieving scoundrels a load of buckshot for a proper send-off. Instead, me and Jefferson just sat there minding our manners till they rode out of sight. Then I headed the team south.

———•———

Around noon I caught the scent of wood smoke coming from the southwest. I pulled the team to a halt just inside a small clearing. Dead pinetops laid scattered here and there amongst stumps still oozing sap. "Smell that, Jeff?"

Jefferson sniffed the air, turned his head a bit and sniffed again. "Sure does. Reckon we's gettin' close to the salt makin'."

"Do tell?" I said, then pointed to the tree stumps and felled tops. "I thought maybe a woodpecker done all that work yonder."

Jefferson throwed back his head and laughed. "You is joshin' me, Eli. You knows ain't no woodpecker done did all that."

We drove on another half-hour or so. The trail got real narrow, brush scraping both sides of the wagon. We come around a bend and yonder sat a boy in the shade of a tall pine. Looked to be twelve or thereabouts. A rusty old flintlock musket laid across his legs. His eyes was closed and his mouth was slacked open. Heard him snoring from where I sat. I looked at Jeff and grinned. "That is some fine lookout they got, ain't it?"

Jeff covered his mouth to keep from laughing out loud, said, "Look like he catchin' lots mo' flies than Yankees, that fo' sure."

"Cain't be much threat of Yankees if they let a young fool like this stand guard," I said, and eased down off the wagon. Picked up a dried pinecone and tossed it towards the sentry. It bounced off his shoulder, but all the boy done was reach up and scratch where it hit. Tried again with a stick. It whacked him square in the chest. His eyes snapped wide open.

"H-h-halt!" he said, grabbing the musket and scrambling to his feet. Pointed it in my general direction but made no effort to cock the hammer.

"I *been* halted a good five minutes watching you snooze."

"P-put your hands up," he said, waving the barrel at me. He

grinned like a egg-sucking possum. "Done catched me a Yankee, I have."

"Put that thing down," I said. "If I was a Yankee I would've done cut your throat."

Well now, that set him to thinking. He lowered the barrel, then jerked it back up. "You my prisoner and I'm taking you in. That nigger too," he said, nodding his red head at Jeff.

"That so? And what if I tell Mister Anderson I caught you sleeping on duty?"

At that, the boy looked right confused. Stared down at his musket for a second or two, then looked up with a cocky grin. "Why, I'll tell him you a damn liar, is what."

I was getting a mite galled by this time. Felt like walking over and thrashing him good. Thought better of it when he thumbed back the hammer he'd just noticed was uncocked. "Get them hands up, both you!"

"Do believe he's got us by the short hairs, Jeff." I raised my arms. Looked over to tell Jefferson to obey but he was already grabbing air. Turned back and faced the boy. "Look here now, I'm here on official business. Got a letter from Captain William Anderson stating such." Easylike, I lowered a hand and patted my breeches pocket.

The boy puckered his mouth and squinted till his eyes was just slits. "That the truth?"

"It is."

"Swear on a stack of Bibles?"

"Point that musket at the ground and I'll show you."

He did, and I did.

The boy took the note and looked it over real good, holding it upside down. "It's Captain Anderson's hand all right," he said official-like, and handed it back to me. He brung the musket to his side, muzzle pointing up, and stood at what I took to be attention, and said, "Reckon you two can pass on through."

"Much obliged." I climbed back on the wagon seat and give him a wave, said, "Best uncock that musket before you go and shoot yourself." Then I whistled to the Morgans and flicked the reins. As the wagon lurched forward Jefferson dern near fell off.

"Put down your hands Jeff, he ain't going to shoot nobody."

EIGHTEEN

A LITTLE FARTHER ON, THE woods give out and yonder was the bay. We was on a sandy bluff some twenty-foot high and it was some sight. I halted the team, set the brake and jumped down off the wagon to stretch my legs and take a good look.

Sunlight danced a jig on the water. Overhead, seagulls was laughing. I could taste salt on my lips. Jefferson come up beside me, all wide-eyed. "It the ocean, Eli?"

"Part of it," I said, not wanting to confuse him. I pointed across to the far shoreline. "See them trees way over yonder? Rest of the ocean is on the other side of them. But it's all connected, so yeah, this is the ocean."

That seemed to satisfy him. "It sure big, like Mama said."

The trail turned back north a short piece, then west and down the bluff. At the bottom the ruts followed the shoreline. Sparse grass and reeds growed in sand white as ginned cotton. The trail cut north again alongside a cove that narrowed the farther along we went. Topped a little rise and there was the salt camp, a hundred yards or so inland under a arbor of great live oaks. Somewheres in the distance I heard the hammering of axes. Here and there thin smoke rose above the treetops.

"There it is," I said, just as two armed men stepped from behind bushes ahead of us. They wore what could pass for Confederate uniforms and carried fine muskets.

"State your business, mister," said one, a man of average size with a red beard and bushy blond hair sticking out from under his slouch hat.

"I'm looking for work. Got a letter from Captain William Anderson proving it."

"Hand it over to Cletus here," he said, then motioned to his partner to go get it.

I'd put the captain's letter in my shirt pocket so it wouldn't look like I was fishing for a weapon in case I needed to show it again. I give it to Cletus, a regular scarecrow. Stood near six-foot tall and might've weighed all of a hundred pounds toting a sack of wet cotton. He handed the letter to his comrade who looked it over, right-side up mind you.

"You be Malburn?"

"I am."

"And that is your slave?" he said, pointing at Jefferson.

"Belongs to my family."

He walked to the back of the wagon and looked in the bed, then circled on around and stopped beside the team. Run his hand over the flank of one. Moved to the other horse, checked the teeth, said, "Fine horseflesh." Well, sonny, I'd already been relieved of my provisions that morning. Now it looked like I was fixing to give up a matched pair of topnotch Morgans. Started me to thinking that maybe salt making weren't turning out to be such a profitable undertaking after all. He stroked the horse's muzzle. "Morgans, ain't they?"

"They are."

He give the horse a friendly slap on the neck and handed the captain's letter to me. "Mister Anderson's sure to hire you on with such a fine team. Camp's just ahead."

———•———

"I'll pay you fifteen dollars a month plus keep," Mister Anderson told me. He took a chewed cigar out of his mouth and pointed it towards the open door. "I offer that much only because you got a good wagon and strong horses."

Well, sonny, I'd watched my daddy do business with merchants and neighbors and such, so I'd learnt a thing or two. Like how not to get hornswoggled by the likes of Big John Anderson—the name he introduced hisself by when I halted the team in front of the clapboard shanty he used for a office. The name fit. Anderson was a big man, dern near wide as he was tall, which was considerable. Weighed three hundred pounds if a ounce, was my guess. Looked like he was fixing to bust the buttons off the white poplin suit he wore.

His offer was a insult and he knowed it. So I said, "Do tell? I done me some asking around when I rode in, Mister Anderson. Fifteen dollars and keep is what you pay new hands. Them without such a fine team and stout wagon, that is. You asking me to work for nothing?"

When he heard that his ruddy face turned a shade redder. Took off his straw hat and fanned hisself. "You're a brash young whippersnapper, Mister Malburn. If I didn't know of your good family, I'd send you packing. But I can always use another wagon to haul. Twenty-five then, not a dime more."

"You said my wagon and team was worth fifteen. Way I figure, that adds up to thirty dollars and keep."

His jaw clinched tight. Took the cigar out of his mouth and spit, said, "See here, Malburn, you . . . oh, never mind. Thirty dollars then, but for that I get the use of your slave."

"No, sir, Jefferson works only for me."

"Now see here!"

I tapped my head and lowered my voice. "He's a mite touched, sir. Oh, he's a good worker, strong and all, but if he ain't handled right—"

"Fine, fine, you work your own darkie then," Anderson said. "It's all the same to me. Now, I got business to attend to." He waved me towards the door. "Go see Boss Miller. He'll get you started."

John Anderson's saltworks was a right big operation, and a first-rate one at that. In a year and a half it had growed from a dozen workers living in tents into a regular town of more than a hundred. Near half was slaves, most of 'em Mister Anderson's own. There was thirty-some buildings built from rough-sawn pine lumber—long barracks for the workers, storehouses, livery and blacksmith shop, smokehouse, kitchen and a well-stocked general store. Even had a church with a belfry. Seemed like everthing a real town would have, it was there.

They fed us breakfast and supper in the mess hall, a long open-sided pole building with rows of rough tables and benches. The slaves had their own place to eat at one end, so I was always careful to sit where I could keep a eye on Jeff. Noon meals we ate on the go, usually cold biscuits or cornbread with slab bacon or saltfish.

Whites and nigras weren't allowed in the same barracks, and I couldn't trust Jefferson off by hisself with a passel of strangers. So we slept in our tent beside the wagon for a week or so. Later on I paid Mister Anderson three dollars for enough lumber to build a small shack at the edge of camp. Used our tent for a roof, and the wagon tarp to fashion a door. Weren't much to look at, but it kept us dry and most of the skeeters out.

The salt camp was a right busy place. Wagons come and went all day long like worker ants. Some hauled seawater, others carried firewood from the woods. Now and again supply wagons come in loaded with goods from St. Andrew or Marianna.

The first month or so me and Jefferson worked as water haulers. We loaded six big empty barrels on the wagon bed and drove the team to the shoreline. A line of slaves strung out from behind the wagon into the shallow bay. They passed buckets full of salt water along the line and handed 'em up to two other slaves who emptied the buckets into the barrels. Took dern near a hour to get a full load. Sometimes Jefferson would wade out and take hisself a turn in the bucket brigade. I told him it weren't his job, but he took it as fun and wanted to help. Seemed he found the company of other slaves to his liking. Even made a friend or two.

When our barrels was full we hauled the water the hundred yards or so to the salt furnaces. It was a right hard pull for the Morgans, the ground being so sandy. But I made sure to work 'em slow and easy. At the furnaces other workers tapped the barrels and siphoned the seawater into holding tanks. When our barrels was empty, off we'd go again. Made eight or ten such trips a day, beginning at first light and working till the sun played out.

Anderson had built eight big salt furnaces and a dozen or so smaller ones. The big furnaces was maybe twenty-foot wide and twice that long. They had brick foundation walls three-foot high, with stout poles supporting a pitched roof. All the sides was open from the walls up to the roof. A long brick kiln run down the middle for most of the foundation's length. At one end was a big firebox. A chimney stood at the other end. On top of the kiln sat five sheet-iron boilers. Each could hold some three hundred gallons of seawater. The smaller furnaces was built much the same but used iron kettles for boilers.

Anderson's works turned out four hundred or more bushels of prime salt a day. Best in the area I heard tell, on account of all the fresh water creeks feeding into the bay thereabouts. At twelve dollars a bushel it was a right profitable business he had going.

Not just any fool with a kettle could do it, though. Salt making was a tricky affair, I soon learnt. When seawater evaporated it left what was called yellow salt in the boiler. This yellow salt weren't fit for curing meat or fish. Had to be refined to get the bad salts out, and Big John Anderson was a master at it, double- or sometimes even triple-boiling the crystals till the salt was pure as snow. His salt was the finest produced in all of West Florida, and much in demand.

On Sundays Anderson kept the furnaces operating with a small crew. Most everybody else got the day off unless bad weather set things back. All week Jefferson looked forward to the nigra church services Sunday mornings. Weren't nothing that boy liked better than singing hymns and memorizing Scripture.

Around midweek or so he'd start asking, "Tomorrow Sunday, Eli?"

"Nope, it's four more days yet."

Next day he'd be asking again, and so on till I could finally tell him that tomorrow was indeed Sunday. His face would light up at that. "Praise the Lawd, tomorrow we goan sing and pray!"

While Jeff was off getting religion I tended to the horses and looked after the wagon. That salt water was hard on axles and wheels. Took a heap of cleaning and fresh grease to keep the wagon sound.

Weren't all work, though. Sunday afternoons we'd wade the shallows netting blue crabs to boil, or gathering up bucketfuls of oysters and scallops. Jeff started a collection of shells that caught his fancy. Some nights when we weren't too tuckered we'd grab a lantern and go floundering with gigs I bought at the general store. Other nights we just lazed around our shack, reading, writing letters home, mending clothes or whatnot.

It was on one such night in mid-July that everthing changed. The day had been hot and muggy and thunder rumbled across the bay all afternoon. After supper, me and Jefferson walked over to where the Morgans was tethered in a little clearing a short piece behind our shack. The wind had picked up considerable and the air was cool. The black sky rolled with thunder and here and there lightning lit up the clouds.

I handed Jefferson the lantern. "Make sure them stakes is tight in the ground," I told him. "Don't like the looks of this storm. I'm going to hobble the horses lest they get spooked and try to bolt." I done one horse with no trouble, but a flash of lightning set the other to stomping and rearing his head before I could get his second leg bound. "Hold him still so I can get this hobble tied," I said to Jeff.

Jefferson set down the lantern and wrapped his big arms around the Morgan's neck. "Whoa, be easy," he whispered to the horse, "it just some ol' thunder. Ain't goan hurt you none."

With Jefferson's help I soon had the other Morgan hobbled. I picked up the lantern and we headed back towards our shack. Two loud claps of thunder shook the sky, one after the other.

"We best hurry," I said. Before them words was out of my mouth I heard screeching like a panther. Then a loud *boom!* shook the camp. Another come right behind, lighting up the night.

Jefferson grabbed my arm. He was shaking all over. "L-Lawd a'mercy Eli. Ain't never seed no lightnin' like that!"

Another boom and screech cut through the dark. I seen a flash this time, coming from out in the bay. "That ain't lightning, Jeff," I said as the church bell went to clanging. "It's a Yankee gunboat!"

NINETEEN

TURNS OUT ALL THE BELL ringing was a signal to the Confederates thereabouts that the Yankees was raiding. I'd wondered how come they never rung it for Sunday services. Didn't wonder no more.

Shortly after the shelling started, a passel of Captain Anderson's men come busting through camp. They spread out up and down the shoreline. Unlimbered two cannons they brung with 'em and returned fire. Me and Jefferson hightailed it to a gully near our shack and watched the fireworks from there. It was some show, sonny. Anderson's boys swapped fire with the Yanks for the best part of a hour. A landing party might've come ashore because muskets and pistols went to raising Cain west of camp.

It's a fortunate thing me and Jefferson had built our own shack because one of them Yankee shells landed on the slave barracks and set it afire. Heard some poor fellers screaming and goose bumps went to crawling all over me.

Finally the Yankee gunboat give it up and chugged on down the bay. Me and Jefferson stayed put and watched the barracks burn long after the ruckus give out. Wondered what all harm might've come to our side, but what's done is done. I weren't about to go gallivanting around camp in the dark to find out. But Big John Anderson's saltworks had been found out, that's a fact.

At daylight a storm come in off the gulf. We hunkered down in our shack to wait it out. Thunder went to cracking and Jefferson went to shaking, thinking the Yankees was on us again. Took some hard talking to convince him it was only nature raising hell. It rained a gullywasher for a hour or so. The wind blowed down a couple of trees, but our shack held together and kept us dry.

After the storm let up, I sent Jefferson to fetch our breakfast and noon rations while I got the team harnessed and hitched to the wagon. Just finished hooking the short rein between the bits when I heard rustling behind me. Looked over my shoulder and seen Boss Miller walking up. I never was one to fault a body for his looks, mind you, but Boss Miller was some ugly, inside and out. Which is how come I remember him so after all this time. Looked more like a boar hog than a human. I ought not say such, because I like pigs. But the truth is the truth. He had these squinty little eyes and a pug nose and fat jowls that jiggled with ever little move. His ears was pointed and stuck out from his bald head. What few teeth he owned was all brown and rotted.

"We got niggers to bury," Boss told me, digging at his crotch like he had fleas. Quit his scratching long enough to pull a plug of tobacco out of his breeches pocket. "Them goddamn Yankees kilt four of Mister Anderson's slaves last night."

"That so?" I said, watching him bite off a big chaw. "I'm sorry to hear it."

"Hell, they was just no-account niggers." Boss run a thumb under one suspender strap and went to scratching again. "Bunch of others took to the woods. Hear tell Anderson's boy has got patrols out hunting. Might take a day or two but we'll get 'em back."

Heartless scoundrel. Four poor fellers dead and he acted like it weren't nothing but dead skunks or such. I had a mind to beat some more ugly into that face of his.

"You off water detail for now," Boss went on before I could find my tongue. "Need your wagon to haul them dead niggers up to the graveyard. When you done hitching your team, pull over by the slave quarters. Got 'em laid out yonder."

Now I didn't much cotton to playing undertaker, sonny. Fact is, the dead spooked me a mite. Didn't even want to look at my own daddy when he was laid out, but Mama went and made me. I grabbed the reins from the wagon bed and snapped one end to near Morgan's outer bit ring, said, "Well, Boss, I didn't sign on to dig no graves."

Boss Miller squinted them beady little eyes till they was near shut. Then he busted out laughing, his jowls a'shaking. "Hell boy, with all the darkies 'round here you think I'd let a white man plant a nigger? Hell no, let 'em bury they own. They's slaves with shovels waiting. Be quick now, 'fore the sun gets up. Ain't nothing stinks worser'n a dead nigger been laying in the heat too long."

The cemetery sat on a little hill a quarter mile inland from the salt camp. Seemed a right peaceful place for eternal rest. Birds was singing, and a steady breeze off the bay kept the morning heat tolerable. All the pines on the hill had been cut down but there was enough scrub oak and hickory and such scattered about to find shade.

The nigra section was off by itself on the backside, maybe eight graves in all, marked with cedar shakes head and foot. Some had seashells and bits of colored glass scattered on top. I sat on the wagon in the shade of a hickory and watched while Jeff and three of Mister Anderson's slaves dug the graves. A sad bunch, them grave diggers was. Soon as they started digging they went to singing:

"Now if you should get there befo' I do, God's goan trouble de water; Tell all my friends I's comin' too, God's goan trouble de water."

Jefferson liked to drove me crazy singing that song the next few weeks. Reckon that's how come I still remember it after all these years.

I kept my shotgun propped agin the wagon seat for show. Boss Miller had give Anderson's slaves a stern talking to about running off. Said I had orders to shoot 'em dead if they so much as twitched a toe towards the woods. He might just as soon saved his hot air. If one of them slaves took a mind to hightail it out of there, so be it. Boss Miller could go hang his sorry self.

Nearby under a magnolia, the four dead nigras laid side by side, wrapped head to toe in blankets. They had been in full shade when the digging started, but now one of the bodies and most of another was in the sun. Thought about dragging 'em back into the shade, but I seen Jeff and the others was shoulder-deep by then and almost done.

Old Preacher Jubal was stretched out in the shade of the wagon, snoring away. On the ride out he told me he had belonged to Anderson's family for three generations. Claimed to be a hundred and two years old. With all them wrinkles and that cotton patch hair, I didn't doubt he was ever bit that or even more.

Made the mistake of calling him "Reverend" Jubal once, and he was quick to set me straight for it. "Ain't nothin' *reverend* 'bout me or nary other sinner," the old man told me. "The Good Book say, 'Holy and reverend be *His* name,' meanin' the Lawd our God Hisself and Hisself only."

Preacher Jubal was feeble of body but still strong of voice. Sunday mornings his "amens" and "hallelujahs" rang out all over the salt camp. Jefferson dern near worshiped that old man, just loved listening to his fire and brimstone sermons. "He a real man of God fo' sure, Preacher Jubal is," Jefferson would tell me after he come back from church. "He say we goan walk on streets of gold someday, them what loves the Lawd. Say them what wicked in they way's goan burn in everlastin' lake full of fire. 'Magine that Eli. Oh Lawd, 'magine that."

When the graves was ready, I shook old Jubal awake. He put on his black frock coat and hat while Jefferson and the other grave diggers helped theirselves to the water bucket. They rested in the shade for a spell, then toted the bodies over to the graves and lowered 'em in the ground.

We gathered at graveside for the service. Preacher Jubal opened his dogeared Bible and spouted near ten minutes worth of Scripture. Cain't say whether he was reading or reciting, but them words rolled out of his mouth right smooth. Tears cut muddy streams down the slaves' dusty faces. Right touching, it was. Come dern near to crying my own self.

When Jubal was done he closed the Good Book and prayed for another five minutes or so. After a chorus of "amens," the old preacher led the others in singing some hymn I never heard before. Best I recollect, it went something like this:

"There is a balm in Gilead, to make the wounded whole; There is a balm in Gilead, to heal the sin-sick soul," or some such. Jeff sung right along, knowed ever word. That boy could be right smart at times if he set his mind to it.

Finally old Jubal seemed satisfied that he'd done his heavenly duty. He moseyed on back to the wagon and rested while Jefferson and Mister Anderson's nigras filled in the graves.

———•———

The camp was swarming like a beehive when we got back from the burying detail. Workers was busy tearing down the smaller salt furnaces and stacking the kettles and lumber onto wagons. At the storehouses, other wagons was being loaded with barrels of salt. I dropped Jubal and Mister Anderson's other slaves off at the mess hall, then me and Jeff headed on towards our shack.

When I drove by Anderson's office, he stepped outside and signaled for me to stop. He walked over to the wagon, chomping a unlit cigar like usual. "The Federals are raiding the coast from West Bay to St. Joseph, Malburn," he told me. "I got two thousand bushels to move by sundown."

"Do tell?" I said. "Well, I reckon my team can handle six barrels a load."

"Your Morgans can handle ten easy. You won't have to push 'em far, half-mile at most. We're hiding the salt inland till them damn Yankees settle down. Then we'll worry about moving it on north."

"You shutting down the operation?" I wondered if I was fixing to be shed of a job.

Anderson took the cigar out of his mouth and grunted, said, "Hell no, just spreading things around some. There's too much money to be made." Then he made a face like he was sucking a lemon. "Besides, our brave boys up north need this salt. Can't feed an army without salt, you know."

That was a fact. The Yankee blockade had dern near shut down goods being imported into the Confederacy, salt included. What little the blockade runners did manage to sneak through was way pricey. Without the salt that Anderson and others was making, there weren't no way to cure the pork and beef to feed our army. Still, I figured Big John Anderson was a heap more concerned with keeping his own pockets full than our soldiers' bellies. "Yes, sir," I said, "but what about the Yankees? I don't much cotton to ducking cannonballs and bullets. Not for thirty dollars a month."

Anderson's face turned red. Pointed his cigar at me, a string of brown spit dripping off it. "Now see here you young whippersnapper, this ain't the time to be bucking for a raise. I need every wagon I can get. I got boilers to move, plus all that prime salt. We agreed on your wages."

"That we did, and I aim to keep my end of it, but I ain't working my horses to death for you or your salt. I'll haul six barrels a load and you'll get a full day's work out of me and my team."

Big John didn't argue, just told me to get the wagon on over to the storehouses and start moving salt.

For the rest of that afternoon and on into the night, me and Jefferson hauled salt inland to different hiding places Mister Anderson had set up. Made a dozen trips all told. Trails was easy for the most part and the footing good for the Morgans, so I upped the loads to eight barrels. A squad from Captain Anderson's command rode along as guides. Felt right safe with them guarding us. Being near a full moon, we had little trouble following the trails even without torches to light the way.

Long about midnight the job was done. Anderson's salt was hid here and yonder, and the Yankees would have theirselves a time trying to find it. Back at camp me and Jefferson seen to the horses, then went straight to bed. Didn't even bother eating, we was so tuckered.

Next morning at first light Mister Anderson set crews to work building small furnaces up and down the coast. Hammers and axes went to drumming all through the woods thereabouts. They was hid good too, mostly in live oak groves. Unless the Yankees come ashore they'd have a heap of trouble spotting 'em from the bay.

At breakfast Boss Miller come by my table and told me to rest the team a few more hours then report for water hauling after the noon meal. Mister Anderson had already put the eight big furnaces back into operation. They was too big to try to move, Boss said. They'd keep 'em going till the Yankees destroyed 'em or give up the war, whichever come first. Meanwhile, most of the salt making would be done at the new furnaces scattered around the bay.

For the rest of the summer, me and Jefferson went back to our old job hauling seawater to the big furnaces. The Yankees didn't raise no more ruckus in them parts and things soon settled down. It was right dull work, but at the time it beat farming, which was all I'd ever knowed.

We kept busy crabbing and fishing and such in our spare time. Even managed to sell some of our catch to them that was too busy or lazy to fish for theirselves. Made sure I done all the haggling for our seafood business, lest goodhearted Jeff give away our profits.

Jefferson kept on with his regular churchgoing. Took to singing hymns all day long that he learnt from Old Jubal. He also struck up a right close friendship with Nebo, one of Mister Anderson's slaves that had helped with the grave-digging detail. Come to find out Nebo was Preacher Jubal's great–great-grandson. Old Jubal was grooming Nebo in the ways of the Lord so he could take over when the old preacher finally give up the ghost and passed on to his Heavenly reward.

Before I knowed it, summer was over. By early October the weather cooled off right nice. Things was going smooth as a shoat's belly the morning Big John Anderson sent word for me to come to his office. "You are a bullheaded young man, Malburn," he told me, "but you're a hard worker and I like your grit. I'm putting you on the Marianna run."

I walked out of Anderson's office grinning like a egg-sucking possum. I was being trusted to deliver salt inland to Marianna. The job paid ten dollars more a month too. Felt right proud of myself. I was sixteen years old now, and knowed it all. Had the world by the short hairs. Been on my own the whole summer, working hard, earning a fair wage, taking good care of Jefferson and the team. Yes, sir, I felt right proud.

Know what the Bible says about pride, sonny? I'll tell you. "Pride goeth before destruction, and a haughty spirit before a fall." It's right there in Proverbs, chapter sixteen verse eighteen. Look it up if you a mind to. Yes, sir, the Good Book says them that's proud and haughty is headed for a fall. That's a fact. And I was headed for a big one.

TWENTY

NEXT MORNING WE SET OUT at daylight from the saltworks with five other wagons and a squad of Captain Anderson's men riding guard. Being as I was new to the job, my rig was last in line. Didn't think much of it till the dew burnt off and the dust kicked up. By noon, me and Jefferson had eat so much dust we was dern near the same color.

Took three days of hard pushing to reach Marianna. Nowadays you can make the same trip in that motorcar of yours in two hours or so. Time sure has changed things, sonny, that's a fact. Late the first day we made the old Marianna-St. Andrew road. Weren't much of a road in them days, but the footing was sound and the teams fared well. A ways inland the flat piney woods give way to rolling hills covered with hardwoods. The weather was right pleasant. There was a cool breeze out of the north, and along the creek bottoms leaves had started showing their fall colors. Best thing was there weren't no signs of Yankees anywheres about.

We kept to the main road for the next two days. The guards was right busy riding off here and there looking for signs of bushwhackers or Yankees. When our train was a couple of miles west of Marianna, we turned onto a narrow pig trail that run roughly northeast through some of the thickest woods you ever did see. A greased boar hog couldn't root through them brambles growing on either side. The trail, such as it was, snaked downhill the last quarter mile or so. Got so steep I had to rein back on the Morgans and work the brake hard to slow the wagon. Finally we come to a flat clearing beside the Chipola River. That was the end of the line for my first and last salt run, sonny.

I no sooner pulled the team to a halt before a passel of workers come out of the woods and went to unloading the wagons. They made quick work of it too, sliding the barrels down skids, then rolling 'em into caves nearby. You'd never knowed them caves was there, they was hid so well in the ravines alongside the river. Later on, the barrels would be loaded onto big freight wagons and hauled on north to River Junction up by the Georgia border where the Flint and Chattahoochee rivers run together to form the Apalachicola. From there steamboats would ferry the salt upriver to Columbus.

After our wagon was unloaded we unhitched the Morgans and staked 'em out near the riverbank to browse and rest a spell. It was a mite chilly, but me and Jeff stripped down and took us a dip in the Chipola to wash off that trail dust. Once we was scrubbed clean we stretched out in what little sunlight snuck through the trees and ate our dinner of smoked mullet and cornbread. Then we hitched the team and headed back up the trail for Marianna.

Mister Anderson had give each of us drivers a list of supplies to haul back, so once our salt was delivered we split up and it was ever man for hisself. If the Yankees was to stop us on our return trip, why, we was just hauling lumber and flour and such back to the family farm at Econfina. The Morgans was right frisky when we headed out, having got shed of the heavy load they'd been pulling the last three days. They dern near trotted up that pig trail like it was flatlands. We come to the main road and turned east. Made town in less than a hour.

I'd been to Marianna with my daddy a few times, but it was Jefferson's first trip. As we drove into town he dern near got a crick in his neck gawking at all the fine, highfalutin homes and buildings lining the streets. To Jeff, the salt camp was a big city, so this must've seemed like something straight out of a fairy tale. He pointed towards one particular grand two-story house with tall columns and fancy porches. I still recollect his very words.

"Lawd, looky yonder. It like the heavenly mansion Preacher Jubal say Jesus goan make fo' them what believes in Him."

"Do tell?" I said. Then I decided to have myself a little fun. "Why, Jeff, I do believe that there could be the very one. Look yonder at the sign." I pointed towards a street post on the corner that was marked with crisscross signs: *Jefferson* and *LaFayette*.

Now Jefferson had learnt enough words through the years to recognize his own name when he seen it. His jaw dropped open and his eyes growed wide as Mama's fancy china saucers. He leaned over, whispered, "You reckon? Fo' sure?"

I nodded, trying my best to keep a straight face. "Reckon so. Signs don't lie."

Jeff hunched up stiff as a starched collar and stared straight ahead as we rode on past the house. Ever now and then he snuck a quick peek back towards his heavenly home like he was afraid he'd turn into a pillar of salt if he chanced to stare too long. When we was finally out of sight of the house he let loose a long whistle, said, "Lawd, Eli, 'magine that. 'Magine that."

Mister Anderson had give me and Jefferson permission to visit our folks for a few days before returning to the saltworks. We'd been gone some five months and Jeff had took to moping lately, which weren't like him at all. The salt camp had been right exciting, but I knowed he missed his folks and the farm. Fact is, even though I thought I was all growed up at the time I was a touch homesick myself. So we left Marianna and set out for home. Only took us a day and a half as I recollect. The load of supplies for the camp weren't near heavy as the salt we'd hauled up, so we made good time.

When we crossed the bridge over Moccasin Creek and started up the steep hill it felt like we was home. Through the trees I could see the mill Mister Lucas Porter had built years before. Folks from all over the Econfina Valley hauled their corn to the mill for grinding. Thought about stopping by to pay my regards, catch up on any news the Porters might have about their son Joe and the other boys fighting up north, but decided agin it. I was chomping at the bit to get on home.

Passing the mill reminded me it weren't but a couple of years back when me and Hamp Watts and Annie Gainer had gone swimming together for the last time in the mill pond back of the spillway. Took a heap of coaxing to get Annie in the water that day, even though she'd swam with us a hundred times before. That was around the time Annie first took a shine to my brother, mind you. We finally sweet-talked her into it, but she made me and Hamp swear we wouldn't breathe a word to nobody. Reckon Annie figured she was too growed up to be mixing with the likes of us. Fact is, she was and we all knowed it.

Me and Hamp closed our eyes while she stripped down to her unmentionables and waded in up to her neck, but I couldn't help sneaking myself a little peek. Ooh, she was some sight, sonny. Annie had sure enough sprouted into womanhood. Couldn't shake that heavenly vision out of my mind. Fact is, I didn't try to. Dreamt about it for weeks afterwards. Shames me to this day I done such, but seems the Devil had me by the short hairs back then.

The Morgans dern near broke into a gallop once we topped the hill and passed by Porter's Cemetery. Acted like they smelt the homeplace though we was still a good four miles out. I had to rein 'em back. They'd been worked hard lately and weren't no sense chancing having one pull up lame now. Reckon they was as eager to get home as we was.

Jeff had been singing up a storm since he woke up that morning. It weren't at all unusual for him to be singing, but he'd been spouting them hymns one after the other till my ears was dern near played out. "Jeff," I said, "you done sung up a whole month of Sundays. You best save some for later."

He just looked at me and grinned, said, "Cain't he'p it, Eli. I goan see Mama and Daddy today. They's joy in my heart and it gots to come out else I bust wide open." And went right back to singing.

Well now, how could I argue with that? Fact is, I was feeling right chipper my own self. It was as purty a October day as God ever made, and we was almost home. Had money in my pockets, and now that I was a man of some means I intended to woo sweet Annabelle Gainer away from brother Daniel.

Yes, sir, dern near felt like singing myself if I could've carried a tune.

TWENTY ★ ONE

WHEN MAMA STEPPED OUT ON the porch to hug me home I knowed right off something was wrong. The sparkle was gone from her eyes. Bad news was wrote in ever wrinkle. A chill run through my belly. Thought for sure some Yankee had done sent Daniel to meet his Maker. When she told me, no, it was Hamp, I felt woozy and dern near passed out. Set down on the steps to catch my wits. I was mighty relieved Daniel was safe mind you, but at the same time I grieved something fierce over Hamp. His death spoilt my homecoming. All the joy, all my highfalutin plans, was snuffed out.

Next day Annie come by for a visit. She looked different, all gussied up and ladylike, nothing like the pigtailed tomboy me and Hamp had palled around with since we was scarce tall as cypress knees. We sat in the shade behind the barn, hugged and cried a spell, comforting each other and recalling the good times the three of us had shared and such.

Next thing I knowed we was kissing. Don't recollect who it was first kissed who, but it went on a spell and weren't neither one of us keen to stop. Finally did, though. Annie's face was all red, like she'd been working out in the sun all day without a bonnet. She touched her cheek and looked at me like I'd slapped her, then hightailed it for the house. Well, sonny, I ain't never had such a feeling in all my born days. My innards was all shaky like I was fierce hungry or some such. I was sorely ashamed for what I'd done, for ever thinking about stealing Annie away from Daniel. How could I have thought about doing such, what with him off fighting the Yankees? Annie loved my brother. They was betrothed and I was just going to have to bear it. Owning up to that fact sure didn't make it no easier, mind you. It was like swallowing a big dose of quinine, but I aimed to live with it best I could.

After Annie left I found my daddy's stash of corn liquor Mama kept around for medicinal purposes and went to drowning my sorrows. Staggered around like a no-account drunkard the next few days, guilt gnawing my innards. Couldn't eat, couldn't sleep. Couldn't shed my mind of Annie, and hated myself for it. Laid awake nights wondering how come I'd let Hamp go off to the war by hisself. Remembered how he'd tried talking me into going, how I'd told him no, I weren't having none of it. Way I figured, Hamp might be alive yet if I'd been there with him. Tried to recollect his face the last time I seen him when he rode off with Tom Gainer. Drawed a blank, and that shamed me even more. I was dern near low as a body could get. But I reckon the good Lord was watching over me. Finally passed out from all the whiskey. First I'd slept in days.

Know what I done when I come to, sonny? I'll tell you. Swore to God I'd leave the next day and deliver Mister Anderson's supplies to the salt camp. Then I'd up and join the Confederate Army and go fight alongside my brother and friends. Promised Hamp I'd kill myself a passel of damn Yankees to avenge what they done to him. Meant it too, sonny, ever word. That's a fact.

TWENTY ★ TWO

FIRST LIGHT NEXT MORNING I made ready to set out for the saltworks. It had turned a mite chilly overnight, with patches of frost here and there. The Morgans snorted clouds while I hitched 'em to the wagon. I was double-checking the load of supplies to make sure it was fast when Jefferson come moseying up. Looked at me like I'd slapped him upside the head. "You goan leave me home, Eli?"

I told him there weren't no sense in him coming, as I was just delivering Mister Anderson's supplies and I'd be back in four-five days at most. Well, sonny, Jeff dern near throwed a fit. We was partners, he said, and it weren't fair to leave him behind. Told me how his mama's eyes had lit up when he give her the fifty dollars I paid him for his share of the summer's work. Said I'd best let him come along, or he'd just saddle his daddy's mule and follow me anyways.

I seen a new spark in Jefferson's eyes that morning. He'd done a heap of growing up since we first left home to work at the salt camp. So I told him we was partners for sure, and if he wanted to come along it was just fine by me. And since we was partners, he'd best see to the water barrel and feed bags while I finished with the supplies.

When everthing was done we said our goodbyes to the folks. We climbed up on the wagon, then I whistled to the Morgans and flicked the reins. They stepped out right lively, like they was glad to be on the trail again. I knowed Jeff was. He hummed a tune while he ate one of the ham biscuits his mama packed for us. Didn't miss a note between bites neither.

Looking back, letting Jefferson come along was near the worst decision I ever made in this whole long life of mine, sonny. I regret it to this very day. But I weren't no prophet, mind you. What's done is done and there ain't no going back. That's a fact.

———◆———

Late the next afternoon we was still a good five miles from the camp when I seen smoke rising above the treetops and out over the bay on the north wind. Way more smoke than what should've been coming even from Mister Anderson's biggest furnaces. I pulled the team to a stop. "Something ain't right, Jeff," I said, pointing towards the smoke clouds.

Jefferson stared at the sky for a minute. "Reckon lightnin' done set the woods afire?"

Well now, that made sense. Told you he had a good head on his shoulders when he took a mind to, didn't I, sonny? A storm had blowed through during the night. Lit up the sky with lightning. Likely a tree got struck and started a woods fire. Weren't really the season for it, cool as it was, but it had been dry in these parts lately. "Why, Jeff, I do believe that's what happened." Felt better already. Figured things was just fine at the salt camp. We'd mosey on along and keep our eyes on the smoke in case it shifted towards us.

But believing something don't make it so, that's a fact. And when we come across a body two-three miles farther on, I knowed for sure things had gone to hell. It was a Confederate soldier, facedown in the trail. I jumped off the wagon to get a closer look. Flies went to swarming when I rolled him over. Dern near made me gag. I coughed and spit. Thought I recognized him as one of Captain Anderson's men, but couldn't come up with a name. Poor soul had been gut-shot. From the look on his face he must've suffered something fierce before he died. Figured he'd been dead a day or two. He was stiff but weren't swole up much. No buzzards or hogs or such had got to him yet. Stunk a mite though—the bullet had scrambled his innards.

Weren't no pistols or rifle to be found, though Captain Anderson's boys always packed heavy. I spied his horse down the trail a ways, browsing on gallberry bushes. I caught the little roan mare and tied her to the back of the wagon while Jefferson fetched the shovel. We took turns digging a proper grave under a magnolia alongside the trail.

It give me the willies to do it, but before we buried him I went through his pockets in case there was any letters or tintypes or such I might return to his family. Found a jackknife and a few two-dollar Confederate graynotes, but nothing that told me who he was.

After the burying I made a cross out of two pieces of dried oak and hammered it into the ground at the head of the grave. Set his slouch hat on the cross hoping somebody might come along and recognize it and know what become of him. Then Jefferson recited a few verses and sung a hymn and we went on our way.

I had a bad feeling I couldn't get shed of. Thought about turning the wagon around right then and there and hightailing for home. Don't know why I decided to go on to the salt camp. Sense of duty, I reckon. Had a wagonload of supplies belonging to Big John Anderson and I felt obliged to deliver the goods. I'd give my word. Couldn't stomach the thought of him taking me for a common thief. Well, sonny, doing what's right sometimes carries a steep price, that's a fact. And I was fixing to pay it.

We hadn't made another mile when I seen somebody coming up the trail, maybe fifty-sixty yards ahead. It was near dark and I couldn't see if he was armed or not. I handed Jeff the reins and fetched my shotgun from behind the seat. "Now, Jeff, just keep 'em moving steady. If I tell you to stop, hold 'em tight and set the brake hard." Weren't sure how the Morgans might cotton to a shotgun blasting over their heads. Didn't want 'em to bolt. Figured we could use the wagon for cover if things got hot.

Jeff give a quick nod and tightened his grip on the reins. When we got a mite closer I seen it was a tall skinny nigra stumbling towards us. A few seconds later Jeff grabbed my arm. "Lawd, Eli—it Nebo!"

He tossed the reins to me and jumped off the wagon and run towards his friend. Poor Nebo must've been some scared. He dropped to his knees and covered his head with his hands and went to begging, "He'p me, Lawd Jesus, don't let 'em beat me no mo'!"

Heard Jefferson tell him, "It me, Nebo, Jeff! Ain't nobody goan beat you."

Took a spell, but Jeff finally got Nebo calmed down. Poor soul had a bloody knot upside the head big as your fist. One eye was dern near swole shut and his lower lip was split open. He was powerful thirsty so we give him water, then I unpacked the liniment I kept for the Morgans and seen to his wounds.

I was itching to find out what had happened at the saltworks but figured we'd best make camp while there was still light. Found a clearing behind a thick stand of scrub oaks a ways off the trail. While Jefferson and Nebo pitched the tent I unsaddled the mare and unhitched the team and seen they was fed and watered. Then I tethered 'em along one end of the clearing.

Couldn't risk a fire, so our supper was venison jerky and whatever cornbread and fatback was left over from breakfast. Nebo ate like he ain't seen food in days. Between bites he told us what had happened at the saltworks.

Two days ago at dawn the Yankees struck from the north. Weren't no cannon fire to warn the camp this time. Way I figured, the Yankees must've come ashore some miles west, then marched northeast a ways before turning south. There was so many bluecoats, Nebo told us, that Captain Anderson's men never had a chance. They stood their ground for a while, but finally give it up and retreated. What workers and slaves was able hightailed with 'em.

Old Preacher Jubal was too feeble to run away, so Nebo stayed behind to look after him best he could. Them damn Yankees went to burning and looting the camp. Took pickaxes and sledgehammers to the boilers. Dumped and scattered ever bushel of salt they found in the warehouses. Poured coal oil inside the buildings and set 'em on fire. "Look like de fire 'n brimstone Granddaddy Jubal always be preachin' 'bout," was how Nebo told it.

Well, sonny, when them scoundrels went to set fire to the church, old Jubal weren't having none of it. He stood fast in the doorway, waving his old Bible and commenced spouting hellfire and damnation to them bluecoated devils. They tried to talk him out of the church but he told 'em he weren't leaving the Lord's house long as there was breath in his old body. Finally some officer give the order to "Get that old nigger out of there."

Jubal was so riled and full of the Holy Ghost it took three men to drag him outside. Nebo tried to stop 'em and got pistol-whipped for his trouble. Meanwhile, other Yankees torched the church. When the old preacher seen the smoke and flames he was madder than a pack of wet bobcats. Shook the Good Book in that officer's face and cried out for the Lord to rain down his holy wrath on ". . . these here bluecoated Philistines."

That's when some cowardly son of a bitch went and bashed in poor Jubal's head with a rifle butt. Last thing Nebo seen before passing out was his great-great-granddaddy laying flat on his back, eyes fixed on Heaven.

When he come to, the camp was deserted. Poor Jubal was dead. Nebo feared the Yankees might come back, so he took to the woods. Been wandering around lost and half out of his head ever since, till we found him.

Well, sonny, much as I hated it I knowed what had to be done. Couldn't blame Nebo for running off and leaving old Jubal laying there, seeing what the Yankees done to him. But somebody had to see Jubal got a Christian burial, and I reckoned that somebody was me.

Hardly slept a wink that night. Woke up at sunrise and checked the sky. The fire had died out during the night, but the wind had shifted and the smell of burnt woods was right strong. We broke camp without bothering to fix breakfast. Fact is, knowing what was coming I weren't the least bit hungry. But Jeff and Nebo ate the last of the jerky and shared a apple.

Nobody said much as we rode along. Nebo's head was aching and Jeff was grieving for Preacher Jubal and weren't in no mood to sing. The cold spell that come through earlier had played out. By midmorning it went from warm to hot. It pained me to think what this heat was doing to Preacher Jubal's body. Tried to put it out of my mind but it kept coming back.

A hour or so later we turned onto the pig trail that led south through the piney woods to the salt camp. Closer we got, the more the woods was scorched. My eyes went to watering and my throat was raw from the smoke and dust the Morgans kicked up. Saplings and palmetto bushes looked like burnt skeletons. Thought I heard a hawk calling and looked up. Didn't see no hawk, but a flock of buzzards was circling high.

When we come to the outskirts of the camp I stopped the wagon near where our shack had stood. It was burnt to ash. I told Jefferson and Nebo to stay with the team while I looked things over. Had the good sense to carry my shotgun and slicker with me.

The camp was ruint, sonny, worse than I'd reckoned from what Nebo told us. Ever building had dern near burnt to the ground. All the boilers was punched full of holes, their brick foundations busted to rubble. Salt was scattered everwheres, tramped underfoot by horses and soldiers. Here and there smoke rose up from the bare earth like it come from the very pits of Hell. Place smelt like death itself.

I heard a grunt and looked towards where Mister Anderson's office had stood. My belly heaved and the bile rose up my throat when I seen a big wild boar rooting the innards of a burnt body. I hollered, but weren't sure if any sound come out or not. The hog pulled his bloody snout out of the poor soul's belly and looked my way, then went back to feeding like I weren't no mind at all.

I raised the shotgun to my shoulder and cut loose with one barrel. The boar squealed and run off a ways, then stopped and snapped his tusks at me. I cocked back the other hammer and run towards him hoping to scare him off. That old hog weren't having none of it. He grunted and charged. Them tusks looked big as Bowie knives and sharp to boot. Weren't no trees or such to be had so I steadied myself and took aim. Only had one chance so I held my fire till he was maybe fifteen-twenty foot away. Couldn't miss from that range, sonny. The load of buckshot caught him square in the head. He turned a flip and fell in a heap of smoke and dust. His hind legs went to kicking, then he snorted blood and died.

Jefferson and Nebo come running up. I hollered at 'em to

get on back to the wagon and mind the horses like I told 'em. Didn't want them seeing or smelling what that hog had been up to. Figured poor old Jubal might've suffered the same or worse. Them boys sure didn't need no part of that.

I reloaded the shotgun and headed for the church, dreading ever step I took. The church had been done in like ever other building in the camp. Only thing left standing was the stone pilings. Seen the bell on its side amongst the ruins. I stopped in my tracks and my innards went all cold when I seen a flock of buzzards on the far side of the church. I run at 'em, waving the shotgun over my head, and they scattered. Two-three took off, the rest lifted their wings and hopped away.

If I had eat any breakfast I'd've lost it right then and there, sonny. I bent over and threwed up what little bile was left in my belly. Weren't for his clothes I wouldn't have recognized poor Jubal. He was swole up something fierce. His frock coat was open. Vest buttons looked like they was fixing to pop off. The buzzards had eat most of the flesh off his face and hands.

Soon as I quit retching I covered the old preacher head to toe with my slicker. Held my breath and tucked the ends under best I could. Then I walked back to the wagon to fetch rope and a blanket to finish the job.

———————

We laid Jubal to rest in the shade of a cedar tree not far from where we'd buried Mister Anderson's slaves a couple of months before. I'll spare you the sad details, sonny, except to say if Jubal was looking down on us he'd been right proud of his great-great-grandson. Nebo opened Jubal's Bible—which we'd found laying near his body—and preached as fine a sermon as ears ever heard. Weren't a dry eye to be had.

I borrowed one of Mister Anderson's boards from the load in the wagon and used my ax to cut a grave marker. Carved Jubal's name and the year in it with my jackknife. Weren't much, but it would have to do. The three of us promised we'd see to it the old preacher got a fitting headstone when times was better. Took quite a spell sonny, but I kept that promise. It's there yet, if you a mind to go see.

There was still two-three hours of light left so we set out for home. I wanted to get away from that place quick as I could. If we pushed hard and burnt ever bit of daylight I figured we could make the farm by day after tomorrow. For the first time in months I didn't feel much growed up. Fact is, I was played out and homesick to boot. Knowed I'd just been home, but things seemed different now. Couldn't wait to see the family and the farm. My salt making days was done. I'd had myself a bellyful of dead bodies and burials and such.

I planned to get in touch with Mister Anderson when things settled down a mite. Way things had worked out, I figured there weren't no rush to return Nebo and the supplies. I knowed Aunt Nettie and Uncle Nate would take Nebo in and treat him like he was their own flesh and blood. Him and Jefferson was dern near brothers now anyways.

As for me, well, I'd lost Hamp and Annie, maybe some of my innocence too. But things was looking a mite better. I'd be home soon. Figured I'd rest up a spell, then ride over to Chattahoochee and sign up. If things worked out I'd be with Daniel and the boys up near Chattanooga in a month or so. Last I heard they had the Yankees holed up thereabouts.

Yes, sir, I had things all planned out. Know what the Good Book says about man and his plans, sonny? I'll tell you. Proverbs twenty-seven, verse one: "Boast not thyself of tomorrow; for thou knowest not what a day may bring forth."

Them's sound words, that's a fact. I was fixing to learn it firsthand.

TWENTY ★ THREE

A LIGHT RAIN COME DOWN during the night. I stepped outside the tent at dawn to do my business and felt a cool wind blowing out of the north. Heard honking and looked up to see a flock of geese winging south through a red sky. Took that as a sure sign it would be a dandy day for traveling. I seen to the horses while Jeff and Nebo got a fire going. Planned to put a heap of miles behind us by dark, so we fried enough fatback and cornbread to see us through the day.

When breakfast was done I saddled the mare and kept a eye on Jeff while him and Nebo hitched the team. I'd put Jeff in charge of the wagon for the trip home, and he was strutting around like a barnyard rooster. He'd done a heap of growing up since we'd been out making our own way in the world.

It had rained enough to keep the dust down so I trailed along behind the wagon keeping a eye on things. Jeff done such a good job handling the team, I soon quit fretting and enjoyed the ride. That little roan was some fine filly, sonny. A touch on the skinny side but purty as she could be. Well broke too, young as she was. Minded the slightest touch of rein or knee. The one time I coaxed her to a gallop it felt like I was sitting in a rocking chair, her gait was so smooth.

By noon we'd made a good seven-eight miles. Didn't want to push the Morgans too hard with their load, so I give the mare a nudge and we trotted on ahead to look for a place to rest a spell. Ten-fifteen minutes later I come to the first of two shallow creeks we had to ford. Figured this would be as good a place as any to stop. I walked the mare to midstream where it was about knee-deep to let her get a drink before we headed back to the wagon. Of a sudden she raised her head and snorted. Two men come riding out of the trees on the far bank. When they cleared the shadows I seen they was wearing Yankee blue and packing iron. Both was mounted on fine bays.

They had me by the short hairs, sonny. I'd left the shotgun with the wagon. Not that I would've used it, mind you. Didn't have no crow to pluck with them. Just wanted to get home. I patted the mare's neck, whispered, "Well, this is a fine howdy-do I done got us into." She tossed her head and whinnied like she weren't arguing the fact.

When the Yankees reached the creek I said, "Halloo," and sized 'em up, wondering what I was in for. The lead rider had a bulldog face and was built like a whiskey barrel. The other was a rail, but just as ornery looking. Decided I'd best play ignorant. Worked up a grin and said, "You boys lost? Ain't seen you in these parts before."

They weren't in no neighborly mood. The stout one, who I seen was a sergeant from the stripes on his sleeves, pointed at me, said, "He look like secesh to you, Jacob?"

Jacob the Rail pulled up alongside his partner, one cheek bulging and eyes squinting at me from underneath his kepi. He let fly a stream of tobacco juice towards me. I watched it splatter in the creek and wash downstream. "That horse is," he said. "I can smell Rebel stink from where I sit. Bet a month's pay on it."

Well now, I'd looked that mare over good, head to hoof. Weren't nothing about her seemed the least bit military—saddle, tack, or whatnot. Figured the poor soldier me and Jefferson buried had outfitted hisself from home best he could like most Confederate cavalry done in them days. Way I seen it, this Yankee was trying to bluff me. I had dealt myself a poor hand, but I reckoned I'd best call. "That so?" I reached down and patted the mare's neck again. "Just how much they pay you boys for soldiering? Hate to be taking your hard-earned money, but this mare belongs to me."

From the scowl on his face Jacob didn't take too kindly to my words. The sergeant neither. He spurred his horse and rode up beside me, eyeballing things real close. I held steady while he circled me. He stopped when he come around to my other side. Waited there a minute scratching at his scruffy whiskers, then said, "He's not armed, Jacob. What do you make of that?"

The rail crossed one of his long legs over the pommel of his saddle, tongued the chaw to his other cheek. "Horse thief . . . deserter. Maybe both," he said, and spit again.

Things was getting a mite uneasy, sonny. I'd heard tell they shot deserters and strung up horse thieves. And this Jacob feller seemed like he'd be right pleased to oblige me with a pistol ball or a tight noose or both. I didn't much fancy either fate, so I said to the sergeant, "Look here, mister, I ain't no deserter or horse thief, and I ain't looking for trouble. I got a wagonload of supplies back down the trail a ways I'm taking to my mama's farm."

The sergeant's eyes lit up when he heard that. He looked over at the rail, then back to me. "Is that a fact . . . just who is driving your wagon?"

I seen now I was in a real pickle. Some months back Mister Lincoln had went and issued his proclamation to free all the slaves in the Confederate states. Course, we didn't pay it no never mind, being Jefferson Davis was our president and we was a separate country and such. But these Yankees might see things different. If they was to find out Jeff was my slave, weren't no telling what might happen. Decided I'd best bend the truth a touch. "Friend of mine, works for the family, and his helper," I said, which weren't the whole truth but it weren't no out-and-out lie neither. Hoped they'd take me at my word and be on their way. Should've knowed better.

The sergeant scratched his chin whiskers again, all the while staring at me. I could dern near feel his eyes burn through me. He said, "Jacob, go fetch the rest of the squad. We might could use some company when this young man's friends show up with that wagon."

The rail grunted like he was disappointed he didn't get to shoot me on the spot, then turned his horse and rode off. The sergeant told me to walk my horse out of the creek and dismount. I did what he said, him following along behind. I tied the mare to a tree and sat on a rock near the creek. The sergeant sat his horse, keeping one eye on me and the other on the trail. I tried sweet-talking him a spell, thinking maybe if I got on his good side he might let me be on my way, but he weren't having none of it. Told me I'd best shut my trap if I knowed what was good for me.

Jacob the Rail was back in fifteen minutes with a dozen or so more bluecoats. I seen then they was all armed with fancy carbines. About half of 'em dismounted and strung out along the bank. The others crossed the creek and disappeared into the woods on either side of the trail. I thought about the shotgun, hoped Jefferson wouldn't do nothing foolish.

Fifteen-twenty minutes later I heard a sound in the distance. I listened hard, straining to hear over the babbling creek. The noise got louder. It was Jeff and Nebo, singing one of them spirituals they liked so. A minute later the wagon come into sight heading towards the creek. I stood up and waved, hoping Jeff would see me and know I was all right before he seen any Yankees. But it weren't to be.

"Why, them's niggers!" Jacob the Rail shouted just as his comrades across the creek stepped out of the woods onto the trail.

Of a sudden I heard a scream. Seen Nebo jump off the wagon and hightail it into the woods. Jefferson was grabbing sky, and even from where I stood I could tell he was praying up a storm.

Then somebody hollered "Halt!" and a shot rung out.

TWENTY ★ FOUR

THINGS HAPPENED QUICK AS GREASED lightning then, sonny. The Morgans bolted and throwed Jefferson off the wagon. They come racing down the trail, ears laid back and eyes wild with fear, and hit the creek at a full gallop. One of the rear wheels struck a rock and the wagon bounced up and come down so hard it broke the axle. Back end of the wagon collapsed and drug along the creek bottom, dumping lumber and sacks of flour and cornmeal into the water. That slowed the team enough so I could grab ahold of a halter. Took some doing but I managed to dig my heels in and bring 'em to a halt.

During all this ruckus come more gunfire. Thought for sure them damn Yankees had went and shot poor Nebo, maybe Jeff too. Finally got the Morgans calmed down enough to chance a look back down the trail. I was mighty relieved when I seen Jeff still standing there with his hands over his head, that's a fact. Felt even better when Nebo come walking out of the woods a minute later with his hands up and a couple of Yankee carbines pointing at his back.

They marched Jefferson and Nebo at gunpoint down the trail and across the creek. One of the guards ordered 'em to sit agin the bank and warned 'em not to move or else. Sergeant Bullard—I'd heard another Yankee call him such by then—rode up and told me to hand over the team to one of his men. "Now get over there with the darkies," he said. Looked a touch less friendly than he did before this fracas started, so I figured I'd best do what I was told and be quick about it.

Nebo was sitting hunched over with his legs crossed and his head down. Weren't sure if he was praying or just done give out in body and spirit. Jefferson was shaking like he had the palsy, his face the color of cold wood ash. When I sat down beside him he looked at me with them big sad eyes, said, "Is they goan shoot us?"

I looked up at the two young fellers guarding us. They weren't paying us much mind, half-standing, half-leaning on their rifles. Fact is, they seemed right bored with the whole affair. I knowed Jeff was some scared so I worked up a grin. "Reckon not, Jeff." I pointed across the creek. "If them boys wanted you shot seems they would've done it over yonder." That seemed to comfort him a mite. I lowered my voice, said, "Unless one of them Yankees asks you something direct, you and Nebo let me do the talking, hear? Don't do nothing or say nothing to rile 'em. I'll do what I can to get us out of this fix."

Another hour or so passed during which time the Yankees collected what sacks of flour and meal and such weren't ruint when the load spilt into the creek. I heard sawing and hammering coming from up the trail a piece. A spell later here come the Morgans, pulling the wagon which now was a two-wheeled cart. A work party went to stacking the cart high with sacks and lumber. When it was loaded I watched the Morgans haul that cart on up the trail till they was out of sight. Didn't know it then, sonny, but that was the last time I ever laid eyes on them fine horses. Never had another such team in all these years. I miss 'em to this day.

Sergeant Bullard come over and told us to get on our feet. I stood up and brushed the sand off my breeches, wondering what was coming. Tried to look steady but my insides felt like thin ice. Couldn't get shed of what Jacob the Rail had said earlier about me being a horse thief or a deserter or both. Jefferson and Nebo looked like they was too scared to move so I told 'em to mind the good sergeant and get off their backsides, which they done.

Sergeant Bullard looked at me hard, then pointed at Nebo, who was standing behind me. "One of my men says he saw this darkie at the saltworks we destroyed a few days ago. Says he attacked a soldier who was trying to save an old nigger from a burning building."

I felt the ice in my belly start crawling up my throat. Knowed we was in some deep brine if I couldn't talk our way out of it. "That so? Why, he must be mistaken," I said, trying to sound convincing. "Nebo's been with me for more'n a week getting these supplies over by Eucheeanna. Jeff here too."

The sergeant turned and called out to some feller I'd seen skulking about a while, eyeballing the three of us from a ways off. When he come over, Bullard pointed at Nebo, said, "Private Simms, are you sure this is the darkie you saw at the saltworks?"

The feller stepped a touch closer to look at Nebo. Said, "It's him, Sergeant. This nigger's the one that attacked Corporal Hines. Hell, I ought to know. I whopped him upside the head myself."

Well, sonny, I had to come up with something quick or we was goners. "That ain't so," I said. "One of the horses kicked him the other day when he was digging a rock out of its hoof."

Sergeant Bullard looked at me, then his man, and back at me. "Will you swear to it, Simms?" he said, all the while keeping his eyes locked on mine.

"It's him, Sergeant," Simms said. "I swear it on my dear ma's grave."

Bullard grunted, then said to the guards, "I'm placing this man in custody for suspicion of harboring slaves and aiding the enemy. See to it him and these contrabands don't escape."

Next thing I knowed some other bluecoats come walking up toting rope. For a minute I thought they meant to string us up and I dern near shat my breeches. Turns out they tied our hands behind our backs, then strung a longer rope around our waists so there was maybe five foot between us when we walked single file. Reckon they figured it would be a heap more trouble with us hitched together if we tried to hightail it.

For the rest of that day and the next two, they marched us west. Kept to the piney woods and palmettos for the most part, but there was seagulls flying here and there, so I knowed we weren't far from the coast. Tried talking to the guards now and again to pass the time. Figured I might get wind of where we was headed and what they intended to do with us. But Sergeant Bullard didn't much cotton to me jabbering with his boys. Said I'd best hold my tongue or he'd have me gagged.

Twice a day they untied our hands so we could eat and answer nature's call if we had to. I never was a real modest soul, mind you, but the three of us standing there trying to make water or worse in sight of all them Yankees weren't much fun, if you get my drift. Come night they tied our feet too, even though there was two soldiers guarding us at all times. The sand gnats and skeeters dern near eat us alive being as our hands weren't free to swat 'em away. It was some miserable, that's a fact. Hated myself all over again for letting Jefferson come with me to deliver Mister Anderson's supplies. My sense of duty or honor or whatnot had landed us in deep stew and there weren't nobody to blame for it but me.

The third morning we turned south. After a ways I seen a big Yankee camp in the distance near the shore of what I took to be West Bay, being we'd been traveling westward a fair piece. A passel of soldiers was meandering amongst the tents, tending cook fires and cleaning weapons and such. Others was marching in formation up and down the beach. They looked right smart going through their drills, all lined up in a tight column of fours, stepping together like a long blue caterpillar.

We followed a path through sand dunes and saw grass that led towards the camp. It was Jeff who noticed first. He looked back over his shoulder at me, said, "Eli, them soldiers what's marchin'. They's colored!"

I squinted my eyes agin the sunlight glaring off the water and took a closer look. Jeff was right. Except for the officer marching alongside the column waving his sword around and spouting out commands, them Yankees was all nigras. Never thought I'd ever see such a sight. A army of nigras. Didn't quite know what to make of it so I said, "Do tell. I never heard of such, but you're right, Jeff. They're sure enough colored."

I'm not sure if Jeff heard me, because he was busy pointing out his discovery to Nebo. Them two jabbered back and forth until we was well inside the camp. Then Sergeant Bullard come riding up and told the guards to untie the hitching rope from around us. When that was done he ordered one guard to march Jefferson and Nebo off to some other part of the camp.

When Jeff heard that he looked at me with them wide eyes and his chin went to quivering. I seen he was scared so I worked up a grin. "You and Nebo go on and mind what they tell you. I'll be along soon as I get this mess straightened out."

Fact is, I was a mite scared myself as I watched 'em walk off, but I didn't let on. You see, sonny, I was ever bit mad as I was scared. When they was out of earshot I looked up at Sergeant Bullard, sitting on his horse staring after 'em. "Just what is going on here, Sergeant? For three days you've kept me and them boys tied up like some ornery mule team, marching us all over hell and creation. I ain't harboring no slaves like you said, and I ain't no Confederate soldier. You done ruint my wagon and stole my horses and supplies. All I want is to—"

"You'll have your say soon enough, Malburn," Bullard said, stopping my little speech before it got good and started. Then he nudged his horse and moved on around a row of tents and out of sight, leaving the other guard and me staring at each other.

"Well ain't he a fine howdy-do," I said, mostly to myself.

"You best shut that smart trap of your'n, Reb," the guard said. He was a ugly cuss, maybe a head taller than me, with bad teeth and pimply skin to match. I reckoned him to be a year or two older than me, fresh off some dirt farm up north.

Well, sonny, I'd dern near had a craw full of damn Yankees and their cantankerous ways. I looked that feller in the eye, knowed I could whip him and any two like him. So I said, "Put down that rifle and untie my hands and let's see who shuts up who."

For a minute I thought he might just oblige me, then Sergeant Bullard come walking up with another Yankee who I took to be a officer from the sword hanging from his belt and the fancy yellow bars on his shoulders. He was a average size feller, but the blond curls dangling from under his kepi and a dandy waxed moustache made him stand out like a leghorn rooster in a flock of crows. Figured him to be in his mid-twenties or thereabouts. He looked me over a minute, said, "I am Captain

Edward Tracy, Company A, Second United States Colored Infantry. The contrabands in your possession have been placed under my immediate command."

Well, sonny, I was a mite confused, being he was ever bit as white as me and saying he was a captain in the colored infantry. And it was the second time I'd heard that highfalutin word, contrabands. Still didn't know what it meant and I told him so.

The captain looked at Sergeant Bullard like he expected a explanation for my ignorance. "The prisoner was informed of the charges against him at the time of his arrest, Captain," Bullard said. "Harboring runaway slaves and aiding the enemy."

That's when it come to me. "Contrabands? You mean Jefferson and Nebo? Why, Captain, they ain't runaways. They're both free men, work for my family up Econfina way." Which was a lie of course, but it was the best I could come up with at the time.

Captain Tracy looked down the front of his uniform and brushed away a speck of dust or some such, said, "I see. And can you produce papers showing they are free men of color?"

He had me there. Best I could do was try to bluff my way out. "Sure can. They're back at the farm in my daddy's desk. I can have 'em for you in two-three days if you loan me a horse." I nodded at Sergeant Bullard. "His men took my mare and team."

Bullard looked at the captain and shook his head. "The prisoner is lying, Captain. There's witnesses that'll swear to it, if you'll permit me, sir."

"Indeed?" Captain Tracy said. "Well, lead on Sergeant, lead on."

With that, the good sergeant motioned to the guard, who stuck the barrel of his carbine in my back to prod me along. We followed the sergeant and captain down a long row of tents, then turned and walked a fair piece down another row of the same till we come to a bigger tent with the United States flag and a couple of other banners flying over it. When we got there Sergeant Bullard told the guard to wait outside, then followed me and the captain through the open flap. Took my eyes a minute to adjust, but when they did I dern near fell over. Sitting next to a table grinning like a hog in slop was none other than Boss Miller hisself!

"Halloo, young Malburn," Boss said. His two lower teeth stuck out of his mouth like yellow tusks. "I hear tell you been hiding runaway niggers."

For the first time in a long while I was speechless, but Boss had sure enough found his tongue. "How did the run to Marianna go?" he went on. "Hear tell you boys had a little trouble on the way back to the saltworks. Lost them fine Morgans and your wagon, did you?" He slapped his thighs and laughed so hard he dern near busted a gut.

Well, sonny, this was some hard nut I was in and there weren't no cracking my way out of it that I could see. So I done the next best thing. I grinned at Boss Miller and said, "Why, Boss, these Yankees must be some kindhearted fellers seeing as they let a shit-eating boar hog such as you in the same tent with 'em."

Boss come off that stool like somebody'd stuck a branding iron to his butt. "Why you smartass bastard!" he said, grabbing for my neck, "I'll rip your damn head off and—"

I was ducking out of Boss's way when I heard somebody shout, "You'll do nothing of the sort, Mister Miller!" Looked up and seen the sergeant bear hug Boss and shove him back onto his stool. Then the same voice said, "Another outburst like that and I'll have you placed in irons."

I had dropped to my knees and rolled onto my side dodging Boss. Now I stood up, which weren't all that easy being as my hands was still tied behind my back. Looked over at Sergeant Bullard and said, "Much obliged for saving my hide."

He grunted and said he'd just as soon let Boss have his way with me and to keep my smart remarks to myself if I knowed what was good for me. A right friendly sort, the sergeant was. Probably kicked his own dog ever chance he got.

That other voice spoke up again, sounded almost kind and fatherly this time. "The charges against you are quite serious, young man. It would be in your best interest to cooperate." The voice belonged to a feller sitting behind a table not far from where Boss Miller sat sulking on his stool. Hadn't noticed him before, what with Boss's tomfoolery. Looked to be about around forty, sort of squat with dark hair and a dandy black moustache and goatee. From the fancy gold leaves on his shoulders I figured he must be some important officer.

Well, sonny, the hands was all dealt and I weren't holding so much as a high card. But I still had grit stuck in my craw knowing Boss had sold out Big John Anderson. So I looked that officer in the eye, said, "Do tell? Why should I do that when you're rubbing elbows with that lowlife scum sitting beside you?"

You should've seen Boss when he heard that, sonny. Tickles me to this very day to think of it. His eyes bulged out and that ugly face of his dern near turned purple, he was so mad. Started to come after me again, so the officer had Sergeant Bullard escort Boss outside the tent so he could get on with business. Couldn't keep from grinning at Boss as he stomped out.

Things went a mite smoother once Boss was out of the way. The officer introduced hisself as Major Edmund Weeks, commanding officer of the Second U.S. Florida Cavalry. He even went so far as to apologize for Boss Miller's rudeness, as he kindly put it. And when Sergeant Bullard come back inside, the major had him untie my hands.

I stood there rubbing the feeling back into my fingers and staring at the rope burns that was cut into my wrists. "Much obliged, sir," I said, "but what about Jefferson and Nebo?"

Major Weeks pulled a cigar out of his coat pocket and bit off the tip. Struck a Lucifer match with his thumbnail and lit up. He looked at Captain Tracy, who all this time had been standing by doing nothing more than fiddling with the ends of his moustache. "Captain Tracy, I believe the contrabands are in your care?" the major said.

The captain took a step forward and stiffened up. "Yes, sir. They've been interrogated and both have volunteered their services. They've been assigned to Company A, Major."

Well, sonny, when I heard that you could've pushed me over with a feather duster. My knees went weak and my stomach knotted up tight like I'd eat a bellyful of green persimmons. What would Uncle Nate and Aunt Nettie say when they learnt I'd gotten their only boy enlisted into the army—the Yankee army, at that?

So I said, "But Major, that ain't right. Why, Jefferson ain't never been away from home or family before." I tapped my temple. "He had the ague when he was little and is a mite squirrelly in the head. Besides, his poor mama and daddy need him back at the farm." Figured I was pissing upstream, but I was desperate.

Major Weeks sat back in his chair puffing on his cigar for a minute. Then he frowned like he'd swallowed a dose of quinine. Stood up and leaned on the table with both hands. Looked me in the eye, said, "The game is up, Mister Malburn. We know you've been employed at John Anderson's saltworks for several months. Do you deny it?"

Well, sonny, my 'coon was treed and I dern well knowed it. I was still half-expecting to face a noose or a firing squad so I figured I'd best play on his sympathies. "It's true, sir. I was working at the salt camp for the summer." I hung my head, done my best to sound sorrowful. "But I was only trying to earn some money for my poor widowed mama and my young sisters."

Sounded right convincing to me, but the major weren't having none of it. He shook his head, said, "You are in serious trouble, young man. Producing salt for the Confederacy constitutes aiding and abetting an enemy of the United States of America." He walked around the table and stood right in front of me, went to rocking back and forth on his heels. Smelt the cigar strong on his breath when he said, "Did they not tell you salt laborers are subject to the same laws as those in direct service to the Confederate Army?"

Dern near felt the limb cracking under me then, and knowed it'd be some hard fall. "No sir, Major, nobody told me any such a thing."

The major grunted, then walked back behind the table and sat down. "I'm afraid ignorance is no excuse for breaking the law. Rebellion against the United States government is punishable by imprisonment, or worse."

I was some scared now, that's a fact. I'd heard tell about Yankee prison camps and didn't cotton to living in such.

"There is one way out of this, Mister Malburn."

My ears perked up when I heard that. If there was something that could keep me from hanging or out of prison camp, I was sure game to hear it.

"I assume you grew up in these parts and know the area well?"

I nodded that I had and did, wondering just what he was

fishing for.

"You appear to be a bright young man," the major said. "You have a sharp mind if I'm to believe Sergeant Bullard's report, and you certainly have gumption. All the makings of a fine soldier. I could use the services of a good scout who is familiar with this country."

I seen it coming now and didn't like it one bit. Made my belly flip just thinking about my brother and my friends off fighting up in Georgia or Tennessee or wherever they was at the time. Them Yankees had me by the short hairs and they was tugging hard. Didn't want to hear what I knowed was coming, but what about Jefferson? I might be able to keep a eye out for him now and again if things worked out. "Just what is it you getting at?" I said.

Major Weeks stood up straight and tall as he could manage. "Mister Malburn, I'm prepared to drop all charges against you if you'll take the oath and swear allegiance to the Union."

And that there, sonny, is how I come to be a Union man.

Calvin Hogue
June 1927

TWENTY ★ FIVE

IT WAS SIX-THIRTY BY the time Elijah escorted me out the front door onto the porch. The sun had dipped below the treetops and evening shadows lay halfway across the yard as I walked to my roadster. I swung open the door and a big yellow fur ball leapt past me and dashed across the yard to the porch.

Elijah slapped his thighs and laughed. "General Sherman loves motorcars, sonny. You ain't careful, he'll be hitching a ride home with you."

I recovered enough to return a halfhearted laugh. Then I brushed cat hair off the seat, climbed in and cranked the car. "Thanks again, Mister Malburn," I called as the motor sputtered to life. "I'll see you next Saturday."

The old man spit a stream of tobacco juice onto the grass and waved. "If the barn don't burn or the creek don't rise," he said, then disappeared through the doorway with General Sherman at his heels.

I turned onto Malburn Road and sped toward Daniel's house. I was a half-hour late and hoped the old Confederate veteran would be understanding about the time, but I wasn't betting my paycheck on it. I wondered if I should mention to Daniel that I'd spent the afternoon with his brother.

Along the way I noticed a stone chimney standing just outside the grasp of a large oak in an overgrown pasture. The sight of it stirred my curiosity. Elijah had mentioned the ruins of Jefferson's family cabin. *"But that story comes later,"* I recalled him saying, and wondered just what story those ruins had to tell.

My stomach growled, reminding me I'd missed lunch. I hoped Daniel's offer to feed me supper was still good, but I was a bit apprehensive about what the main course might be. I'd heard country folks in these parts were rather fond of possum and raccoon, among other wild fare. I wanted to be a gracious guest but doubted I could stomach such delicacies, hungry as I might be.

I needn't have worried. An old battered pick-up I hadn't seen before was parked in the yard. And when Daniel's door opened, there stood Alma Hutchins wearing a flour-dusted apron and a big smile. "Well hi there, sugar," she said, friendly as ever, and gave me a hug. "My, if you ain't a sight for sore eyes. Come on in. Uncle Dan's done beat you to the table." When I stepped inside to the delicious aroma of fried chicken, my stomach relaxed and I forgot all about possum and raccoon.

"I want to thank you again for carrying Uncle Dan home the other evening, Calvin," Alma said as I followed her down the hallway. She stopped short of the kitchen door. "I don't know exactly what y'all have been up to," she whispered, "but the old boy's had a spark in his eye all week. It's been a while since he asked me to cook him a decent meal."

We walked on into the kitchen where Daniel sat at the table eyeing a platter of golden brown chicken. When he looked up and saw me, he growled, "You late, boy."

"Now Uncle Dan, don't be rude to company," Alma said, like she was scolding a difficult child. I envied the way she so easily put the old codger in his place.

"Ain't being rude," he said, glancing at Alma then back at me. "Feller says he'll be somewheres, he ought to show up on time is all. Supper's getting cold."

"Sorry, sir," I said, and reached across the table to shake his hand, "I let the time get away from me."

Daniel's one clear eye burned through me. "Humph," he

grunted, and shook my hand. "I ain't getting up. These old bones been giving me fits lately."

Alma told me to have a seat, and then scurried about the kitchen placing bowls of mashed potatoes, gravy and black-eyed peas on the table. "I got to get on home and feed them boys of mine, else they'll be fussing like wet biddies," she said. "Y'all need more sweet tea, it's in the icebox, and there's more cornbread in the warming oven." She grabbed her purse off the counter top and kissed Daniel on the cheek. "See you at church in the morning, sweetie. Y'all eat up now. You're both nothing but skin and bones." Then with a parting smile she was out the back door. Watching her go, I felt like my safety net had been taken away.

Daniel spooned a helping of mashed potatoes onto his plate and passed the bowl to me. "Been visiting my brother today, I hear." He must've read the surprise on my face. Before I could come up with an answer he said, "One of my grandyoung'uns seen your motorcar parked in Eli's yard."

It seemed the old man had eyes everywhere. I couldn't move a finger in the Econfina Valley without him knowing about it. "Yes, sir, I was there today," I said, feeling my face begin to flush. "I hope that's not a problem." Suddenly I was angry at myself for being apologetic, and mad at this irascible old goat for making me feel like I always had to walk on eggshells. As though I were doing something wrong by trying to record his family's saga for posterity. "I told you from the beginning that I intended to tell both sides. I can't very well do that without—"

"Hold on there," Daniel said, waving a half-eaten drumstick like a conductor's baton. "Don't go getting burrs in your breeches, boy. I got no squawk with you talking to my brother. That ain't what I meant at all."

Daniel leaned back and pulled a pint bottle out of his overalls. He set the whiskey on the table and winked with his good eye. "Help yourself, Calvin. Goes real good with Alma's fried chicken. Best in three counties, heh-heh."

Daniel Malburn
September 1863
Dark Night at Chickamauga

TWENTY ★ SIX

I HAD NO SOONER STARTED towards the fight when what was left of my Company K pards come stumbling out of the smoke back across the Chattanooga Road. They was a pitiful sight to behold, gospel truth. Looked like the elephant had tromped all over 'em. Took a spell to find Joe and Yerby. I was mighty relieved they was still amongst the living.

Before I could bring myself to say anything about Hamp, Yerb took off down the line looking for him. Joe commenced jawing but I couldn't make out hide or hair of what he was saying, being I was still half-deaf and scatterbrained from that shell.

Later on I learnt just what a fracas I'd missed after that blast cold-cocked me. Our boys pushed the Yankees hard some two hundred yards past the Chattanooga Road. In all the smoke and confusion the different companies of the Sixth Florida got mixed together. Still, it looked like they had the bluebellies routed when of a sudden there come a furious fire from the trees beyond. The boys stood their ground for a spell and give the bluebellies everthing they had. But things finally got too goldamn hot and they fell back a piece to the cover of a ditch that run across the field parallel to the road. Years afterwards, when me and Joe attended the dedication of Chickamauga Battlefield, we learnt it was a Indiana regiment armed with repeating rifles that put a halt to our attack.

Our boys held their own in that ditch and swapped fire with the Yanks, giving ever bit as good as they got till a enemy battery managed to flank 'em. The Yankee gunners aimed their cannons down the length of the ditch and let loose a enfilading fire of canister that cut the boys to pieces. The losses was terrible. Finally, them that was able retreated back across the road. That's when I met up with 'em.

I fell in with the others and we headed back across that blasted cornfield towards the tree line where we'd formed our line of battle earlier in the day. It was near sundown by then, and the battle was mostly played out. The Yankees stayed put, and we weren't game to push the issue no more. It ain't that the Yanks had whipped us, no sir. But both dogs had wounds aplenty to lick after the day's fight.

Everwhere you looked was the dead and wounded, men and horses both. Along the slope where the fight had been the hottest you could've walked a hundred yards in ever direction and never touched the ground. Made me sick seeing all them bodies and parts of bodies. The screaming and groaning nearbout drowned out what guns was still firing. Poor as I could hear, it still made my skin crawl. Stretcher bearers scurried here and yonder to treat what poor souls they could manage. It was some awful sight, like walking through Hell itself. To this day I cain't get shed of it.

We'd just crossed the split-rail fence and halted when Yerby come walking up to me and Joe. The look on his face told me what was coming, but I dreaded hearing it all the same. "You seen Hamp?" he says. "I cain't find him nowheres."

"Might've got caught up with one of the other companies," says Joe. "You know how mixed up things was out yonder."

It was then I seen a hunk of Yerby's right ear had been shot off and was bleeding something fierce. "Yerb," I says, pointing at his ear, "you been shot."

Yerby reached up and felt it. Looks at his bloody hand and says, "Oh." Touched it again. "Well hang my ear. Where's my brother?"

Joe pulled the stopper out of his canteen. "Last I seen of him was before we charged them batteries this side of the road," he says, swigging down the last of his water. "I lost sight of everbody in the smoke afterwards."

Then Yerby looked at me. I turned away and stared into the trees back of us. "Danny?" he says, and from the way he said it I knowed he'd seen it in my eyes.

Of a sudden I felt dizzy and sat down. Laid my Enfield across my legs and wiped at the dust on the stock whilst I pondered what to tell him.

"Danny?" he says again, barely a squeak.

I tried to swallow but my throat was too dry. "He's gone up, Yerb," I says. "Hamp is dead."

It nearbout gutted me, but I managed to tell Yerby and Joe how Hamp had been shot dead beside me whilst charging that Yankee cannon. What I couldn't bring myself to say was how poor Hamp's body was blowed to pieces and that there weren't nothing left to bury. Truth be told, it ain't never right to lie, but I couldn't make myself tell my pards the horrible thing I seen. So I said Hamp was shot through the heart, that he was dead before I got to him and didn't suffer none. That much was gospel.

Yerby took it hard. When me and Joe tried to comfort him he shook free and walked off into the woods a piece. Sat down with his back agin a tree, just staring at the shadows. We let him be with his grieving.

The sun finally give up and night closed in. Nighthawks buzzed in the smoky sky and whippoorwills called from the woods. Joe had just built a little fire to boil coffee when Yerb come walking up toting our mess's tin lantern. "Get your spare candles," he tells me and Joe. "Let's go find Hamp."

Well, sir, I knowed there weren't no use in doing such. Hamp was gone, and I sure didn't cotton to stumbling around that field of death in the dark. Off in the distance we could still hear the moans and screams of the wounded. "Yerb," I says, "we cain't do Hamp no good now. Pickets out yonder will be shooting at anything that moves. Besides, chances are the stretcher bearers or Yanks done took care of him anyways."

Yerby turned on me like a stepped-on rattler. "If it was your brother laying out there you'd go looking for him," he says. "Course, you ain't got to worry none about that, do you, Eli being the yellowbellied coward he is."

Well, sir, them words stung something fierce. It couldn't have hurt no more if Yerby had stuck his Bowie knife through my heart. Hamp had been like my own brother, and I knowed Eli weren't no coward. He was back at the farm looking after the family because I'd told him it was his duty to do such.

Before I could talk, Joe says, "There ain't no call for that. Danny ain't done—"

"Shut your mouth if you know what's good for you, Joe Porter," Yerby says, then shoved Joe so hard he fell on his butt.

Now, Joe was a head shorter than Yerb and skinny as a rail, but what he lacked in size he more'n made up for with grit. He spit out his chaw of tobacco, jumped up and lit into Yerby. Them two commenced scrapping like two hounds over a soup bone. They was all arms and legs rolling in the dust and dark till I finally got betwixt 'em. Took a licking doing it.

"This ain't right, boys," I says, straining to keep 'em apart. "Come on now, we're pards."

Yerby had fire in his eyes and I figured him and me was fixing to go at it, but of a sudden he went limp. I seen a passel of our comrades had gathered around to watch the festivities. Then Tom Gainer come busting through the crowd. Had a bandage on his left arm just above the elbow. "What's this about?"

I turned loose of Joe and Yerb. Picked up my slouch hat and dusted it off. "Nothing, just wrassling."

Tom looked us over and frowned. "You boys didn't get enough fight from the Yanks today?"

Nobody spoke up, so he says, "Well, it seems a shame to waste all that spare pluck you got, so you best use it on picket duty tonight. And put out that fire."

Then Tom walked over to Yerby and put a hand on his shoulder. "I'm truly sorry about Hamp," he says. "He was a brave soldier and died doing his duty. You can take comfort in that."

Yerb didn't say nothing. Seemed all the fight had finally leaked out of him. After Tom and the other boys scattered, Yerb picked up the lantern and fiddled with the candle till it was upright in the holder. "I'll find out where Tom wants us to go," he says without looking up, and walks off.

———————•———————

We crossed the rail fence and felt our way into the cornfield. Most of the wounded near our lines had been recovered, but farther on there was a passel of dead laying around for us to stumble over. Here and yonder we heard some poor soul cry out. They seemed a far piece off, but it still raised my hackles. Weren't long before Joe found a shell crater big enough to hold the three of us. A wagon that had lost its rear wheels was laying on its side at the edge of the hole. We decided that was a good place to hunker down for picket duty. We weren't near as far out in front of our lines as we was supposed to go, but if Gen'ral Tom Gainer wanted pickets any closer to the Yanks, well, sir, the way we figured he was more'n welcome to lead the way.

It was as dark a night as you ever seen, and Lord, it was some cold for September. I could barely see my hand in front of my face, it was that dark. A north wind was blowing and I knowed frost weren't far behind. Here and yonder the woods glowed a eerie red. Shells had set fires up and down the battlefield during the day's fight. Unearthly screams cut through the dark. Later on we learnt that scores of poor wounded souls too hurt to escape got burnt alive.

Joe volunteered to take the first watch, which suited me fine. I was tuckered and my head still ached something fierce. I was mighty glad we'd brung our blankets. I unrolled mine and wrapped up. Joe sat up where he could see out of the hole. He rested his Enfield across his legs and bit off a fresh chaw. Yerby commenced sharpening his Bowie knife on a rock he'd picked up somewheres.

I shut my eyes but couldn't sleep. At first I blamed it on Yerby drawing his blade across the stone. Then I figured it must be the musket fire cracking here and yonder from edgy pickets. But it weren't either, truth be told. It was the wounded that kept me awake. Even with my poor ears I could hear 'em moaning and crying out. It give me gooseflesh and I covered my ears with the blanket but couldn't shut out that terrible sound. Some was yelling for their pards to come get 'em. Others was calling out to God or their dear mothers. Most all was begging for water. It was a pitiful thing to hear. I ain't forgot it in all these sixty-some years. Never will, I reckon.

After a while, Joe whispers, "Lord a'mighty, cain't we do something to help?"

Yerby give a quick laugh and says, "Let the bluebelly bastards suffer."

"Why, that ain't Christian," Joe says. "Besides, some of 'em might be our boys."

"Well go on then, you want to get your fool head shot off. Serve you right."

Well, sir, there was something in Yerby's voice that bothered me a mite. It weren't like him to talk such, not to his pards anyways. I started to say something, but let it go. Figured it was all a part of his grieving for Hamp. I pulled the blanket around me tighter and finally fell asleep.

Seemed like I'd just drifted off when Joe shook me. I knowed right away something was up. Figured the Yanks might be probing about. I sat up. "What is it?"

"Yerb's gone."

Well, sir, that woke me up quick. "What?" I hoped I'd heard wrong. I looked around and sure enough, Yerb weren't there. In the distance I could still hear them poor suffering souls begging for help. "Where'd he go?"

"Well if I knowed that I wouldn't of bothered you," says Joe. "It was his watch. I just woke up and found him gone. Lord, I wish them fellers would hush."

"Maybe he went to piss," I says, trying to sound hopeful.

"He ain't pissing. He's gone, blanket and all. I'm scared, Danny."

Well, sir, this was just jim-dandy. Yerby off to who-knows-where. All them wounded and their God-awful wailing making our skin crawl. Trigger-happy pickets on both sides itching to plug anything that moved. Seemed like the pits of Hell itself, except it was goldamn near to freezing. Then it come to me. "He's gone looking for Hamp."

"Why, that's crazy," says Joe. "In this dark?"

"He ain't been right in the head since I told him about Hamp. You seen that for yourself."

"Reckon so, all the same, he—"

Of a sudden some poor soul let loose a bloodcurdling scream.

"Look yonder!" Joe says.

I squinted hard towards where the scream come from, seen a flame flicker for a second, then go out. The smoke and mist hanging over the cornfield give the light a ghostly look. I judged it to be a hundred yards away, but it was hard to tell. A second or two later it glowed again and went out just as quick.

Joe grabbed my arm. "Reckon what that is?"

"Well, it weren't no firefly. Somebody might've lit a match."

"They begging to get shot, is what," says Joe.

"I cain't argue with that," I says. Only a fool would go and strike a match in this dark with all the itchy-fingered pickets out yonder. Yes, sir, only a fool . . . or a crazy man. "Say, did Yerb bring the lantern?"

"Don't recall, but that ain't nowheres near where you seen Hamp get kilt."

"No, but we best go check it out anyways. Cain't chance letting Yerb go and get his fool head shot off just because he ain't thinking straight."

We snuck out of our hole and commenced crawling towards the right front where we seen the light. It was slow going, what with keeping our rifle barrels out of the dirt and doing our best not to crawl over bodies. It took a spell, but we finally made it to where we thought the light come from. "See anything?" I whispers to Joe.

"Shh . . . hear that?"

I held still as a treed squirrel. Didn't hear nothing but far off gunfire. My ears was ringing some yet, and what I could hear sounded all hollow. I leaned over close to Joe. "What is it?"

"Don't know. Wait . . . there it goes again."

I still couldn't hear it but I seen a log or something a few yards away. I crawled ahead to check it out. I put my hand out and felt wool. It moved and I jerked my hand back. Gooseflesh climbed all over me. "Over here," I says.

Joe crawled over beside me. By then I heard what sounded like gurgling coming from the poor soul laying there. "This feller's still alive."

"Where you hurt, pard?" says Joe.

There weren't no answer, just more gurgling.

"Look here," I says, "I'm going to strike a match so's we can see where this poor feller's ailing."

"You crazy?"

Well, sir, it was a fair enough question, but it weren't right to just leave the feller be. "He's bad hurt. We're obliged to do what we can to help him." I fished a match out of my breeches pocket and got ready to strike it with my thumbnail. "Now look him over real quick 'cause I ain't keeping it lit but a second."

Joe huddled up close so's to block out as much light as we could. I held my breath and struck the match. It flared and right off I seen the wounded feller was a Yankee. Then my stomach curdled and I nearbout puked.

"Lord a'mighty," Joe says, way too loud, "his throat is cut!"

TWENTY ★ SEVEN

THE POOR SOUL'S THROAT WAS laid wide open, ear to
ear. He'd done bled out like a slaughtered hog. His eyes was
rolled back so there weren't nothing but the whites showing. He
kept gulping for air like a fish out of water, but all he got for his
trouble was bloody bubbles out of his throat.

"Lordy," says Joe, "you don't reckon Yerb—"

"Don't go saying such. Maybe somebody stuck this feller
with their bayonet." That must be what happened, I told myself.
I sorely wanted it to be so. After all, I had kilt a Yankee officer
with my own bayonet that very afternoon. But truth be told,
I knowed it weren't so. This feller would've been long dead if
somebody had slit his throat open during the fight.

Of a sudden I felt a cold hand grip my arm and I shivered.
In the dark it felt like the Grim Reaper hisself had ahold of me.
It took ever bit of grit I had not to jerk away, but somehow I
managed. The dying Yank commenced shaking all over. A
rattling come up from his lungs and out his throat, then he
turned loose of my arm and went still. I put my hand on his chest
to make sure he was dead. His jacket was soaked through with
blood and his chest felt warm, but there weren't no heartbeat

that I could tell. "He's gone up."

Joe commenced whispering the Lord's Prayer. I rubbed my bloody hand in the dirt and offered a quick silent prayer to go along with Joe's reciting. Joe was just finishing up when another glimmer of light cut the dark a short piece a ways. It no sooner died out than rifles barked and spit flame to our front. Balls whizzed overhead. A second later there come a answering volley from behind us. Lucky for me and Joe them pickets was all aiming high.

"Lord a'mighty, everbody is trying to kill us," says Joe.

"They ain't shooting at us. I seen that light again." I put my hand close to Joe's face and pointed towards our front where the light come from. "Over yonder, maybe forty-fifty yards. That must be what's got 'em all antsy."

We stayed put for a spell, shivering from the cold and the wailing of the wounded and dying. I wanted them pickets to settle down a mite before we chanced moving. I looked for the moon to judge what time it was, but the smoke and clouds was still too thick to see it. A minute later the light glowed again, this time to our left. Just like before, it flickered for a second, then went out. Me and Joe hunkered down next to the dead Yank, waiting for the pickets to have a go at it, but nobody fired.

Well, sir, I'd had a bellyful of waiting around playing hide-and-seek with whoever or whatever was making that goldamn light. Maybe it was fireflies after all, I told myself. With all the smoke still hanging over the cornfield, and tired as I was, my eyes might be fooling me. Then I remembered the poor Yank. Sure weren't no firefly that slit his throat. Much as I dreaded it, I had to find out.

I told Joe to sit tight. Decided to leave my rifle as it would only slow me down and Joe might could use a extra quick shot if things got hot whilst I was gone. I rested it agin the dead bluebelly's leg to keep the barrel out of the dirt. I made sure the pistol I'd took off the Yankee officer was still tucked in my belt, then crawled towards where I'd last seen that light.

I weren't more'n halfway there when somebody cried out for help. The light shined again and my blood went cold. There weren't no time to lose. I jumped to my feet and run for all I was worth, hoping my eyes was playing tricks. But I knowed I'd seen the flash of a knife blade.

Why I didn't trip over a body or get shot down by pickets in them last few yards, I'll never know. When I got close I pulled out the Colt's. "Don't do it, Yerb!" I says.

Them words no sooner left my mouth when I stumbled over something and sprawled flat on my belly. That's when I seen Yerby had been using his hat to cover the candle lantern and shade out the light. A rough circle of yellow lit up the ground where it sat.

"Keep back!" says Yerby. I could barely make out the shape of a poor whimpering Yankee laying next to him. Yerb was on his knees, leaning over the feller. He had ahold of his knife with one hand, the other'n was clamped over the Yank's mouth.

"Let him be, this ain't right," I says, expecting any second to get shot from all the ruckus we was raising.

"What ain't right? They kilt Hamp, didn't they?"

"But that was war, a fair fight. This here is murder."

"Bible says 'a eye for a eye.' "

"Thou shalt not kill," I says back. "I cain't let you do this."

I could barely make out Yerb's face, but I ain't never forgot the way he grinned at me. Pure evil, it was. Then he says, "You going to shoot me, Danny?" and puts the blade agin the Yank's throat.

My hand commenced shaking as I lifted the Colt's and cocked back the hammer. "If I have to."

TWENTY ★ EIGHT

CAIN'T SAY HOW LONG ME and Yerb stared each other down, but it seemed like a week in Hell before he says, "Why Danny, I do believe you would." He moved his knife away from the Yank's throat.

Truth be told, I don't know if I could've pulled that trigger or not. Me and Yerb had growed up together. Killing him would've been like killing family. I eased the hammer down and rested the pistol butt on the ground to stop my hand from shaking so. I was sick inside, tired of this whole goldamn mess. "Just leave him be," I says. "He ain't to blame."

Yerb looked at the bluebelly a minute, then back at me. "Well hell, this one is good as dead anyways," he says, still grinning. "Been gut-shot." He took his hand off the Yank's mouth, then put the knife back in its scabbard and crawled a few feet away.

The poor wounded soul commenced groaning and begging for water. We had filled our canteens from spare ones took off the dead after the fight, so I slipped the pistol under my belt and uncorked mine. I crawled over to the Yank and lifted his head to give him a drink.

"You wasting good water," Yerb says.

I looked over at him. It was too dark to see his face, but I could feel them cold eyes staring back at me. "We got to help this feller. You'd want the same for Hamp."

Yerby give a mean laugh. "Why, I was trying to help him. Put him out of his misery, same I'd do for any suffering cur."

Muskets commenced spitting fire back and forth across the cornfield. I hunkered down best I could next to the Yank, but none of the balls come near. It kept up right hot for a minute or two. Wondered if a night attack might be in the works, but the firing soon died down to a few scattered shots, then finally quit. By the time all the ruckus settled and I looked up, Yerb was gone.

The wounded Yank was a mite out of his head by then. He commenced thrashing about, begging me not to kill him. I told him to hush, that I didn't mean him no harm. Finally got him quieted down and was giving him a drink when Joe come stumbling out of the dark toting a Enfield in each hand. He dropped to his knees beside me, blowing like a winded horse. "Lord a'mighty, is Yerb shot?"

"It ain't Yerb, it's a Yank. He's bad hurt."

"Well, where is Yerb? I swear I heard y'all jabbering from over yonder."

"He took off when them pickets got riled," I says. "Thought I told you to stay put."

Joe handed me my Enfield. "It weren't me they was shooting at. I figured you done kicked up a nest of bluebellies and could use some help."

"Well, this feller can use all you got. He's gut-shot."

We set about doing what we could for the poor soul. The clouds had thinned a mite, and the moon give off just enough light to see a arm's reach. I fished my jackknife out of my breeches and cut the straps of the Yank's knapsack. Joe helped me ease it out from under him. We propped his head on the knapsack, then unrolled his blanket and covered him with it.

I was giving the Yank another drink when somebody calls out, "Halloo there, Reb, what are you up to?"

Well, sir, hearing that voice sent a chill up my back. It weren't far off, no more'n thirty yards or so, sounded like. Me and Joe grabbed our rifles and hugged ground shoulder-to-shoulder behind the wounded Yank. I squinted towards where the voice come from. Couldn't see nothing but dark and shadows.

Before I could work up a answer, the voice calls out again, "Speak up, Johnny. We heard you poking about."

Joe grabs my arm and says, "What we going to do?"

"Hold on a goldamn minute and let me think."

We was in one jim-dandy of a mess. Weren't no telling how many bluebellies was out yonder. I didn't cotton going to no Yankee prison camp, so the way I seen it we could either fight it out or skedaddle. Trouble was, them Yanks had the drop on us. If we was to make a run for it they'd likely shoot us down. I worked up my grit and says, "Who wants to know?"

"Fifty-eighth Indiana."

Then it come to me. "Hey, Yank, we got one of your pards here. He's bad hurt. We'd be obliged if you'd come fetch him."

That struck their fancy. They commenced jawing amongst theirselves for a spell, then one of 'em calls out, "Can we trust you boys not to shoot?"

Seems them bluebellies thought there was more of us than just me and Joe. Seeing the tight spot we was in I figured there weren't no harm in bluffing a mite, so I says, "Them that's with us won't, you got my word."

The Yanks talked it over a spell longer, then one calls out, "All right, Johnny, we'll be along directly."

We didn't no more trust them Yanks than we would a cottonmouth on a trotline, so we left the wounded Yank for his pards and God to look after and lit out whilst the getting was good. Weren't no more we could do for the poor soul anyways. Once we was a safe distance from them Yanks, we stopped to look around and get our bearings. By then the wind had cleared out most of the smoke in that part of the field and we was able to spot the wrecked wagon next to the shell hole.

We crawled like fiddler crabs the last fifty yards or so to the crater so's we wouldn't draw fire from any pickets that might be nearby. Well, sir, there was Yerb, leaning agin one side of the hole with his hat pulled over his eyes, snoring away like he was back home safe in his own bed.

Joe whispers, "Hey, Yerb," but I hushed him up quick and told him he best get what sleep he could, that I'd keep watch till sunrise. Tuckered as he was, Joe weren't about to argue with that. A minute or two later he was fast asleep.

I fetched my blanket and crawled over to the wagon and leaned back agin it. Laid my Enfield across my lap so's it would be handy should any bluebellies come poking about. Truth be told, right then I didn't care if one come up and shot me through the head. Poor Hamp was dead. Yerb had gone plumb crazy with grief. He'd murdered that Yank in cold blood. Most likely that weren't the only one neither. I recollected the look in his eyes when I shoved the Colt's in his face. Seemed then there weren't a plugged nickel's difference betwixt me or that Yank in Yerb's mind.

I got to thinking what I was going to do come morning. Should I tell Tom what Yerb done, or just keep it betwixt me and Joe? And what about Yerb? We'd been pards all our life, but in one black day things had sorely changed. Weren't for sure I even knowed who he was no more.

I shivered and tugged my blanket up tighter but it didn't help a whole heap. Reckon my gut was ever bit as cold as that north wind. Figured I might never get warm again. After a while I give up trying. I stared out into the dark, trying not to think, and waited for sunup.

———•———

Before daylight we headed back to our lines. Me and Joe done our best to act like things was fit, but Yerb weren't buying it. We decided to let it be for a spell. Figured Yerb might come to his senses if we give him time to chew on it.

We reported in to Tom. The supply wagons had come up during the night so we drawed our rations and commenced frying up our bacon and cornbread. Yerb took his share and ate but never said a word, just kept staring out across that goldamn bloody cornfield.

Near midmorning orders come down to move out. We marched west till we struck the Chattanooga-LaFayette Road, then followed it north a piece. After a spell we halted and spread out in a line of battle alongside a shady lane near a farmstead. We was guarding some artillery positioned at the farm from Yank cavalry that was rumored to be prowling about. Spent a goodly part of the day resting in the shade whilst laying on arms. That was jim-dandy by me. I'd had a bellyful of fighting.

I managed to sleep a mite and commenced dreaming about home and my Annie. When I woke up I was sorely homesick. Reached inside my shirt and took out Annie's tintype. Right then I'd have give everthing in the world to be home with her. Then the thought struck me how just yesterday young Hamp was admiring Annie's picture and confessing as to how him and Eli was both sweet on her. Thinking about poor Hamp nearbout broke my heart, so I wrapped the tintype back in its kerchief and put it away.

Them goldamn Yanks was still hankering for a scrap, and our boys was game. It was some hot fracas. All day long cannons boomed and muskets rattled. From the sound of things, the fight was moving roughly northwards.

Well, sir, that bluebelly cavalry never did show, and by late afternoon our shirking come to a end. The Yanks was making a fierce stand on a ridge of high ground to the northwest up by the Snodgrass farm. Orders come to move out at the quick march. We lit out in column of fours up the road and was soon eating dust and choking on all the burnt powder and smoke from the wood fires.

We kept on north for a half-hour, then turned onto another road heading roughly west. The sun had set and it was getting cooler, but I was sweating like a plow mule in August. Joe was on my right, chawing his tobacco and muttering prayers betwixt coughing fits. On my left, Yerb just stared ahead, jaws clenched tight but mum as a deaf mute.

By the time we finally hooked up with the Confederate lines, the battle had petered out some. Our officers got their orders and we commenced stumbling through ravines this way and that till we halted and formed a line of battle at the foot of a steep ridge. Couldn't see ten foot in any direction, dark as it was and with a heavy mist rising.

Things had got so quiet it was plumb eerie. Up the hill we could hear voices and the rattling of gear, but nobody seemed to know if they was friend or foe. Here and yonder muskets spit flame and a cannon fired but there weren't no particular order to it. Then come the shouting of orders and we commenced uphill at the double-quick with the Rebel Yell rising from a thousand throats.

Halfway up that hill we took a volley and a few of our boys was hit. We halted and fired one back, then charged forward ready to give 'em the steel. Well, sir, it was all over before it got good and started. Them Yanks was skedaddling like swarming ants, but we captured a whole passel, right near a thousand as I recollect. Then a cheer went up that beat any I ever heard before or since. Seemed like the whole countryside for miles around was alive with our victorious jubilation. The Battle of Chickamauga was over.

During the charge up that hill, company lines had got mixed up some, so I commenced looking around for my pards. Weren't long before I seen Joe walking towards me. I raised my Enfield over my head. "Whoowee, Joe Porter, we whipped 'em good!" I says. But when Joe got closer I seen the look on his face and knowed something weren't right.

"Come quick, Danny. Yerb's been shot."

The Sixth Florida had took that hill and captured all them Yanks whilst losing only a handful of dead and wounded, but Yerby Watts was amongst them unfortunate few. Well, sir, I'll spare you the gory details, but he had caught a ball in his right leg that shattered the bone halfway betwixt his knee and ankle. I sent Joe to find Tom Gainer, then fetched my cherished kerchief and tied it tight as I could above the wound to stop the bleeding. Figured Annie would forgive me for putting it to such a noble use.

I seen Yerb was hurting something fierce but all the while he never uttered a peep. I kept telling him he was going to be all right, that they would fix him up and he would be home before he knowed it. Might just as well been jawing to the tree he was sitting agin.

In a few minutes, Joe come back with Tom. Tom squatted down and said a few words to Yerb, then took me and Joe aside and told us where the regimental infirmary was being set up at a farm near where we had turned off of the LaFayette Road.

"You best get him there quick," Tom says. "That leg's got to come off."

Reckon we knowed that from the get-go, but we weren't

about to let on to Yerb. Truth be told, he most likely knowed it hisself. Poor Yerb had lost his only brother, and now they would have to take his leg. Tom had give Yerb a canteen that held a pint or so of whiskey. He commenced drinking whilst me and Joe used our ramrods and some haversack straps to fashion a splint of sorts for his leg. Then we helped Yerb up on his good leg, slung his arms over our shoulders and headed down the hill.

It was slow going till we found the road. It had turned downright cold, and ever breath we took still stunk of spent gunpowder and bitter smoke. In spite of the cold and foul air, crickets was chirping and fireflies lit up all around. Seemed that only mankind out of all God's creation had gone mad.

Hundreds of our boys had been kilt or wounded that day in the terrible fighting around the Snodgrass farm, so there was a whole passel of suffering souls being helped along. We fell in amongst 'em. Some carried lanterns or torches that made the going easier. Me and Joe was tuckered from two days of fighting, but we managed well enough. We stopped now and then to catch our wind and let Yerb drink more whiskey. After a spell he'd drunk enough so's his pain was tolerable. Weren't long before them corn squeezings had loosed up his tongue a mite too. He kept jawing about how he was going to kill the whole damn Yankee army once his leg was healed up.

We finally made the LaFayette Road. Wagons loaded with wounded crowded the road, raising more dust to add to our misery. We kept to one side and tried to shut our ears to all the suffering. When the hospital finally come into view, Yerb was near passed out. Well, sir, that proved a merciful thing, for a terrible sight stopped me and Joe dead in our tracks.

"Lord a'mighty," Joe says, "look a'there!"

I gawked in horror as a leg come sailing out a window and landed on a grisly pile of amputated limbs. My gut froze. Through all these long years I ain't been able to shake that terrible sight from my memory. Joe turned his head and puked, wiped his mouth with his free hand. "Lord a'mighty," he says again.

I fought off being sick my own self, then says, "Come on, let's get this done." We carried Yerb on up to the house through a passel of wounded boys that was sitting or laying about the yard. A red-eyed orderly took a gander at Yerb's leg, told us to lay him on the long porch where a heap of other badly wounded unfortunates waited their turn for the surgeon's knife. Here and yonder other orderlies made their way amongst the wounded, giving them water and what little aid they could.

Joe spied a place by the front wall that give some protection from the wind and we eased Yerb down gentle as we could. He was stirring some by then and his teeth had commenced to chattering. There weren't no blanket to be had, so I took off my jacket and spread it across his chest and shoulders.

Of a sudden Yerb's eyes flew open wide and wild as a spooked horse. He raised up and grabbed ahold of my shirt with both hands so tight, I feared it would rip. "They ain't taking my leg!" he nearbout screams. "Don't let 'em cut off my leg, Danny! You won't let 'em, will you?"

"Oh, Lord Jesus!" Joe mutters. He turned away and commenced reciting the Lord's Prayer.

Well, sir, it felt like that north wind had swept inside my very bowels and turned my blood to ice. Yerb had put me in some hard fix and there weren't no good way out that I could tell. "Now, Yerb," I says, "it don't look that bad, but it ain't up to me."

Yerb jerked me down with the strength of a madman till we was face to face. "Goddamn you, Daniel Malburn," he says, "don't let 'em take my leg. You owe me that! You owe me!"

Yerb kept cussing and raising a ruckus till two orderlies come to see what the fracas was about. I was shook and don't recollect all the details, but somehow or other they got Yerb to calm down and turn me loose. One of them fellers told me and Joe they would take care of our pard, that it was best for all concerned if we got on back to our company. So that's what we done.

By the time we made it back to our lines, I was done in, but bone-tired as I was, sleep escaped me. The two days at Chickamauga weighed on me like a grist stone. Weren't but two nights ago me and Joe and the Watts boys was camped below Dalton's Ford, young Hamp itching to finally get in a real scrap and see the elephant. Well, sir, he seen it all right. We all did. And that elephant had tromped all over us.

Now poor Hampton Watts was dead, kilt the day before his sixteenth birthday. Yerby Watts had suffered the loss of his brother and a leg. He was so eat up with grief and hatred I feared he would never again be the pard I'd growed up with.

It was just me and Joe Porter now. What was to become of us? Figured there weren't no way I would survive this terrible war and see home and loved ones again. I hoped and prayed Joe would, but I wouldn't have give a plugged nickel for his chances neither.

Well, sir, it's a merciful thing the good Lord don't allow us poor mortal souls to know the day or hour of His ways. Because if I'd knowed what lay ahead, I might've chucked it all in and lit out for home right then.

Calvin Hogue
July 1927

TWENTY ★ NINE

UPON RETURNING TO MY ROOM at Mrs. Presnell's boardinghouse the night of the Fourth, I found a note tacked to the door. I had just dropped Jenny off at her place after enjoying a cookout and fireworks display on the shores of North Bay near the village of Lynn Haven. I unlocked the door, pulled the lamp chain and read the note.

Monday, July 4
Dear Mister Hogue:
A Mrs. Alma Hutchins telephoned for you this afternoon. She asked that I relay a message. Mister D. Malburn has taken ill and is currently a patient at Adams' Hospital on Magnolia Avenue. She did not offer any further information, nor did I inquire, as I did not wish to appear nosey.
Sincerely, Mrs. Presnell

A sinking feeling hit the pit of my stomach. My weekly serial on the Malburn brothers was proving to be popular with readers of the *Pilot*. What if Daniel was too sick to continue, or worse, what if he died as he'd earlier predicted? My project would be ruined!

A wave of guilt swept through me as I realized how selfish that sounded. It wasn't just the Malburns' saga I stood to lose, it was the brothers themselves. During the past weeks I'd grown quite fond of both irascible old gents. I'd last seen Daniel two weeks ago. He'd looked pale and said he was feeling a "mite peaked," so we postponed the interview until this coming weekend. Elijah, however, had been agreeable to an unscheduled session, and we'd spent several productive hours together as he related more of his wartime adventures.

I glanced at the clock on my nightstand. It was almost eleven. There was no need trying to find out more information on Daniel at this late hour, and Uncle Hawley was expecting my story to be on his desk first thing in the morning, so I busied myself writing the article on Lynn Haven's Fourth of July festivities.

———•———

First thing Tuesday morning, I placed a copy of the article I'd written in Uncle Hawley's in-box. He wasn't due in the office for another half-hour, so I sat in his chair and dialed the operator from his desk phone. When the operator answered, I asked that she put me through to Adams' Hospital.

"Adams' Hospital," a lady's voice said. "How may I help you?"

"Yes, could you give me the condition of Mister Daniel Malburn? I understand he's a patient there."

"Are you a relative?"

"No, just a friend. I'm Calvin Hogue. Mister Malburn's niece left a—"

"Oh, you're that writer for the newspaper," she said. "Miz Hutchins said you might be calling. Hold on, please."

I heard the jingling of someone picking up the receiver. "Calvin, that you, sugar?"

"Yes, ma'am. How is Daniel?"

"Well, he's running a fever and having bad coughing fits. Doc Adams thinks it's a touch of pneumonia. Uncle Dan's on vapors to help with his breathing, and some sort of sulfa drug."

Pneumonia! The word made me shudder. I wasn't all that

knowledgeable about medicine, but knew enough to realize that pneumonia was very serious, often deadly, in someone as old and frail as Daniel Malburn. I glanced at the frivolous Fourth of July article I'd placed in Uncle Hawley's in-box and wondered if I'd be submitting any future installments of the Malburn chronicle.

"Course he's ornery as a old plow mule and fussing up a storm," Alma said, "so I reckon he's not feeling too poorly."

Hearing that lifted my spirits somewhat. I could almost feel Alma's cheerful smile coming through the telephone line. "The doctor thinks he'll be okay, then?"

Alma chuckled. "It'll take more than a case of the croup to put that mule-headed man down, sugar. He might put on like he's got one foot in the grave sometimes, but I figure the old boy's got a couple of good years in him yet."

Hearing that, I felt a "whole heap" better, as Daniel himself might say. Alma's optimism was beginning to rub off on me. I was almost confident now that the Malburns' story would live on. Better yet, so would a dear friend.

THIRTY

IT WAS FRIDAY BEFORE DOCTOR Adams allowed Daniel to have visitors other than immediate family. By then the fever was gone and his lungs had cleared enough to where he was breathing normally and coughing only occasionally.

I had explained the situation to Uncle Hawley on Tuesday, and when I approached him Friday morning for permission to visit Daniel that afternoon, he was his usual gruff self. "Well what you standing there wasting time for, boy?" he said. "You got a story to write, then get on with it. Can't be letting our readers down."

I picked up Jenny for a quick lunch at McKenzie's Diner. After dropping her off at the courthouse, I drove the few blocks to Adams' Hospital. The smell of alcohol and other medicinal odors greeted me as I entered the building and walked over to a portly, gray-haired nurse sitting at a large metal desk. The wall behind her was lined with stacked filing cabinets. A large ceiling fan circulated what little fresh air entered through two open windows.

The nurse was busy writing in a ledger. I cleared my throat to gain her attention. "Hello. I'm here to see Mister Malburn.

Room Eight, I believe?"

She looked up, eyes frowning over thick spectacles. "Down that hall, turn left, second room on the right," she said, pointing over my shoulder with the pen.

My thank you was met with silence. I followed her directions, smiling and nodding to another nurse I passed in the hallway who offered a friendly smile in return. Daniel's door was standing halfway open. I checked the patient's name on the door to be sure, and knocked lightly on the frame.

"If you ain't here to stick me or poke me, then come on in."

I stepped into the room. Daniel was sitting up in bed, resting against pillows. "Good to see you, sir," I said, setting my satchel on a nearby table. "How are you feeling?"

"Well tarnation. Calvin!" The old Confederate seemed genuinely pleased to see me. "I ain't gone up yet, just tuckered from laying in this hospital all week."

"You're looking well," I said. He was still pale and appeared to have lost a little weight, but his good eye had that old sparkle back. "Are they feeding you okay?"

"Humph. Wouldn't slop my hogs with it." He turned his head and coughed a couple of times, then pointed to a picnic basket on the dresser. "Alma's seeing to it my gizzard don't growl, heh-heh."

We made small talk for another few minutes, then I figured it was time to get down to business. "I've got the rest of the day off from work, if you feel up to talking."

Daniel glanced around the room. "Well, sir, cain't do no plowing whilst I'm stuck in this bed, so I reckon I'm game. Truth be told, I'm a mite antsy to get on with it."

"Good." I walked over and opened my satchel. I took out my pad and pencils, then reached for the half-full Mason jar. I held up what remained of the moonshine Daniel had given me after our first session. "Brought along a little something to whet the whistle," I said, grinning. "Good for what ails you."

Daniel Malburn
October-November 1863
Chattanooga

THIRTY ★ ONE

I WON'T WASTE A WHOLE heap of time recollecting how General Bragg squandered our great victory at Chickamauga. When the last of the Yanks skedaddled from the Snodgrass farm, General Longstreet was antsy to give chase and finish off the whole bluebelly army. But General Bragg seen things different. Bragg figured we'd whipped the Yanks soundly, that we'd best sit tight a spell and lick our own wounds, which was considerable. And being as he was commander of the army, that's what we done.

With the hounds called off, the Yanks crossed the Tennessee River to Chattanooga and commenced fortifying their works. After a spell, General Bragg finally seen fit to move the army north, and we took up positions on Missionary Ridge and Lookout Mountain overlooking Chattanooga.

For the next month we kept the bluebellies penned up there. They was in a bad fix, gospel truth. Couldn't leave their works without risking our artillery, and our cavalry harassed their supply lines till them poor fellers was nearbout to starve.

It was powerful cold up on them rocky ridges, and when it commenced to rain, things got downright miserable. What clothes we had was thin and ragged, and if a body had shoes without holes he was truly a blessed soul.

Weren't much fighting going on to speak of. Ever now and again our artillery would swap a few shells with the Yanks. Here and yonder pickets or skirmishers would get into a little scrap, but it weren't nothing to write home about. Most our time was spent trying to stay dry and warm and scrounging up enough food to keep our gut from growling. Truth be told, we was nearbout bad off as the Yankees. Word was, there was stores aplenty a few miles back at Chickamauga Station that General Bragg somehow didn't see fit to give us. That didn't help matters none, rumor or truth.

Towards the end of October, some twenty thousand fresh bluebellies showed up from the west, and after a hot fight, pushed our boys back at Brown's Ferry on the Tennessee River. That give the Yanks control of the river west of Chattanooga and opened up their supply line. A few weeks later that goldamn Yankee General Sherman come marching into their works with another twenty thousand troops. We knowed then something big was stirring.

That Yank army was something to behold. They was nearbout a hundred thousand strong now, well fed and equipped, whilst we numbered forty-some thousand pitiful hungry scarecrows. At night their campfires looked plentiful as the stars in the sky, and daytimes they would prance around and parade whilst their bands played all sorts of fancy music. It was a right impressive sight to see. But if it was a fight they was hankering for, we was more'n game to oblige 'em.

Don't recollect the exact day, but it was sometime during the last week of November when the Yanks struck our lines below Missionary Ridge at a place called Orchard Knob. Us Florida boys was strung out a ways behind the knob in a skirmish line at the base of the ridge. Around high noon drums went to beating and bugles commenced blowing and here come the bluebellies marching towards us like they was on parade!

For an hour or so the Alabama boys that was picketed alongside and atop Orchard Knob figured the Yanks was just strutting and putting on a show. Then more bugles cut loose and them bluebellies commenced charging with flags flying and bayonets glittering. Them poor Alabamians was sorely outnumbered, but they give the Yanks a goodly dose of shot and steel before their works was overrun. Them that could fell back to our works at the base of the ridge whilst we cut loose volley after volley to cover their retreat. The Yanks kept at it the rest of the day, but the fight finally petered out when dark and the weather set in.

Next day the Yanks struck all along our lines. The fight was hot and heavy to our left up on Lookout Mountain. The clouds had set in and we couldn't see a goldamn thing, but from the sounds of it our boys was in a real tussle. In the center where we was, it seemed the Yanks couldn't make up their mind what they was up to. Here and yonder a fight would break out for a spell, and then sputter. To the right, things got hot for a hour or two, but the fighting quieted down by dark.

Later that night, a eerie thing happened, something I ain't forgot in all these years. Of a sudden the clouds parted and a full moon lit up the sky. Frost shined silver on rocks and bushes far as the eye could see. Then the moon commenced to disappear like a biscuit being eat, bite by bite. Soon it was gone except for a faint glow around the edges. Ain't ashamed to say that there eclipse chilled me nearbout as much as the cold. Most of the boys took it as a omen of sorts. Weren't sure if it was for good or bad, but it didn't make sleeping no easier.

Didn't know it then, but the Yanks had pushed our boys slap off of Lookout Mountain that day. That fight was what come to be called the famous Battle Above the Clouds. The valley to our left was plumb crawling with Yanks spoiling to get on with the fight come morning. And after a bitter cold and wet miserable night, that's just what they done.

THIRTY ★ TWO

WELL, SIR, NEXT MORNING ALL hell broke loose. Early on, the Yanks struck our right at Tunnel Hill something fierce. The main road and railroad south to Atlanta run through that pass, and if the bluebellies captured it, the Army of Tennessee would be done in for sure. Our boys there, led by the gallant General Patrick Cleburne, beat back attack after attack and held on throughout the long day and night of fighting.

Around midmorning the Yanks struck our center. We throwed 'em back again and again, but by early afternoon they broke through somewheres down our line and commenced to roll up our flank. Weren't no choice but to fall back to a second line of works a piece farther up the ridge.

It was some hot scrap scrambling up that ridge with them Yanks close on our heels. Balls was whizzing and snapping like mad hornets in ever direction, ricocheting off rocks and trees and kicking up dirt at our feet. The boys on up the ridge kept blasting away at the Yanks, doing the best they could to buy us time to make it to the works.

Here and yonder some poor soul cried out and fell. A passel of our boys give it up and surrendered. Me and Joe Porter stuck close, using whatever boulders or trees was handy for cover on our way up the steep ridge. Ever now and again one of us would turn and fire, then reload on the run whilst the other done the same. More'n once them bluebellies called out for us to surrender, but we kept going. Seemed like a month of Sunday sermons before we finally stumbled into our works.

For a spell me and Joe laid in the bottom of the trench like two broke-down horses, trying to catch our breath. The boys manning the works kept firing and reloading fast as they could.

Joe turned his head and puked, wiped his mouth with a filthy sleeve and says, "Lord a'mighty, I thought we was done for sure."

I checked my rifle, seen there was a fresh cap on the nipple, then got to my feet. "We best give these fellers a hand or we will be yet."

Me and Joe took a place in line and commenced firing at the Yanks swarming up the ridge like ants to a picnic. "Ain't never seen so many Yankees in all my born days," Joe says whilst reloading his Enfield. "They's thicker than the flies on that dead mule back at Chickymauga."

"I ain't going to argue that." I pointed my barrel through the head log, seen a patch of blue through the thick smoke and fired. Commenced to reload and seen I had maybe six or eight balls left in my pouch. "Say, Joe, you got any lead to spare?"

Joe squeezed off a shot, then hunkered down and checked his pouch. "Got maybe a dozen."

I looked at Joe, but he knowed what I was fixing to say and beat me to it. "Reckon we ought to borrow some from them boys then," he says, nodding towards a couple of poor souls laying nearby who had gone to meet their Maker.

Well, sir, I weren't never one to plunder from the dead, specially them wearing the same uniform as me, but we was in a bad fix and them poor souls had no more use for it, so we done what had to be done.

The fighting went on for what must've been a good two hours and still the Yanks kept coming. Our rifles got so hot we had to let 'em cool down lest the powder flashed when we poured it down the barrel. We took to throwing rocks at the Yanks whilst letting our rifles cool. Some of the boys grabbed stout limbs and used 'em to pry loose big boulders that went crashing down the hill like great bowling balls. The ridge was so steep in places our artillery couldn't aim low enough, so the artillery boys commenced lighting fuses and tossing live shells down the hill by hand. It was a mighty fierce scrap, gospel truth.

Late afternoon, word come down the lines to fall back to the works atop Missionary Ridge. Our flanks was being rolled up, and there just weren't no stopping the bluebellies. So we crawled out of our works and commenced another running fight towards the top of the ridge. It was nearbout a repeat of what we done earlier in the day. Scores of our boys was struck down, a passel more was captured. Somehow luck was holding tight to me and Joe. We made it to the works, took our place in line and commenced to fight.

Throughout the day's fight, companies had got mixed together amongst all the confusion and retreating. Me and Joe was fighting alongside fellers we didn't recognize, but they was still mostly Florida boys from Colonel Finley's brigade, or Alabamians. Towards dark orders come for a general retreat. That was jim-dandy by me. I'd had more'n a bellyful of this fight. Truth be told, I was plumb sick of this whole soldiering business. All I wanted was to go home and marry up with Annie and live in peace. Let the Yanks have this goldamn worthless pile of rocks.

Then word come that us Florida boys weren't leaving just yet. We was staying put a spell to entertain the bluebellies so the rest of General Bragg's army could escape. Well, sir, them was words I didn't much cotton to hear. Figured me and Joe was goners for sure. There was only so much luck to go around, and I figured ours was just about plumb used up.

We was ordered to fall back a ways to a narrow pass where a road cut through the ridge. We took up positions amongst the rocks on either side of the road. Once the Yankees gained the ridge they'd have to come through that pass to follow Bragg's retreat.

It was near dark when the first of the Yanks come marching towards the pass. We waited till they was nearbout on us, then we cut loose with a volley that sent 'em skedaddling. They come at us again and again, but our position was a good one and with the cannons we had with us we managed to keep 'em at bay.

After a spell, scouts reported that the Yankees was trying to flank us, so we pulled back to yet another position that had been picked out beforehand for just such a situation. We'd barely got settled when the bluebellies come a calling. Our cannons cut loose with canister and we commenced to give 'em volley after volley till they fell back again.

It was nearbout midnight before the Yanks finally give it up. We was plumb tuckered, but we had done the job. The Army of Tennessee was saved, leastways what was left of it. It was a hour or two before dawn when we lit out to catch up with the rest of our army.

"Joe," I says, blowing frost with ever breath as we hoofed it down the road towards Georgia, "this soldiering business is getting a mite tough to chew. What say we just keep on walking south till we hit Florida?"

Joe tongued his chaw to his other cheek and spit. "How far you figure it is to home?"

I swapped shoulders with my Enfield. "Don't rightly know; five or six hundred miles I reckon."

Joe give a little laugh and spit again. "Hell, the way them Yankees been hounding us, we'll be home in a week."

Calvin Hogue
July 1927

THIRTY ★ THREE

A FEW DAYS LATER, DOCTOR Adams discharged Daniel from the hospital on the condition that he spend the next couple of weeks under Alma's watchful care. Hearing the good news, and after getting permission from Uncle Hawley to take the day off, I offered my services to drive Alma and Daniel to her home in Bennet.

"Why that's real sweet of you, sugar," Alma said, flashing her warm smile. "That'll save my Hiram a day off from the mill, and spare me and Uncle Dan from getting a sore backside bouncing around in that old truck of ours. But you got to promise you'll stay to supper."

Except for the tight squeeze fitting the three of us in the roadster, the ride to Bennet was uneventful. Despite the warm day, I put the top up to keep the wind off Daniel. We passed the time with small talk until Daniel dozed off.

"It's just past the Marianna turnoff, sugar," said Alma when we reached the outskirts of Bennet. "That big ol' place yonder on the right."

Alma's house was a large two-story affair. There were two wings connected by a dogtrot, fronted by a wraparound shaded porch. The faded white paint was chalked and peeling in places, but the wood appeared to be in good condition. The porch was nicely accented with numerous potted plants and flowers in hanging baskets.

"Watch your step, sweetie," Alma said to Daniel as we helped him up the steps and onto the porch. The front door stood open. Alma pulled back the screen door and held it. "Y'all come on in, and don't mind any mess my boys may've left."

She led the way through the huge parlor to a bedroom at the front of the left wing. "I got your bed all ready," she said, pulling back the quilt and fluffing up a couple of large feather pillows.

Daniel eased onto the bed and leaned back into the pillows. "Where's my pipe? I ain't had a smoke in—"

"Now, Uncle Dan, you know good and well what Doc Adams said. Your lungs got to clear more before you can go back to that pipe. You want a chew, sweetie, or some snuff? Hiram's got both."

"Humph, goldamn doctors. Never wanted to go to that highfalutin hospital noways."

After Daniel was settled down, Alma led me back into the main wing of the house. "This old place ain't much to look at Calvin, but it's home."

I looked around the big parlor with its high ceilings and comfortable furnishings. The mantel above the stone fireplace was crowded with framed photographs and old tintypes. "It's a fine house. Reminds me a lot of my grandparents' home up in Pennsylvania."

Alma smiled and looked around like she was seeing the place for the first time. "It's been in Hiram's family for many a year. These front rooms here used to be the general store. But that was years ago."

I walked closer to the fireplace and glanced at the photos and tintypes. One tintype in particular caught my attention. An attractive young man and woman stood side by side wearing what looked to be wedding attire. Both had dark hair and appeared to be in their late teens or early twenties. The man was clean shaven, and his wavy hair was combed back showing a high forehead and intense dark eyes. The young woman's hair was piled atop her head with lovely ringlets curling down to her shoulders. She was beautiful, with striking dark eyes, high cheekbones and full lips.

"You don't recognize him, sugar?" Alma's eyes sparkled, enhancing the ever-present smile.

I studied the tintype more closely but drew a blank. "No, should I?"

Alma laughed. "Well, you sure ought to. You spent plenty of time talking with him lately. That's my daddy, Elijah Malburn."

When Alma's words finally sunk in, you could have—to borrow a phrase I'd heard from Eli—pushed me over with a feather duster! For the moment, I was speechless.

Alma picked up the tintype and gazed at it. She stroked a finger across the image. "This was taken on Mama and Daddy's wedding day, April twenty-second, eighteen sixty-six. Mama was nineteen. Daddy turned nineteen that August."

I remembered back to when Alma had introduced herself at the reunion: *"I'm Alma Hutchins, nee Malburn."* But the Malburns were such a large extended family that I'd never put two and two together. "And, your mother was . . .?"

"Annabelle," said Alma. "Wasn't she just beautiful? Mama was a Gainer, from the William Gainers. Her brother Tom fought with Uncle Dan in the Confederate Army. Tom was married to their sister, Sara." Alma placed the tintype back on the mantel. "I'd best quit reminiscing and see to supper. Them boys of mine'll be getting home anytime now.

"Oh, I nearly forgot, sugar. After supper I got a box of letters and other whatnot you'll be wanting to see."

——————◆——————

I left Alma's with a full stomach and an invitation to supper following my interview with Daniel the following Saturday. Best of all, I had discovered another important piece of the puzzle that was the Malburn brothers' story. Annabelle Gainer. Sweet Annie. Dan's Annie, or Eli's Annie?

It was beginning to come clear that far more than the war had wedged between Daniel and Elijah. I could hardly wait until I could go through the letters that Alma had given me. It would be a long week.

Daniel Malburn
Winter 1863-64
Dalton, Georgia

THIRTY ★ FOUR

WELL, SIR, ME AND JOE'S walk back home got cut a
mite short when General Bragg halted the retreat at Dalton,
just a few miles below Chattanooga. We took up positions on
Rocky Face Ridge. It run roughly twenty-some miles north to
south betwixt us and the Yanks. Rocky Face was a mighty fine
defensive position. It was so steep a mountain goat would have a
time climbing it. The few passes that cut through it could be held
by a handful of well-armed soldiers. We commenced fortifying
Rocky Face with strong works and waited for the bluebellies to
show.

Seems the Yanks had had theirselves a bellyful of fighting for
a spell. Here and yonder a skirmish broke out, but they never
did strike us in force. Reckon they didn't fancy attacking up that
ridge. Weren't long before our cavalry reported the main body
of Yanks had pulled back to their works at Chattanooga. That
was some welcome news, but we kept our eyes peeled anyways.

Over the next several days a passel of stragglers found their
way to our position on Rocky Face Ridge. Amongst them was
some Company K boys, including three of me and Joe's pards
that had joined our mess after Chickamauga. Orville Cowart and

Goose Hutchins was both Bennet boys. They was first cousins, but a body would be hard put to know it by looking at 'em. Orv was maybe five foot three in his shoes and nearbout as big around. He weren't fat, just built like a cannonball and strong to boot. His pa run the local blacksmith shop and livery.

Goose, whose given name was Charles, was a good foot taller than Orv and thin as a fence rail. He had this long neck and big beak of a nose, so folks natural took to calling him Goose when he was just a young'un. Goose's family owned the general store in Bennet. If you ain't guessed it yet, years later Goose become Alma's daddy-in-law. She married up with his youngest boy, Hiram, around nineteen and ten, if I remember rightly.

The other feller was Billy Yon. He was a skinny redheaded young'un, seventeen as I recollect. Billy had joined up same time as Hamp Watts, but come down with the ague before Chickamauga and missed that fight. His folks worked a small farm north of the Gainer plantation, up near the Alabama line.

After a spell, word come that General Bragg had resigned and General Joe Johnston had took command of the Army of Tennessee. We also learnt we was staying put at Dalton for the winter, so we commenced building winter quarters. The boys took turns guarding the ridge whilst others cut down trees to build log huts to shelter us agin the cold weather that was already setting in. Weren't long before our mess had ourselves a right snug log cabin, with split wood floors and a mud and stone fireplace to boot.

General Johnston had inherited hisself one miserable army, that's the gospel. But "Ol' Joe," as we come to call him, didn't waste no time putting things right. When we first got to Dalton, most the boys was in rags and a goodly number was barefoot to boot. A passel of fellers had lost or throwed away their rifles during the fight and retreat, and we was all nearbout starved. Weren't long till General Johnston had trains rolling in from Atlanta with new uniforms, shoes, weapons—nearbout everthing a army could need. And food—well, sir, we ain't eat so good in a blue moon. It weren't no time at all till the Army of Tennessee was a whole different critter than that miserable bunch of scarecrows that stumbled into Dalton.

It was some cold winter, but the days we weren't manning

the works on Rocky Face Ridge or marching and drilling, we kept right snug in that cabin of ours. Many a night was passed sitting by a warm fire playing cards or reading or writing home and such. Weren't long before the trains brung us something we treasured more'n all them fine supplies we sorely needed. One morning towards late December, Joe come back from fetching our rations toting a handful of letters from home. Since Chickamauga mail had been scarcer'n hen's teeth, so us boys took to that mail like fleas to a hound.

I put my Annie's letter in the pocket next to my heart and opened the one from my mama first. It was dated sometime early in November of 'sixty-three. I don't recollect the exact date; it got smudged out over the years.

Things was fine at the farm, Mama wrote, and everbody was getting on tolerable, what with the war being on and all. They was all sad to hear the news of poor Hamp's passing, but took comfort knowing he was with the Lord. What I read next was more'n a mite troubling.

Elijah and Jefferson was home from the saltworks a few days this month past. Your brother was sorely grieved upon learning the tragic news regarding Hampton. Those two was so close.

I fear something may have befallen Elijah and Jefferson. They left to deliver a load of supplies to the saltworks and was to return in a few days' time. It has been near two weeks and there is no word of them since. Aunt Nettie is worried sick, as am I. I pray they are only delayed and will arrive home soon.

Now a feller off soldiering has worries aplenty without fretting about folks back home. Just looking out for hisself and his pards is a bellyful. My mama being worried sick over both her sons didn't make the load I was toting any lighter. But knowing my brother, I was more mad than worried. Figured him and Jefferson was off somewheres having theirselves a high time and would get on home when they took a mind to.

My heart commenced beating a mite faster as I opened Annie's letter. The pages was scented with her favorite lilac toilet water. I breathed in her scent and unfolded the pages. Inside was a square of finespun cloth that had been stitched about the edges. In the center was the red outline of Annie's sweet lips where she had kissed it.

I looked around to make sure none of the boys was watching, then I put my lips to her sweet kiss. Nearbout felt like crying, I missed her so. I weren't never much of the praying sort, but before I commenced reading Annie's letter I asked the Lord to watch out for all the folks back home, specially my Annabelle.

"And Lord, if you see fit, please take care of me and my pards too," I says. "Reckon you know how sick we are of this war and all the killing. I'd be much obliged if you seen to it we get home safe."

Well, sir, the Good Book says, "Ask and it shall be given you." I never put much stock in the Bible in them days, but I was sure hoping the Lord would make good on his word. Didn't know it then, but it weren't two weeks later me and Joe Porter would be on our way home!

THIRTY ★ FIVE

NOT LONG AFTER HE TOOK command of the army, General Johnston commenced granting furloughs. That sure set right with the boys and put "Ol' Joe" in fine favor. Orv and Goose had been on leave with Tom Gainer before Chickamauga. Me and Joe hadn't been home since we joined up in March of 'sixty-two, so we was the first amongst our mess to get furlough. Soon as I learnt the good news, I wrote home to Mama and Annie.

In mid-January, me and Joe boarded the train at Dalton and headed south towards Atlanta. It was a bitter cold day with gray skies and a biting wind, but we was happy as spring robins. Didn't have no overcoat, but we wrapped up tight in our blankets and made do.

The train stopped for a spell at Resaca to take on water and other soldiers. Then the whistle blowed a time or two and we chugged on south. "This is fine country hereabouts," says Joe, looking out the window towards a valley ringed by low hills. "I'm a mite sick of them mountains."

The train was just passing through the covered bridge that spanned the Oostanaula River. "Joe Porter," I says, "if I had a dollar for ever bellyache I heard you utter, I'd be a rich man for sure."

Yes, sir, we was in fine spirits as we watched Resaca disappear behind us. We was leaving the war and soldiering behind, for a spell anyways. A few more days and we'd be home.

Weren't no way of knowing that we'd be passing this way again some four months later. Things wouldn't be near so gay then.

————◆————

A few days later, me and Joe stepped off a steamer at the landing in Chattahoochee. We was mighty glad to be back in our home state. We slung our blanket rolls and walked over to the Confederate detachment that was stationed in Chattahoochee. We showed the clerk our furlough papers, then signed a ledger for the use of two horses, tack and saddles and enough rations for the ride to Econfina.

We rode till well after dark, then camped along the road a few miles north of Marianna. At dawn we was saddled up and on our way. Passed through Marianna at midmorning, stopping just long enough to rest and water the horses and woof down a hot meal at a local eatery.

We rode hard the rest of the day and made camp well after dark a couple of miles north of Porter's Mill. Joe was almost home, but he didn't want to raise a ruckus showing up at night. We built a fire, ate the last of our rations, then stretched out on our bedrolls trying our goldamndest to fall asleep. Reckon Joe was too excited being so near to home and all. After a spell I heard him stir, then sit up. "Danny, you awake?"

"I am now," I says, rubbing my eyes and scowling at him across the dying fire. "What's so all-fired important you went and ruint my good dream for?"

"I'm scared."

"Joe Porter, there ain't no Yankees in these parts. And if there is, well hell, we'll just up and surrender to 'em and be done with it. Go to sleep."

"That ain't what I mean."

"Well, just what is it you *do* mean?" I says. "I ain't up to playing riddles at this hour."

"You ever think how things will be when we're home?

Our folks and all? We ain't the same now. Things is different somehow."

I chawed on Joe's words a minute. Truth be told, I'd done a passel of thinking about just such my own self. The war had changed us, the hard living and killing. All the suffering and death we seen had built a wall inside us that shut out part of ourselves from others. We had growed hard, old beyond our years. "Hell, you're just tuckered. A few days sleeping in a featherbed and eating that good cooking of your ma's and you'll be the same Ol' Joe Porter that left home two years ago.

"Now, shut that trap of yours and get to sleep, else I'll up and shut it for you."

THIRTY ★ SIX

I TURNED MY HORSE ONTO the wooded road that led down to our farm on Econfina Creek. The sky was clear winter blue. Chimney smoke rose above the tall pines and naked hardwoods. Somewheres in the distance I heard the mournful lowing of cattle along the creek. After two long years, I was home.

Of a sudden a feeling swept through me, that same cold fist that squeezed my gut when we was commencing to march agin the enemy. I felt like turning around and skedaddling back to Chattahoochee. I halted the horse and dismounted. Figured on walking the rest of the way to give myself time to get ahold of my wits. This was my home. The war and soldiering was far away. Weren't nothing or nobody here for me to fear. I drawed in the good cold air and smelled wood smoke and piney woods. I weren't used to so much riding. It felt good to stretch my legs. Started feeling a sight better.

I walked past Uncle Nate and Aunt Nellie's cabin and seen a fine crop of collards growing in their winter garden. Weren't nothing stirring about their place but chickens. I figured Nate and Nellie would be up at the house by this time. Soon the road narrowed into a lane bordered on both sides by a limestone and rail fence me and Eli had helped our daddy build when we was just young'uns. The lane curved left and yonder stood the house. The place looked fine, just like I'd remembered it in my dream that first morning at Chickamauga. Even the barn back of the summer kitchen looked freshly whitewashed. Uncle Nate and Eli had done a good job keeping things fit.

I walked on towards the house. Thin smoke was rising from the parlor fireplace and the kitchen chimney, and I caught the smell of baking bread. Here and yonder chickens was scratching up the yard, chasing after whatever bugs they could stir up on a winter's day. A bluetick hound I didn't recollect was sleeping near the big magnolia over by the summer kitchen. He sat up, give a halfhearted "woof" and commenced wagging his tail.

I whistled to the dog whilst I tied the horse to a fence rail but he just kept sweeping the ground with that tail. Untied my blanket roll and swung open the gate that led to the porch. Just as I reached the steps a voice called out.

"My, if you ain't a sight fo' so' eyes!"

I turned and seen Uncle Nate walking down the steps from the dogtrot, his cottony hair and beard shining like snow agin his coal-black skin. "Hey there, Uncle Nate!" I says, and we give each other a big hug.

"Mistah Danny, Mistah Danny," Uncle Nate says, hugging me tighter, "how is you, boy? Yo' mama goan be mighty glad you's home safe." Uncle Nate kept ahold of my shoulders and looked me over, then busted out laughing. "What happen to you, boy? Why, you near dark as me."

I rubbed my cheek and looked at my hand. I *was* a mite filthy. "Reckon it's all that good Georgia dirt and smoke smudge," I says, and laughed. "We don't get much chance to wash up at the war."

Uncle Nate's dark eyes was shining and his yellow teeth showed through the big grin on his face. "Let's get on to the house. Yo' mama and baby sistahs goan pitch a hissy fit when they sees you. Yo' Aunt Nettie goan boil water fo' yo' bath. Don't you worry none, Mistah Danny, we goan clean you right up. Cain't have you lookin' like no fieldhand, no suh."

I slunk down in the iron bathtub till weren't nothing but my head sticking above the water. A layer of brown scum floated on the water. It had took two good scrubbings with Aunt Nettie's lye soap before I got respectable clean. With that chore done, I was letting the hot water soothe me to the bone. From what I had just learnt at breakfast, I sorely needed soothing, gospel truth.

When all the hugging and kissing and carrrying on with my mama and sisters and Aunt Nettie was over with, they set me down to a late breakfast of grits, eggs and fresh sausage Uncle Nate had made the week before. I told 'em Joe's ma had done stuffed me, but Mama and Aunt Nettie wouldn't take no for a answer. I hadn't yet asked about Eli and Jefferson, but everbody seemed in good spirits so I figured they was safe, maybe off working on the farm somewheres. When I did ask Mama bout 'em, she give me a queer look and said they was well. Then she showed me a letter Eli had wrote from Cedar Keys, and said him and Jefferson had joined up with the Union Army. Well, sir, I was nearbout struck dumb hearing that. Plumb lost my appetite too.

Whilst Aunt Nettie was filling the tub, I took the letter from my ma and read it time and again. Eli and Jefferson had got theirselves captured by Yankees that was raiding near the saltworks. They had conscripted Jefferson into the U.S. Colored Infantry and give my brother the choice of joining the Union Army or going to prison camp. Eli up and took the oath so he could watch out for Jefferson. It was his duty to do such, he wrote.

Well, sir, I laid in that tub tussling with my thoughts. My own brother, wearing Yankee blue whilst me and my pards was off fighting the goldamn bluebelly invaders to keep 'em off our sacred Southern soil! How in tarnation could he've went and done such a thing? Weren't it the Yanks that kilt his best pal? I recollected how Eli come home one day when he weren't much taller'n a cypress knee, his thumb sliced open nearbout to the bone. Him and Hamp had cut theirselves so they could swap blood and be blood brothers like they'd heard Indians done.

Now poor Hamp Watts was dead, kilt by the Yankees at Chickamauga. And Eli had up and joined 'em! I knowed

Jefferson was a mite slow-witted at times, but he weren't some helpless young'un. That boy could work ever bit as hard as any man. He knowed right from wrong, his good Christian folks had seen to it, and he knowed how to do what he was told.

No, sir, there weren't no good reason for my brother doing what he done. Much as it pained me, the way I seen it, Eli was a traitor. There weren't no honor in what he done, and sooner or later there was bound to be devil to pay. Prison would've been a sight better than joining up with the enemy agin his own people.

I decided not to let on to the family how I felt about this sad affair. Our mama had troubles enough weighing on her heart already. I weren't going to dump more for her to tote. It was done, and there weren't nothing I could do to change things. But I sure didn't have to like it none.

THIRTY ★ SEVEN

NEXT MORNING AFTER BREAKFAST I washed up and shaved the whiskers off my face. Rummaged through my closet and got out my best Sunday go-to-meeting clothes and tried 'em on. They still fit tolerable, if a mite looser than before I left for the war. It weren't Sunday, but I was calling on my Annie and wanted to look proper.

Yesterday I'd sent word to the Gainer plantation that I was home, and with their kind permission would call on Annabelle around Friday noon. A servant from the Gainer plantation arrived that evening with a note in Annie's own delicate hand, saying she'd be counting the hours till I come. Well, sir, I was plumb tickled to hear that. I reached in my breeches pocket to make sure the small box was there.

When I was done spiffying up, I saddled the horse and headed down the road behind our house to the creek. I crossed the bridge that spanned the creek betwixt the Malburn and Watts' farms. My daddy and Coleman Watts had built that wagon bridge years ago, soon after they settled on the Econfina. It was the finest piece of bottomland in the area, I'd heard my daddy say, so them two decided to split it up and farm on opposite sides of the creek.

Mama told me Yerby was home and doing well as could be expected, what with losing his leg and all, so I decided to stop on the way and visit a spell. I come out of the woods near the creek and seen a couple of Mister Watts' slaves hoeing a field of cabbage and winter greens. I waved to 'em and followed the wagon road the quarter mile up to the Watts house. Wood smoke was rising from two slave cabins nearby, and the sweet scent of curing meat come from the big smokehouse on ahead.

I rode around to the front of the house and there was Yerb, sitting on the porch in a straight-backed chair, crutches and a shotgun propped nearby agin the railing. "Howdy, Yerb."

"Daniel Malburn," says Yerby, his voice sounding cold as the north wind, "still drawing breath, I see. Your ma warned me you'd be coming."

I climbed off the horse and tied him to the hitching post out front of the porch. Opened the saddlebags and took out two jars of peach preserves Mama had put up. "Been in a tight scrape or two, but I'm still kicking," I says, walking up the steps onto the porch. "Your daddy home?" I held up the jars, trying hard not to look towards Yerb's missing leg. "Mama sent these."

Yerb turned his head and spit a stream of tobacco juice over the porch rail. "He's down to Ard's Ferry for supplies. Help is scarce around here nowadays, what with Hamp dead and me crippled. Reckon Daddy's got more work than he can rightly handle."

I set the preserves on the rail and took a seat beside 'em. "What's with the shotgun?" I says, and give a little laugh trying to lighten the mood. "You got a salt lick somewheres out in the yard?"

"Ain't after no deer." Yerby spit again. "Heard there was bluebellies stirring around the bay a while back. Figured any goddamn Yanks come this way, I best be ready."

Well, sir, the silence that followed was as cold as ice. I knowed what Yerb was digging at. His brother was dead, and Yerb was a one-legged cripple, to hear him tell it. And my brother was one of them goddamn Yanks he was so antsy to blast with that scattergun of his.

"Joe Porter is home," I says, hoping that might cheer Yerb some. "He's fit. Says he'll be up to see you shortly."

"I heard the bluebellies sent you peckerwoods skedaddling from Chattanooga," Yerby says, ignoring my news about Joe. "Any more Econfina boys gone up?"

I took a minute recollecting what had happened when the Yanks kicked us off Missionary Ridge. "Earl Hayes is dead, shot through the head. The Ferguson boys both went missing. Word is they was captured. And one of the Hicks twins lost a leg." I flinched. Them words had jumped out before I knowed what I was saying. "Sorry, Yerb."

Yerb give a cold laugh. "Don't you fret none. Us cripples got to stick together. Which of them Hicks boys was it?"

"Jeremiah. He took a ball in the thigh. Last I heard, gangrene had set in. He's in a hospital somewheres near Atlanta."

Yerby laughed again. "Well, their mama won't have no trouble telling which is which, will she? Maybe he'll get lucky yet and die. Better'n being a damn cripple the rest of his years."

I'd nearbout had my fill of Yerb feeling sorry for hisself. And I was a mite tired of toting eggs ever time I was around him. I knowed Hamp was dead and Yerb had lost a leg. But he weren't the only one that had suffered in this war. There was misery aplenty to go around. "Goldamnit Yerb, losing a leg below the knee don't make you a cripple. Old Jessup Miller lost his in the Mexican War and he does right fine on that wooden leg of his. Ain't no reason you cain't do the same if you quit your bellyaching and give it a try."

Yerb's jaws clenched and his face commenced turning red. He stared at me with them cold, hard eyes of his, pure hate shining in 'em. He give a laugh and cut loose another stream of juice that splattered near my shoes. "Them's easy enough words to say, being it ain't your leg they took and it ain't your brother that's rotting in some unmarked grave."

Well, sir, them words stung. I looked down at my shoes, checking for stains. "Just shined these shoes this morning. I'd be obliged if you was a mite more careful where you spit."

Yerb used his good leg to rock back in the chair. He looked out across the yard a spell, then back at me. "This is my porch, reckon I can spit any damn where I please."

I felt my own face burning. I eased off the porch rail and walked towards the steps, then turned around. "There ain't a day goes by I don't grieve for Hamp," I says. "And I hate it that you lost your leg. But weren't none of it my doing. We're pards, Yerb. We growed up together. Why is it you treating me like the enemy?"

Yerb pushed hisself up till he was standing, then took a short hop to the porch rail. Grabbed one of the crutches and leaned on it. "Reckon I'm just a mite bitter. It was goddamn Yankees that kilt my brother and cost me my leg. Ain't nothing going to bring either of 'em back, I know that."

Yerb tongued the chaw out of his cheek and spit it over the rail into the yard. "Thing is, your brother chose to join up with the goddamn enemy, the very same that took Hamp and my leg. Don't see how I can ever forgive that. Don't see how the Watts and Malburns can ever see eye to eye again."

I walked on down the steps, untied my horse and mounted up. "I hate hearing that," I says. "What Eli done shames me, I ain't denying that. But he's still my blood and my brother. And he weren't nowheres near Chickamauga, Yerb. Remember that." Then I turned my horse and rode off.

THIRTY ★ EIGHT

I THOUGHT ME AND ANNIE weren't never going to get away by ourselves. Mister Gainer and his missus wanted to know all the latest news about the war, their son Tom and the rest of us Econfina boys that was off soldiering with the great Army of Tennessee. And sister Sara was worse yet, pestering me to no end for news about her husband.

"Is my Tom well? Is he eating proper? Did he receive the packages I sent? Does he want for anything?" On and on she blabbered till my ears nearbout fell off. I was downright ill of talking about war and soldiering, but I kept mannerly and bore all the palavering and done my duty to be a proper guest.

Took the best part of a hour sitting in that fancy parlor getting grilled like a roasting shoat before Annie come to my rescue. "Now, Daddy, you and Mother and Sara will just have to wait till supper to ask Daniel any more questions," she says. He's come to see *me*, after all." Then she stood up from the settee we was sharing, grabbed my arm and led me out onto their big covered porch.

We set on the porch swing a spell, rocking back and forth whilst holding hands and making small talk. Truth be told, much as I'd wanted to be alone with Annie, I was feeling a mite shy and uncomfortable. Annabelle Gainer had done some growing up in the two years I'd been gone. That loose dress with the puffy sleeves and buttoned-up collar didn't much hide the womanly body underneath. She was downright beautiful. More'n once I caught myself staring where a gentleman ought'n be, and there was a antsy hunger in my groin that shamed me.

But I had important business to get to, so after a spell I mustered the courage and asked Annie to take a walk. We set off down the path through the woods to the big springs on the Gainer property. The green pines shimmering agin the blue sky was a sight to behold. Annie pulled her shawl tight about her shoulders and leaned into me as we strolled along.

We come to the clearing around the springs. The crystal-clear water bubbled out of the main hole like it was boiling hot. It had been a spell since I'd been swimming, and for a minute I had a mind to strip down to my long johns and jump in. The springs in these parts stay around sixty-eight to seventy degrees year-round. Feels mighty cold when the weather's hot, but in the winter a body feel's like he's sitting in a warm bath, that's the gospel.

We took a seat on the flat limestone rock that hung over the mouth of the main spring. We held hands, and after a spell I took the chance to put my arm around Annie's shoulders. She snuggled closer, nuzzled her cheek agin my shoulder. Looked up at me with them big doe eyes, then we was kissing for the first time since I'd rode off for the war.

Well, sir, when we was done my insides was all aquiver. Figured I'd best get on with it before I lost my gumption. I give Annie a quick peck on the cheek and fished the small box out of my pocket.

In Dalton we'd got paid for the first time in months. When I learnt me and Joe was getting a furlough, I'd visited one of the sutlers near camp. Found a fine silver ring with a flowery vine etched around the band. After some dickering, I bought it. It cost me plenty but I figured it was worth ever cent, because I aimed to marry up with Annie whilst I was home.

Annie give a gasp when I opened the box and showed her the ring. She held out her hand and I slipped it onto her ring finger, more'n a mite relieved to see it fit just fine.

"Oh my," Annie says, turning her hand this way and that, looking it over, "it's the prettiest ring I ever saw."

"I was hoping we could get married."

"Of course we will," she says, smiling and still admiring her ring.

I took a deep breath. "I mean . . . soon, whilst I'm home on leave."

Her hand stopped turning. She looked at me, her eyes wide, smile gone. Her mouth fell open like she was trying to let out words that wouldn't come. "Oh my," she finally says, frowning.

Well, sir, it felt like somebody had punched me hard in the gut. Just last night I imagined Annie throwing her arms around my neck and showering me with sweet kisses. Her sullen *"Oh my"* felt colder than the wind blowing agin the back of my neck.

Annie lowered her hands to her lap and stared out across the springs. "I *do* want to marry you, Daniel, truly I do, but—"

"But what? Ain't we been betrothed the past two years?"

"Yes, but—"

I got up in a huff and walked down to the spring. Picked up a flat rock and throwed it over the spring. It skipped two or three times and then sunk like my spirits. As I watched it go under I heard Annie's footsteps behind me and felt her hand on my arm.

"I love you with all my heart, and I do want to marry you. Only, I don't think Mother and Daddy will approve. Not while the war is on."

I turned around and seen tears welling in her eyes. "It ain't their say, is it? What about Tom and Sara? Lest I'm mistaken, the war was on when them two got hitched."

"My brother is twenty-five and Sara's twenty-two," Annie says. "Mother thinks I'm too young, especially with you away at the war."

I felt my hackles rise. "I'm twenty-one come March, and you're seventeen. I'll wager your ma weren't no older when she married your daddy."

Well, sir, we kept at it for a good hour or so, Annie giving sound reason after reason why it would make more sense for us to wait till the war was over before we married, me bucking up at ever point she made.

I finally growed tired of all the haggling. Truth be told, most of what Annie said made sense. There weren't no good reason for us to marry up now, only my selfishness. I couldn't take proper care of her whilst off fighting. And there weren't no arguing the fact that I might not live through the war, though Annie wouldn't hear of such talk. Last thing I wanted on this earth was to leave her a widow woman.

"It's settled then," I says after a make up hug and kiss. "We'll get hitched soon as this war is over and I get home."

Annie give a big laugh. "Even if I have to hogtie you and drag you to the church." The smile was back on her sweet lips.

"I'm holding you to it, Annabelle Gainer." I pulled her close. "Would you keep the ring on till I get back?"

Well, sir, it's been more'n sixty years but I still recollect Annie's very words. She looked up at me, them big doe eyes just a'shining. Then she kissed the ring and touched it to my lips. "I'll wear it for the rest of my days, Daniel Malburn. For the rest of my days."

Elijah Malburn
Late 1863
Soldiering at Cedar Keys

THIRTY ★ NINE

THE DAY AFTER I TOOK the oath, Major Weeks marched his command west along the coast a ways where we met up with a fleet of steamers that was anchored off the shore of West Bay. Spent two days waiting there while other troops come in with more recruits and conscripts, white and colored. Sunrise the third morning we rowed out and boarded the steamers and sailed east.

We was bound for the big Union garrison at Cedar Keys, some seventy-eighty miles east-southeast as the crow flies. We hugged the coastline for the goodly part of a week. Made stops at Hurricane Island on St. Andrew Bay and St. Vincent Island over by Apalachicola. At both camps we picked up a passel more volunteers and conscripts.

Them outposts was part of the Union blockade force aimed to keep supplies and such from coming into the Confederacy. They also served as refugee shelters. Back then, these parts was full of Rebel deserters and conscript shirkers and other such trash. Folks loyal to the Confederate cause didn't much cotton to traitors or their kinfolk, so them with Union leanings looked for protection under Yankee guns.

It was some rough trip once we set out across the gulf for Cedar Keys. It was blowing a gale and them waves must've been eight-ten foot high. Being it was the first time I'd ever been to sea I took a mite ill. Fact is, I was sick as a hydrophobie dog. The colored troops was on a different boat, but I found out later poor Jeff and Nebo didn't fare no better. As I recollect, it took two days to make Cedar Keys. I was more'n a mite glad to set foot on solid ground again, that's a fact.

I hear Cedar Keys is a right purty place nowadays, but back then it was dreary thereabouts, leastwise the army garrison was. Most ever tree had been chopped down to build officer quarters and other buildings a army camp needs. The enlisted troops was housed in rows of tents that stretched along the salt marsh a half-mile or so. The skeeters and sand gnats and flies liked to've toted us off, they was so bad. It was some miserable.

Soon as I could I bought writing paper and pencils from a sutler and sent word to home that me and Jefferson was safe and fit though we was in a unfortunate fix of sorts. Explained best I could how the Yankees had captured us and how they declared Jeff a contraband and conscripted him into the army. How they give me the choice of joining up or going to prison. Told 'em that I went and joined up so I could keep a eye out for Jeff. Swore I'd do my best to get us both out of this mess safe and sound. Didn't believe a word of it at the time, sonny, but figured it might give some comfort to Jeff's folks and the family.

Refugees had built a shanty town just outside the main camp. Them folks was a sorry lot. Most the women and children was barefoot and wore rags. Had to keep a sharp eye on the menfolk else they'd cut your throat and rob you blind. Couldn't trust the young'uns neither. Little scoundrels would steal anything that weren't locked up or nailed down. The lot of 'em was sickly, mostly skin and bones. Seemed there weren't never enough food to go around. The army did what it could to keep 'em fed and doctored, but the troops was often short on rations and such theirselves. Most ever day the ague or some other pestilence took a misfortunate soul or two, refugees and soldiers alike.

I was now a private in the U.S. Second Florida Cavalry, most of which was West Florida or southern Georgia and Alabama boys. Some was right fine fellers, doing what they felt was their patriotic duty to God and the Union and such. But a goodly number weren't nothing more'n common rabble and weren't to be trusted whether they was Union sympathizers or Confederate deserters. Mornings at roll call it weren't unusual to find two-three of 'em had hightailed it during the night.

The first two-three weeks at Cedar Keys was spent marching and drilling and learning other such military hogwash. Quartermaster issued me a spiffy Yankee uniform, a right fine mount with a McClellan saddle and a pair of Remington forty-four caliber revolvers. Never did tote a sword or one of them fancy carbines, but swords was mostly for show anyways and carbines was hard to come by at the time.

I'd signed on as a scout, but being as I could read and write Major Weeks made me his courier too. That was the major's highfalutin word for messenger boy. The major weren't a bad sort, and being his errand boy had its rewards. As such, my quarters and overall situation was a heap better than most enlisted fellers fared. It weren't long before I settled down and got used to the routine of army life. I didn't much cotton to soldiering, but reckoned it was a heap more tolerable than prison.

Jeff and Nebo was members of the Second U.S. Colored Infantry, which was commanded by white officers. The colored quarters was in a separate part of the camp and they done their drilling and such mostly by theirselves. As it turned out, the Second Florida Cavalry and the Second Colored Troops done a heap of soldiering together, so it seems the good Lord was looking out for me and Jeff after all.

Some days was busier than others, and when things was slow and my duties was caught up, Major Weeks give me permission to visit Jeff and Nebo. Them two was in the same squad and mess, which was fortunate. They looked out for each other and stuck together like body and shadow. Weren't likely to find one more'n spitting distance from the other, day or night. Both of 'em took to army life like pigs to slop, which weren't hard to figure since they'd both been slaves and used to doing what they was told.

Made me proud to see Jeff and Nebo doing so good, that's a fact. Cain't say I weren't still worried some, though. Marching and drilling and whatnot is one thing. War is a whole 'nother critter, sonny, that's a fact. And dern if we weren't fixing to find that out.

FORTY

THE NEXT MONTH WE TOOK to the mainland, raiding farms and beating the bushes chasing after bands of Rebels that was herding cattle northward to feed the Confederate armies.

Now I didn't much give a hoot for either side's cause in that dern war, sonny. But I sure didn't cotton to robbing people out of house and home which is what we done to them poor folks that lived thereabouts. "Spoils of war" was what Major Weeks called it. Cowardly thieving and plundering is what it were. What our boys couldn't tote off they made dern sure the "secesh" wouldn't have no more use for it. More'n once a poor woman with half-starved young'uns was left without so much as their milk cow or scrawny chickens to get by on. Them that give our boys a hard time was likely to get burnt out. I vowed early on I weren't going to have no hand in all that evilness, but it shames me to this day that I rode with them that did, white and colored.

Didn't much come of our soldiering neither, seeing how them Confederates knowed the country so well and was slicker than goose grease. Ever now and again they'd circle back and give us a volley, then they'd be gone before our boys knowed what hit 'em. It was like chasing shadows.

Towards year's end we did get in a right hot scrap near the railhead at Station Four, but I was off delivering a message for Major Weeks and missed most of that fight, which was fine by me. Fifteen-twenty colored troops was kilt or wounded, but the good Lord was watching out for Jeff and Nebo that day and neither of 'em got so much as a scratch. I was some glad to find they was safe, and hoped our good luck would hold. But hoping and wishing is near useless as a bucket full of holes, sonny, that's a fact.

———⋅———

Our soldiering come to a halt when winter set in, and it weren't long before Christmas rolled around. Major Weeks give me permission to go visit Jeff for a couple of hours Christmas afternoon. It was the first Christmas me and Jeff had spent away from home and family, but we made the best of it. I give Jeff a new jackknife to replace the one he'd lost chasing Yankees a spell back, and he give me a little Christmas tree he'd cut from a pinetop and decorated with colored buttons and such. Dern near brung me to tears when he done that.

Back at my tent I set the tree on the ammo box I used for a table. Stared at it for a spell, recollecting past Christmases when the family was all together gathered around a tree that dern near touched the ceiling. Them was some happy times and I sorely missed 'em, so much so I went to feeling sorry for myself.

Them good times was gone and most likely wouldn't come again. My daddy was dead, Hamp was dead, my brother was up somewheres in Tennessee fighting for the Confederacy. My sweet Annie was betrothed to Daniel. Me and Jeff was wearing Yankee blue through no fault of our own, leastways that's how I took it. I sure weren't no traitor, but here I was, a scout and courier for the Second Florida United States Cavalry. Reckon that up and made me one after all.

Right then and there I felt like hightailing it out of camp and heading for home. Figured I could pull it off too, sonny. Just saddle up my horse and light out. Any guards stop me I'd tell 'em I was delivering a message from Major Weeks to Station Four or one of the other outposts on the mainland. I'd done just that a dozen or more times the past months. Get shed of the Yankee blues and be home in a week or so. Then I'd join up and head for Tennessee to fight with Daniel and Joe Porter and Yerby Watts and the other boys from home.

Got right stirred up thinking about it. Went to making plans to carry out my great escape, then I remembered Jeff. Weren't no way I could take him along without us getting caught for sure. Chances was good they'd shoot us for being deserters. Least they'd do was throw us in the stockade, which weren't a whole site better, what with all the pestilence and whatnot killing off prisoners near ever day.

Dern Yankee scoundrels had me by the short hairs, that's a fact. Didn't much care what they done with me, but weren't no way I'd risk Jeff's neck to a noose or firing squad or prison. We was stuck at Cedar Keys like a splayed-foot mule in quicksand.

Well, sonny, I finally figured what's done is done. I had got me and Jefferson in this pickle and I'd see we got out of it or die trying. The war couldn't last forever. Me and Jeff would make it home sooner or later. Turned out to be a heap sooner than I expected.

Elijah Malburn
Spring 1864
Raid on Econfina

FORTY ★ ONE

WINTER FINALLY GIVE UP THE ghost and made way for spring. I was glad to see it go too, being as it had rained dern near ever day from January through March. Got a mite tired being wet all the time and plodding through muck to get anywheres. It had been a miserable winter, sonny, that's a fact. Only good thing was, it kept us from doing much soldiering.

One fine morning in early April, Sergeant Bullard stuck his ugly head inside my tent, hollered, "The major wants to see you, Malburn."

I weren't in no mood for company, mind you, least of all Sergeant Bullard's, who always done his best to make things ever bit as miserable for the troops as the winter weather had done. I weren't high on the good sergeant's list of friends, and it galled him to no end that Major Weeks had made me his personal courier. I put down the rag I was using to oil my saddle. Looked him in the eye, said, "Do tell?"

That nasty scowl of his crawled across his bulldog face. "Right away, Private!" he said, loud enough to've blowed out my lantern if it had been lit.

Never did much cotton to getting hollered at, and I knowed

dern well to watch my tongue lest I wind up on one of Bullard's
work details, but he'd done put a burr in my breeches. "Why,
Sergeant," I said, kindly as I could, "where is your manners?
There ain't no need to shout. I'll be along shortly, soon as I finish
cleaning this fine McClellan saddle the army issued me." Picked
up the rag and went back to rubbing oil on the stirrups but kept
a eye peeled his way.

Know what he done then, sonny? I'll tell you. Ol' Bullard
turned three shades of red and come at me bellowing like a boar
hog. "You sorry secesh son of a bitch, I'll—"

Stopped dead in his tracks when I pointed my Remington at
him. "That so? Now, Sergeant, I would sorely hate to shoot you
dead in this tent. It would make a awful mess for me to clean up,
and I'd have to go and explain to the major how you attacked me
and how I was only protecting myself, which a feller has ever
right to do."

His face was red as a festered boil, sonny. He backed up a
step or two and went to spouting all sorts of foul hogwash about
my family heritage and how I weren't nothing but Rebel trash
and such. Kept at it till I had myself more'n a craw full.

I cocked the hammer and stood up. "I ain't never been much
for killing, but if you say one more word about my poor dead
daddy or my dear widowed mama I will pull this trigger sure as
I'm standing here." I pointed to the tent flap with my free hand.
"So I'd be real obliged if you'd shut your trap and get out of my
quarters."

I was only bluffing, mind you, but reckon I was right
convincing because Bullard quit his jabbering real quick. Turned
pale as raw cotton, his jowls went to quivering and he backed
on out of the tent, me following ever step of the way. I weren't
giving him no chance of pulling his pistol on me once he was
outside.

Well, sonny, if looks could kill I'd've been a goner, that's a
fact. You never seen such hate in a man's eyes. Knowed I'd made
myself a enemy for life. He stared me down for a spell till some
of his color come back. Then he hawked up a big wad, spit it at
my boots and stomped off towards headquarters.

I waited for Sergeant Bullard's pot to simmer a spell before
I reported in to Major Weeks. His headquarters was near the

shore in what had been a dandy hotel before the war. It was a fancy two-story affair with gables and a porch on three sides, and a fine view of the Gulf out front. Two guards was marching back and forth across the porch in front of the door. I figured that must've been Sergeant Bullard's doing, because there weren't never a guard posted before our little scrap that morning.

The guards stopped and come to port arms when I got to the top of the stairs. I told 'em what my business was and one told me to stay put. He went inside for a minute, then come back out, said all soldierly-like, "The major will see you now," and held the door open for me.

I was some glad to see Bullard weren't in the major's office. Hoped that would help when I give my side of things. I come to attention and told the major I was reporting in as ordered.

Major Weeks went to shuffling some papers on his desk. I seen they was full of writing that was scribbled in a bad hand which Tom Gainer never would have stood for in his schoolteacher days. The major looked up, then back at them papers. In the few months I'd been the major's messenger boy, I had purty much learnt how to read his mood, least I thought I had. But right then he had on his poker face. Figured that weren't a good sign. Finally he quit shuffling the papers. Held 'em up and shook 'em at me. "I understand there's been trouble between you and Sergeant Bullard. There are some very serious charges here, Private Malburn, not the least of which is threatening Sergeant Bullard's life with your sidearm."

Major Weeks got up and walked over to the side window. I seen him out the corner of my eye, rocking back and forth on his heels and tugging on his goatee, which was what he done when he was galled about something or other. Stood there a minute rocking, then walked back to his desk and sat down. He picked up the papers and stared me straight in the eye the way my daddy used to do when I knowed he weren't going to tolerate no tomfoolery. "I have Sergeant Bullard's report of the incident here. Now I want to hear your account, young man, and I want the truth. Good or bad, nothing but the truth."

So I give it to him, ever detail I could recollect, even the very words the good sergeant spouted when he went to sullying my mama and daddy's good name. When I was done the major had turned near red as Bullard when he was staring down the barrel of my pistol. I took that as a good sign, but figured I had a jawing-out coming anyhow, since Bullard was a highfalutin United States Army sergeant and I weren't nothing but a lowly private and a Southerner to boot.

Well, sonny, I weren't wrong. The major stood up behind his desk and went to giving me a tongue-lashing the likes I ain't had since my daddy caught me and Hamp Watts sneaking a pint of his good corn whiskey. Said he weren't at all pleased with the ruckus between me and the good sergeant, and I'd best learn to show proper respect to my superiors and obey orders and control my tongue and temper. Any more acts of insubordination out of me and I'd find myself inside the prison stockade toting a ball and chain.

Whew, my ears was near burning when the major was done, that's a fact. At first I had a mind to jump over that desk and give him a good thrashing, but I knowed Major Weeks was giving me a fair shake, so I let it be. I knowed he was right too. What's done is done. Like it or not, me and Jeff was in the Yankee army and there weren't no good way out till the war was over and done with one way or the other. I had best start minding my p's and q's. So I told the major I was sorry that things had got out of hand between me and Sergeant Bullard, and that I'd do my best to mind my manners and be a better soldier from here on out. Didn't mean a word of it, mind you, but I figured it was what he wanted to hear.

Well, sonny, after all the palavering, Major Weeks got down to business. Told me the Second Cavalry and the Second Colored Troops was planning a big to-do, and that it was high time I started earning my thirteen dollars a month.

I thought that was right funny, since I ain't so much as sniffed a Yankee greenback since I joined up, but I kept my trap shut. Didn't seem near as funny after the major told me we'd be sailing to St. Andrew Bay to raid the Econfina Valley. That's a fact.

First thing I done after Major Weeks dismissed me was to go find Jefferson and let him know what was stewing. The major had warned me that this was strictly a military campaign and I had best stick close by and not try to contact family or friends if we come near my homeplace. Well, sonny, weren't no way I intended to oblige the good major on that, but I sure didn't want Jeff getting hisself in any trouble. He was doing right fine at soldiering, but I knowed how much he missed his folks. Once we was on the march, I might not get the chance to give him a talking to.

I saddled my horse and hightailed it to the colored camp. Asked around till I found out Jeff's squad was on work detail over by the railroad bridge. Took a shortcut across some dunes to the road that led down to the railhead and found the work party clearing brush alongside the roadbed.

The sun was high and it was right hot for April. Most of them boys had shed their shirts and their backs was slick and shiny with sweat. I seen Jeff up ahead alongside some other feller maybe forty-fifty yards away, swinging a blade through high weeds like he was racing rain to make hay. That boy always was a hard worker.

I rode on past the work party a piece towards a grove of wind-bent oaks. Figured that's where I'd find Jeff's sergeant. Sergeant Able was near the spitting image of Abraham Lincoln, if you can fancy what Honest Abe would've looked like if he'd been born a nigra. Weren't the handsomest feller you ever seen, that's a fact. He had been in the army for near three years and was right proud of them stripes on his sleeves. He could be a cantankerous cuss when he took a mind to, so I had learnt to tote along a little something or other to make him a mite more agreeable.

I walked the horse over to where Able was sitting in some shade with his back agin a scrub oak. Looked to be snoozing, so I made a racket dismounting and tying the reins to a bush. Reached in my breeches pocket and pulled out the fresh plug of tobacco I'd brung. "Be much obliged if I could jaw with Jefferson a spell, Sergeant."

Slow as a gopher, Sergeant Able looked up and pushed the bill of his kepi above his eyes. He seen what I was holding and grinned. I took that to be a good sign and tossed him the plug. He stuck two fingers in his mouth and cut loose a whistle that dern near made my horse bolt. Hollered for Jeff to come quick, then he bit off a big chaw and went back to snoozing.

Jeff come running up toting the sling blade. I got my canteen and we walked off a ways and found some shade. When I went to telling him where we was going, he got right excited, said, "We goan home? Goan see Mama and Daddy and—"

"Now look here, Jeff, it ain't like that. This here is army business. You remember how we went chasing after them Rebels a while back? Raiding them farms and all? That's what we going on, a big march. Won't be no time to get home and see the folks this time."

Jeff looked a mite befuddled. "Why we goan do that? They's our neighbors."

Well, sonny, I told him I didn't cotton to raiding our friends and such at all, but we was in a bad fix and had to do what we was told or else we'd be in a worser one. Done the best I could to explain how we was in the Union Army and how the Union had a beef with the Confederacy and meant to do whatever it took to make us all one country again, and that's why the army was fixing to march through the Econfina.

Now Jeff's mind weren't the most fertile field on the farm, and I ain't sure how much of what I said took root. So I told him he weren't to leave his squad no matter how close we got to home and to obey whatever Sergeant Able or his officers told him to do. "Don't do nothing or touch nothing unless they order you to do it. Just do what you're told. You understand?"

Jeff said he did, and I left it at that. Figured there weren't much could go wrong by obeying orders. That's what soldiering was all about, I told myself. Just do what you're told.

Them was words I'd live to regret, sonny. That's a fact.

FORTY ★ TWO

TWO-THREE DAYS LATER WE boarded a big steamer and set out across the Gulf. There was some four hundred of us in all, near even divided between the Second Cavalry and the Second Colored Troops. Seemed like a heap of soldiers to plunder a small valley where maybe half that many folks lived, what with most of the men off fighting elsewheres. Had a bad feeling in my belly about this whole business. Figured right then and there weren't no good to come of it.

This time the weather was dandy and it was smooth sailing the whole day. Next morning Major Wells called me into his cabin where him and a passel of officers was standing around a map spread out on a table. Felt a mite squirrely rubbing elbows with all that highfalutin brass, that's a fact. The major jawed a spell with his officers, then pointed at the map and asked me which roads did I think would be best for our march through Econfina.

Well, sonny, I felt like a ham in a brine barrel. Telling a lie or telling the truth, there just weren't no good way out. I was pickled. Figured for Jefferson's sake I'd best go with the truth and hope things played out. I studied the map for a minute,

then pointed out the Econfina Road that run from the landing
at Bayhead north up through the valley.

"This here's the best road, Major," I said. "It's about seven-
eight miles from the landing up to the ferry at Bear Creek. You
can cross the wagons and such there."

The major tugged at his goatee while he eyeballed the map.
"And the town of Bennet is located at this crossroads?" he said,
pointing at where the Marianna Road run into Econfina Road.

I give a little laugh. "It ain't much of a town, Major. There's
a general store, dry goods store, blacksmith shop, a couple of
churches and the schoolhouse."

The major grunted, kept looking the map over. After a spell
he said, "Where is the gristmill located?"

I went to sweating when I heard that. I was shamed enough
to be scouting the way for this raid. Now they wanted me to show
'em targets, and them targets was my neighbors and friends. Joe
Porter was one of brother Daniel's best pals, and his folks was as
goodhearted as they come. But what could I do? My 'coon was
treed and the hounds was snapping at my tail. So I pointed just
north of the crossroads and showed him where Mister Porter
had built his mill on Moccasin Creek near to where it feeds into
the Econfina.

It went on like that for dern near a half-hour, I reckon—
Major Weeks asking me where farms and bridges and stores and
such was and marking up his map as I showed him. Figured he
was finally satisfied when he went to palavering with his officers,
giving out orders and assignments and other such military
hogwash.

But I weren't off the hook yet, sonny. Know what the good
major done then? I'll tell you. Turned to me, said, "One more
thing and you may be excused, Malburn. The Gainer place . . .
the largest plantation in the area and you've failed to mention it.
Surely that was a mere oversight. Its location?"

Now them was words I truly didn't cotton to hear, that's a
fact. William Gainer's spread was the biggest and finest for miles
around. He run a couple of thousand free-range cattle along the
creek, and had dern near two hundred slaves working his fields.
Sold more beef and corn to the Confederacy than anybody else
in all of West Florida. But that weren't why I was fretting so.

William Gainer was Tom and Annabelle Gainer's daddy. The Gainer plantation was my sweet Annie's family home! My hand shook like the palsy when my finger touched the map.

———•———

Later on that day out I seen smoke rising high in the northwest, and before sundown land come into view. It was near dark when we landed at Hurricane Island at the mouth of St. Andrew Bay. We stepped off the boat onto a long wharf, then marched along a beach with sand white as fine sugar and made camp for the night. In the moonlight the big dunes behind us looked like snow-covered mountains.

It was a fine place. Three-four years back, me and Daniel and some of our pals from Econfina had spent a week right near that very spot netting mullet during the spring run. Went to thinking about them good times, and how things was so different now. My best friend dead, my brother and the others off fighting who knowed where. Sweet Annie betrothed to Daniel. Me and Jeff fixing to take part in a Yankee raid on our very friends and neighbors. Felt right sorry for myself that night, sonny, that's a fact.

Turns out I had good reason.

FORTY ★ THREE

DAYLIGHT NEXT MORNING WE BROKE camp and marched back to the wharf where we boarded some smaller boats and set sail up St. Andrew Bay. On the backside of the island I seen where all that smoke had come from. The Yankees had captured a blockade runner toting some hundred bales of cotton bound for England. Stacked it up in a big pile and set it afire. More of them "spoils of war" the major was so fond of calling it. Shameful waste is what it was.

Took the best part of the day to make it to Bayhead where Econfina Creek, Bear Creek and Bayou George all run into North Bay. On the way we passed the ruins of Mister Anderson's saltworks where me and Jeff had worked so hard last summer. Weren't nothing stirring from what I could see, only the ruins of busted-up kilns and salt kettles and burnt buildings and such. Wondered what had become of Mister Anderson since that scoundrel Boss Hog went and sold him out to the Yankees. The war was over before I found out the Yankees sent him off to a prison camp where he died. Also learnt his son William, the captain, had been mortally wounded during the raid on the saltworks. That war and all its nonsense sure cost Big John

Anderson and his family a heap, sonny, that's a fact.

Towards midafternoon we reached the upper part of North Bay. Sailed a short piece up Bayou George and landed at the Bayhead settlement, which weren't no more than a deserted fish camp and a few scattered farms at the time. A few years back it had been a right popular summer resort with folks that lived inland coming down to fish and swim in the bay and nearby springs. The war and hard times had took care of that. The general store was still standing, but it was boarded up. It was owned by Amos Enfinger, who lived with his wife on a small farm a quarter mile up the road. Behind the store was twelve clapboard cabins that Mister Enfinger rented out in better times. Ever cabin was named for one of the tribes of Israel. Down near the water a passel of rowboats was chained together upside down between two live oaks. Weren't much else to speak of but a rickety bait shack and a smokehouse. The Enfinger's two boys was off fighting with my brother Daniel, so the place had got a mite run down since I'd last seen it.

Took near a hour to unload the boats onto the pier and get things organized. Captain Tracy had already marched his company of colored troops up the Econfina Road towards the ferry at Bear Creek, so there weren't no chance for me to see Jeff. I hoped he remembered our little talk and wouldn't get a mind to hightail it for home.

While Major Weeks was going over the map and palavering with his officers, I saddled up my horse and accoutrements and such. Put fresh loads in my Remingtons. Hoped I wouldn't need 'em, but if trouble come I wanted to be ready.

Of a sudden I smelt smoke. Looked up and my belly went cold. Colored troops was going from cabin to cabin setting 'em afire. Others was busting up the rowboats with axes. Somebody took a ax to the general store's front door and a squad of coloreds went to toting out boxes and barrels and sacks of goods.

I felt sick, near to retching. This weren't nothing but thievery and plunder, and like it or not I was part of it. Amos Enfinger and his wife was old and could barely scratch out a living on that sorry farm of theirs, what with their boys off to the war and all.

I run over to Major Weeks and busted right in on his little meeting. Pointed towards the store, said, "Major, cain't you stop 'em? Folks that own the place ain't done nothing to bring this on."

Know what the good major said then, sonny? I'll tell you. Puffed hisself up like a strutting spring gobbler, said, "The troops are carrying out orders, Malburn. And for your information, the people who own this place are known to be secessionists. Those cabins, the boats, this store . . . all used to aid and supply the enemy. Cut the roots and the tree will die. Remember that, Private."

Couldn't do nothing but look on while them boys finished their evil. Then it come to me. They was only doing what they'd been ordered, same as I'd told Jeff to do. Knowed right then and there weren't no good would come of all this.

When the colored troops was done doing their duty they formed up in columns of two and set out up the road towards Bear Creek. What goods weren't carried off was burnt or ruint one way or another. Didn't leave nothing standing behind, not even Enfinger's store. I mounted up and took my place behind the major. My throat was tight and my eyes was tearing, but it weren't only the smoke that had me choked up, sonny. That's a fact.

Cut the roots and the tree will die. Couldn't help thinking a whole forest might be done in before this tomfoolery was finished.

FORTY ★ FOUR

IT WAS NEAR DARK WHEN we reached the ferry at Bear Creek. Company A had already secured the ferry, and Captain Tracy had set out pickets to guard both sides of the creek. Jefferson weren't around, so I figured he was on picket duty somewheres.

Ard's Mercantile and Ferry was on the main route from St. Andrew on the coast, inland through Econfina and on to Marianna. Me and brother Daniel had made the trip from the farm to the coast many a time with our daddy. It was the only place to cross Bear Creek for miles around unless you wanted to swim or chance the swamps, and only a dern fool or lunatic would try that. Them waters was crawling with danger, sonny. I'd seen gators near twenty-foot long with my own eyes, and moccasins thick as a man's leg. What with the ferry and store, Mister Ard had hisself a right profitable business going, and he didn't give a tinker's damn who he traded with, long as the money was good.

I seen Mister Ard jawing with Major Weeks but kept my distance, hoping he wouldn't recognize me. Figured there weren't no sense in complicating things anymore than they already was. It was dark as pitch by the time Major Weeks dismissed me.

Clouds hid what moon and stars there was, and thunder was rumbling in the west. I took that as a good sign. I unsaddled my horse and tied him to a picket pin. Spread my blanket under a nearby tree not far from Mister Ard's house where the major had took a room for the night. Laid down and said my prayers for the first time in a spell. Prayed for rain and prayed the major wouldn't call for me during the night to run a message or such. If he did, my goose was good as cooked.

You see, sonny, on the march from Bayhead I had conjured up a plan of sorts. I knowed Mister Ard kept a dugout canoe behind his smokehouse that he run trotlines with for catfish and turtles and such. I'd snuck a look earlier and seen it was still there. My plan was to wait for the camp to quiet down, then sneak away in that canoe, cross the creek and warn what folks I could that the Yankees was coming. Sort of like Paul Revere done back during the Revolution. That might give people a chance to hide whatever livestock or goods and valuables they could.

There was a slough that cut northwest from Bear Creek through the swamp and come out at Econfina Creek. If I could find my way through it in the dark, I'd wind up a fair piece north of where any of Company A's pickets was likely to be. That would save me two-three miles. I'd be needing a horse, but I had that figured out too. If my luck held there'd be enough time to make it to the Watts farm, maybe my own, and get back before sunup.

The major had give the order that no cook fires be lit that night, so I waited till most of the lanterns inside Ard's house and store was doused, and things around camp was settled, to make my move. By then it was raining. Figured I wouldn't need my pistols, so I tucked 'em inside my blanket to keep 'em dry and put on my poncho. Slipped the halter from my horse and retied the rope around his neck, then headed for the canoe. Lucky for me, Mister Ard's hounds had growed used to all the soldiers stirring about and didn't raise a ruckus.

Weren't no moon to judge by, but I figured it was near midnight by the time I paddled into the slough. It was dark as a cave, but I could feel a passel of gators eyeballing me. My skin went to crawling hearing them bulls bellowing back and forth across the swamp. Said a quick prayer the canoe wouldn't dump over and make me gator bait.

Squinted hard through the dark and it weren't long before I
spied the first of the whitewashed tin cans Mister Ard kept tied
to stobs and bushes and such to mark his trotlines. Managed
to follow them cans like trail markers all the way through the
slough, and a half-hour later I was paddling upstream agin the
swift current of the Econfina.

Kept paddling another twenty-thirty minutes till I come to
a clearing on both sides of the creek. Knowed then I'd made
Vickers Ford. Now I had a hard choice to make, sonny. There
was more farms and people living along the east side of the
creek, including my own, which was a good eight miles up the
Econfina Road. Weren't as many farms on the west side, but
the way the creek run I could save four-five miles by following
Williford Road. That road run right by the Watts farm and on
up to the Gainer plantation. Wanted to see my folks some bad,
mind you, but I weren't sure how much time was left before
light. Tussled with that thought a minute, then dug hard left for
the west bank till I felt the canoe slide onto solid ground. I pulled
the canoe up the bank and hid it in some bushes, then grabbed
the halter and lit out for the Cox farm.

Vernon Cox was a second cousin or some such to our family.
He had followed my daddy and Mister Watts down from North
Carolina a few years after they'd settled along the Econfina. Him
and his wife was childless, but they managed to farm a hundred
acres or so, mostly planted in corn. It was smoked hams and
sausage Cousin Vernon was knowed for. Kept his hogs rolling
fat from field corn and sweet acorns they rooted up in the
woods along the creek. Had his own special brine to cure them
hams in. Wouldn't tell a soul what his secret was come hell or
high water. Some years after the war he made a heap of money
selling his recipe for ham and sausage to a meat company up in
Montgomery. But that's another story.

I trotted up Williford Road a ways, then took a shortcut
through a patch of woods till I come to the Coxes' cornfield.
Eased my way through the waist-high stalks till I come to the
backside of his barn. I'd already decided not to waste time
waking up the Coxes and asking the loan of a horse. Figured I'd
just sneak in the barn and borrow one and tell 'em what was up
when I returned it. So that's what I done.

It had been a while since I rode bareback and it took a spell to get the hang of it again. The halter I brung along made things a heap easier. Soon had the horse in a easy gallop making good time up the road towards the Watts farm. By then the rain had near quit and the clouds thinned a mite. The half-moon give just enough light to make out where I was going, and it weren't long till I seen the limestone and rail fence that marked the lane leading to the Watts place. Pulled back on the reins and slowed the horse to a walk. Turned him onto the lane, wondering what I would say when I come face-to-face with Mister Watts.

I dismounted before the Watts house come into view and tied the reins to a stout bush. It was a cool night but I was sweating like the August sun was beating down on me, so I shed the poncho. Walked on up the lane to the porch steps and stopped. Wondered if I ought to go knock on the door or just call out. Decided I'd best knock.

Got to the second step when a loud *click* from behind stopped me cold. I weren't much for soldiering, but I sure knowed the sound of a hammer being cocked when I heard it.

FORTY ★ FIVE

"GET THEM HANDS UP WHERE I can see 'em if you want to live another minute."

The sound of that voice surprised me near much as the hammer click. I put my hands up quick. "Yerby? It's me . . . Eli Malburn."

Figured hearing my name might bring a friendly greeting of sorts, but I was wrong. Weren't nobody talking but the crickets, so I said, "You home on furlough?"

Another minute or so passed. My arms was getting a mite tired holding up the night sky. Then Yerb said, "Keep them hands high and turn around." He sounded mean as a cornered rattler.

"I ain't armed," I said as I turned around real slow, hoping when he seen it was really me things would get a mite more neighborly. I come face-to-face with Yerb. There was a goodly piece of his right ear missing, and I seen he was holding a shotgun under one arm and a crutch under the other. Looked down and seen his right breeches leg was pinned up. Went all cold in my belly when I seen that missing leg. Near fainted right then and there.

I was some shook, sonny, that's a fact. Learnt later that Tom Gainer hadn't told anybody right off that Yerb had been shot the day after Hamp was kilt. Reckon he thought it best to find out how Yerb fared before giving Mister Watts any more grief. Took a spell before I come to my senses enough to hear Yerby was talking.

"So, it's true then. My pa said you run off to join up with the damn Yankees!"

That shotgun was waving in my face and Yerb's eyes looked wild and mean like a cur dog caught raiding a chicken coop. I swallowed hard. "It ain't like that at all. I was hauling supplies for the saltworks and—"

"It ain't?" Yerb reached out and poked me in the chest with the barrel. "*It ain't?* Well what's with that uniform you wearing?"

Well, sonny, I went to explaining to Yerb best I could how the Yankees had captured me and Jefferson, took my wagon and team of Morgans, conscripted Jeff into the Colored Troops and give me the choice of joining up or going to prison. Told Yerb I didn't have no other choice. Said I felt obliged to watch out for Jeff, so I went and took the oath.

Yerby weren't having none of it. He hawked up a wad and spit it towards my boots. "You had a choice all right, bluebelly. You could've joined up with Hamp but you was yellow. You could've went to prison 'stead of being a goddamn turncoat. Hamp is dead and it's them like you that done it." Yerb looked down at his pinned-up breeches, stretched out what was left of his leg, said, "Took this too, damn 'em all to Hell."

I had near give up hope when a lamp flared in the house and the front door creaked open behind me. "What's going on out here?" I heard Mister Watts say. "Who you got that gun on, boy?"

Yerby looked up at his pa with them mean snake eyes. "A goddamn Yankee is what."

"It's Eli Malburn, Mister Watts," I said, feeling a mite relieved. Coleman Watts had always been a good and fair man. Him and my daddy had growed up together and been best pals, just like me and Hamp. But things had been hard for him of late.

He had lost his wife to the fever the winter after my daddy had his accident, and now Hamp at Chickamauga. I hoped all the bad hadn't turned him mean like his oldest boy. "I come to warn you folks that the Yankees is raiding up the Econfina."

Felt a heap better when Mister Watts told Yerby to put down that shotgun and for us to come on in the house. "And you watch what comes out of that mouth of you'rn," he said to Yerb. "Being in the army don't give a body the right to take the Lord's name in vain."

Well, sonny, I spent the next half-hour or so jawing with the Watts. Told 'em what I recollected from Major Weeks' map, where I figured the Yankees was headed and what places they was likely to target. "Way I figure, it'll take 'em two days to get here," I said. "Could be quicker though, so best scatter your cattle and hide what horses and wagons and such you can.

"Let 'em think they got the drop on you. Hide your best goods and let 'em have what they want of the rest. Don't squabble with 'em, else they'll likely burn you out the way they done Mister Enfinger."

Yerby went to spouting off how he would kill any bluebellies that come near Watts land.

"Don't do it, Yerb," I said. "They must be four hundred or more strong, counting all the colored troops. Ain't no way you can stop 'em."

Yerb picked up the shotgun he had leaned agin his chair. "I don't need no bluebelly telling me what to do. Damn Yankees done kilt my brother and took my leg. They ain't taking nothing else, not without a fight they ain't."

Yerby was some hot, sonny, that's a fact. Never seen such a look in a man's eyes. Pure evil it was. This weren't the same Yerby Watts I'd knowed for all my near seventeen years. Seemed the war had took him and give back a stranger.

Mister Watts went to scolding Yerb like he was a knee-high young'un. Them two come near to scrapping like barnyard roosters before Yerb got his feathers unruffled. It took a spell till we got back to business.

We jawed a touch longer, then I said I'd best be getting back. Mister Watts promised him and Yerb would warn my folks and the Gainers and spread the word to what others they could.

When I stood up to leave he shook my hand and said it was a brave thing I done by coming to warn 'em.

Know what he said then, sonny? I'll tell you. Looked me straight in the eye, said, "I don't hold it agin you, you wearing that uniform. And I reckon Hamp wouldn't either."

I ain't forgot them words in sixty-some years, sonny. Meant a heap to me, that's a fact. Still does.

FORTY ★ SIX

IT WAS NEAR FOUR-THIRTY when I left the Watts and hightailed it for the Cox farm. Weren't no lamp shining in the Cox house that I could see, so I put the horse in the barn and lit out through the cornfield towards Econfina Creek. Weren't no time for niceties if I wanted to make camp before daylight. I'd done all I could.

Made good time paddling downstream. By the time I come to the slough the cans was easy to spot in the moonlight. The sky was hinting gray when I pulled the canoe up the bank behind Mister Ard's smokehouse. I flipped it upside down and headed back for the big oak where I'd left my bedroll.

Got near halfway there when of a sudden a voice called out, "Halt! Who goes there?" and a sentry stepped out of the shadows from behind a tree.

Now this was some fine mess I'd stepped in. Made it all this way only to get snared a few yards shy of my blanket. I tucked the halter inside my poncho in case I had to grab sky. "Private Malburn, Headquarters, Second U.S. Cavalry," I said. Sounded right smart to me. Hoped the sentry would be duly impressed too.

"What you got there?"

"This here? Just my poncho." I held it out so he could see.

"It ain't raining."

"No, it ain't, but it has been on and off all night. I don't fancy starting the day off wet."

Took a spell before he said, "Well then, what's the password?"

"Nobody give me no dern password," I said, which was the truth.

The sentry thought that over for a minute. "Then I reckon I got to take you to the Sergeant of the Guard."

Well, sonny, I felt the quicksand sucking at my boots. Had to come up with something, and fast. So I said, "Do tell? Why, that's fine by me, but how about we go see Major Weeks first. Seeing as how I'm his personal courier, I don't think the major will much cotton to being woke up just to find out I been to the privy."

The good sentry thought that over a bit, said, "Reckon you can pass," then shouldered his rifle and marched on towards the creek.

Whew! I had bluffed my way out of another privy hole, that's a fact. Figured my luck was bound to run out sooner or later, but I made it on back to my campsite without any more ruckus. Put the halter on my horse and retied him, then stretched out on my blanket to rest up a hour or so before the major needed me.

I was tuckered but couldn't get to sleep. Kept wondering what the next few days might mean for the Econfina Valley. Would Yerb and Mister Watts get the word out in time? Was there anything else I could've done? Remembered then what my mama used to say when things got muddled: "It don't do a body no good to worry. What will be will be."

Felt a touch homesick thinking about my mama and the twins, Jeff's folks, how near to home I'd been. I sorely missed 'em all. I went to thinking about Annie till I drifted off to sleep.

FORTY ★ SEVEN

NEXT THING I KNOWED THE sun was up and the camp was stirring. Figured I best eat while I could, so I dug some hardtack and a chunk of ham out of my saddlebags. Barely got it wolfed down before Sergeant Bullard come out on the porch of Ard's house and hollered for me.

Didn't waste no time reporting. Since our little fracas I'd kept my nose right clean. Minded my manners and done my best to sound soldierly when talking to Bullard. Figured that was fitting if me and Jeff was to survive all this tomfoolery and get back home. So far the good sergeant had done his part keeping things mannerly too, but I knowed it goaded him something fierce. That plumb tickled me, sonny, that's a fact.

Bullard met me at the foot of the stairs. Handed me a folded paper, said, "The major wants you to get this message to Captain Tracy. He's camped about two miles north on the Econfina Road."

I folded the message in half again and stuffed it in my breeches pocket. "I'll be needing the ferry. Creek's too high to swim my horse across. Besides, there's gators and such."

That ugly scowl crawled across Bullard's face. "Lieutenant

Whitten is waiting at the ferry with a squad," he said. "Report to him immediately. And make damn sure Captain Tracy gets that message."

I saddled up quick and lit out for the ferry. One of Mister Ard's nigras took the reins and led my horse onto the planked deck and tied him to the rail next to the others, maybe twelve-fifteen horses in all. Then him and another nigra grabbed the pull ropes and tugged the ferry towards the far bank.

I reported in to Lieutenant Whitten. He told me I was to accompany him and his men who was delivering two supply wagons to Captain Tracy's camp. After I delivered the major's message, my orders was to ride on with Lieutenant Whitten and his scouting party and show 'em the best place to ford the Econfina. Once they made the crossing, I was to report back to Company A headquarters and wait for new orders.

It took near thirty minutes to cross Bear Creek, unload the horses and haul the wagons and other whatnot up the landing to the road. Then we mounted up and set out at a fast walk. Lieutenant Whitten sent four men on ahead of the wagons, led by my old friend Jacob the Rail who had got hisself promoted to corporal a while back. Two others dropped back a piece to guard our rear. The woods was too thick to put out flank riders, so me and the rest strung along the road ahead of the wagons.

We ain't made a half-mile when of a sudden a shot rung out ahead. Lieutenant Whitten rode up beside me. "Ride up there and find out what's happening!"

He just got them words out when yonder come a second shot, then another'n. The lieutenant got all wide-eyed, hollered, "Hurry!"

I kneed my horse and lit out up the road. Pulled one of the Remingtons out of my belt in case things got testy. Last thing I wanted was to draw down on a neighbor, but recollecting what Yerb had said and that mean look in his eyes had me a mite edgy.

Didn't fancy being a target for some trigger-happy fool, so I slowed my horse to a walk where the road took a sharp curve to the left. Eased on around till I could get a look-see at the road ahead through some branches and still keep hid. Them four boys the lieutenant had sent ahead was all dismounted. They was holding their carbines at the ready and gawking at something laying in the road. Only counted three horses.

"Halloo, boys," I hollered, waving my hat high as I come around the bend so they'd see it was me and not shoot. "You got trouble?"

Jacob the Rail pointed down at the road. "Snake, big 'un."

"Do tell?" I said, and rode on up. Well, sonny, the Rail weren't lying. Diamondback dern near eight-foot long and thick as a man's leg was stretched out in the grass growing between the road ruts. The head was bigger'n a man's fist. They had shot it clean off but it was still twitching and showing its fangs.

The Rail poked at the rattler's head with his carbine. "Bastard spooked my horse. He throwed me and bolted up the road. I nearly landed on top of the damn thing."

"You best not fool with that head," I said. "It'll stay deadly poison for near a day."

Jacob looked up at me like he thought I was joshing, but he quit poking at the head. He found a big stick laying nearby and flicked the head off the road. Then he grabbed the snake by the tail and cut off the rattles and flung the body into the woods. The Rail held the rattles out to show the others and grinned. "I got myself a fine good luck charm here boys, fourteen rows and a button."

Couldn't help grinning back at the Rail. "Reckon you'll be needing it too, Corporal, and right soon. The lieutenant ain't likely to be tickled when he finds out you boys raised all that ruckus over a snake." Then I turned my horse and hightailed it down the road.

When I got back, Lieutenant Whitten had the men dismounted and strung across the road in a skirmish line, with the wagons a short piece behind. I done my best to keep a straight face when I told him about the snake.

The lieutenant's jaw went tight and he dern near turned purple. He turned around and kicked up a clod of dirt in the road, said, "Damn fools!" and walked off towards the supply wagons.

I sat my horse, waiting for the lieutenant's stew to cool down a mite. After a spell he give the order to mount up, then he rode over to me. "Are there any farms or houses nearby?"

The sun was climbing and it was getting hot. I took off my

hat and fanned myself. "You mean in earshot of them carbines?"

"Yes, Private," he said, and from the sound of them two words I could tell he weren't in no mood for tomfoolery.

I put my hat back on, turned in the saddle a mite and looked around. "Well, sir, the widow Tuller's place is half a mile or so over yonder," I said, pointing roughly east. "But she's real old and near deaf. The Miller farm is a little south of the widow's cabin. They got two boys off fighting up north. I wouldn't worry none though. Mister Miller is likely busy putting in his crops. Even if him or his missus did hear them shots, they'd take it for somebody out hunting squirrels or such." It weren't quite the truth, sonny. The widow Tuller *was* eighty-some and near stone-deaf, but Jessup Miller had fought in the Mexican War and would know them shots weren't from no hunting musket. Fact is, them fancy repeating carbines had a sound all their own.

Reckon I was right convincing. Leastways Lieutenant Whitten seemed satisfied with my take on things. He give the order to move out and we headed on up the road towards Company A's camp. About a hour later we come up on a squad of colored boys that Captain Tracy had set out as pickets. Jacob the Rail had found his horse, and him and his boys was resting in some shade waiting for us to catch up.

Lieutenant Whitten jawed with the colored sergeant a spell, then stomped over to Jacob and give him a tongue-lashing to beat holy Hades. I weren't close enough to make out the words, but you could dern near see the smoke coming out of Jacob's ears.

A short ways up the road we come to the camp. I rode over to Captain Tracy's tent and told the nigra guard posted outside what my business was. He stuck his head inside the open tent flap a minute, and then told me to go on in.

I ducked inside the tent, come to attention and snapped a right smart salute to the good captain, who was sitting on a camp stool behind a small table. "Message from Major Weeks, sir."

Captain Tracy took the note and unfolded it. While he read he run a hand through them blond curls. Looked up at me, said, "Stand at ease." He eyeballed the note again, then looked at a map that was spread across the table. "How far is it to the Marianna Road?"

I took my hat off and scratched at a skeeter bite on the back of my neck. "You mean the cutoff, or where it meets the Econfina Road?"

Captain Tracy looked a mite surprised at that. "Cutoff?" He moved some papers covering part of the map, said, "Show me."

I walked around the table and stood next to the captain. Looked the map over. "The cutoff ain't on this map, Captain. It's right about there." I pointed to where the Econfina Road run past the edge of a cypress swamp. "Five-six miles north of here. It ain't much of a road, just a muddy pig trail that cuts north around the edge of this here swamp."

The good captain give his fancy moustache a tug. "I see. How many miles would this cutoff save rather than going on to here?" He tapped his finger on the map where the Ecofina-Marianna roads met.

"Seven, maybe eight," I said. "But I wouldn't try to get no wagons through there, not after a rain."

"And the gristmill? It's located here on the Marianna Road, is it not?" he said, pointing to Porter's Mill, which was half a mile north of the Econfina-Marianna junction.

Well, sonny, them was words I dreaded to hear. I recalled how Major Weeks had circled Porter's Mill on his big map at the meeting on the ship. I smelt trouble brewing, bitter than burnt coffee. "That's right, Captain. The mill's just north of the junction, half a mile or so."

Captain Tracy run his finger up the line of the Marianna Road past Porter's Mill, said, "And just where does this cutoff meet the road to Marianna?"

I looked at the map again. "Somewheres about here." I pointed a inch or so north of what I took to be the Mocassin Creek bridge. "That creek there runs through the swamp and on to the mill."

The captain studied the map a minute or two longer. "That will be all, Private," he said without looking up. "You are dismissed."

I come to attention again and saluted, then walked out into the bright sunlight. I was a mite sick in the belly, and it weren't from nothing I ate. I had just sold out the Porters. Know how that made me feel? I'll tell you. Felt like I ought to be throwed in the same hog waller as that scoundrel Boss Miller.

FORTY ★ EIGHT

AFTER CAPTAIN TRACY DISMISSED ME, him and Lieutenant Whitten jawed a spell, then the lieutenant give the order to mount up and we rode north out of camp. We passed another picket line and headed up the road towards Vickers Ford, which is where I'd told Lieutenant Whitten would be the best place to cross Econfina Creek. That weren't exactly the truth, sonny, but I weren't about to tell him about the bridge my daddy and Mister Watts had built over the creek between our family farms. I aimed to do everthing I could to keep 'em away from there.

"The creek'll likely be up a mite because of the rains," I'd told him before we left camp. "Shouldn't be no problem for men or horses, but getting wagons across might prove touchy."

It was maybe two miles to the ford, but it was slow going. The lieutenant weren't taking no chances getting us ambushed by rushing things. He had put me out front with a couple of other boys as a lead guard. Jacob the Rail and his pards was bringing up the rear. Reckon the lieutenant figured that's where they'd do the least harm in case they come across another secesh snake or such.

It was midafternoon when we come to Vickers Ford. The Econfina was fifty-sixty foot wide there, usually clear and no more'n two-three foot deep. Didn't look near as high as I hoped it would be, three and a half foot or so, but it was running fast and murky from all the runoff. I told the boys to sit tight while I checked things out. Rode down the bank trace to the creek, then kneed my horse in the ribs. He took a few steps into the creek, then stopped and snorted. A crooked tree limb come floating by. His eyes went wild and his ears laid back and he reared on me. I leaned into his neck and waited for the limb to pass, then slapped him hard on the rump and he dern near run the rest of the way across.

I rode up the far trace and looked around. The rain had washed away any marks I'd made last night when I drug the canoe up the bank. The weeds where I'd hid it looked like a deer or some such had bedded down, so I weren't worried none. Other than that, there weren't no sign of the ford being crossed for some time.

It had been hot, but it was clouding up again and a breeze had cooled things off a mite. Thunder rumbled to the west. I rode on up to Williford Road for a quick look-see. Weren't nothing stirring, so I turned my horse and headed back to the ford. Weren't no wooden snakes swimming down the creek to spook my horse this time. Got back across just as Lieutenant Whitten and the others come riding up. I trotted up the trace and met him on the road.

"The ford's in dandy shape for all the rain, Lieutenant. Maybe three-four foot deep, hard sandy bottom."

"Good. And what is down that road?" he said, pointing east where the ford trace crossed Econfina Road.

"The Vickers farm."

The lieutenant scratched at his chin whiskers. "This Vickers, could he be troublesome?"

I give a little laugh. "Vickers and his wife is getting a mite long in the tooth. They got four growed daughters, but best I recollect, all their men is up north with the army. Fact is, most everybody in these parts is off fighting somewheres, 'cept young'uns and old folks."

The good lieutenant give a nod. "Company A is under march.

Wait here and report to Captain Tracy when they arrive. Tell him I've crossed the creek and am reconnoitering north up Williford Road." Then he give his men the order to move out and rode down the trace towards the creek.

When the last rider had crossed I dismounted and dropped the reins to let my horse graze along the roadside. Found a stout oak that would give me shelter and a view up and down the road and sat down to wait. I was some tuckered, sonny, that's a fact. Leaning agin that tree felt near as good as any featherbed I'd slept in. Just about drifted off to sleep when I heard the jingling and clanking of a wagon coming down the road. Jumped up quick as I could, grabbed the reins and led my horse a ways into the woods. Tied him to a sapling, then snuck back to the edge of the road and hid behind some bushes, pistol in hand. Weren't a minute later the wagon come into view. Near fell over when I seen who it was.

I stuck the Remington back in my belt. "Halloo, Sam!" I hollered and stepped out onto the road, waving my hat. It was Samuel, Lucas Porter's most trusted slave. His youngest boy, Artemus, was sitting beside him.

Sam's eyes went wide. He yanked the reins, said "Whoa there Bell, whoa Flo," and brung the team of mules to a halt. Sam stared at me for a mite. "Mister Eli? Well, I be."

"It's me," I said and walked over to the wagon which was stacked high with sacks of meal. I said howdy to Artemus and he nodded back. "Where you headed, Sam?"

Sam took off his straw hat and scratched at his graying hair. "We's takin this load to Mister Ard. What you doin' here? I heared you done jined up wid de Yankees."

I shook my head. "It ain't like that. Me and Jefferson got ourselfs captured and drafted into the Yankee army."

Sam looked a mite confused, but there weren't no time for explaining or social palavering. "Look here," I said. "You best turn this wagon around and hightail it back to the mill. There's Yankees just down the road a piece, coming this way quick."

Sam looked down the road and shook his head. "Mister Lucas say to take this load to Mister Ard, say I's to bring back a load of supplies, say—"

Sam always could talk the fleas off a hound, but there weren't no time for jawing, so know what I done, sonny? I'll tell you. I pulled a Remington from my belt and pointed it at Sam. "Cain't let you do that, Sam. You turn this wagon around now and get on back home!"

Sam's eyes got big as saucers when he seen that pistol. Artemus, who was a big man near twenty and strong as a ox, went to shaking. "Do what he say, Pappa, 'fo he shoot us!"

Sam shook his head and muttered something I couldn't make out, then whistled to the mules and flicked the reins. They made a wide turn using both sides of the trace and headed back north.

I ran to catch up to the wagon, said, "Listen, I didn't mean no harm back there. But you got to get word to Mister Porter. Tell him the Yankees are coming for the mill. Hide what goods and such you can. There ain't no time to waste."

Then I slapped one of the mules hard on the rump. "Go, Sam!"

When they was out of sight I took my jackknife, cut down a leafy branch from a oak and went to wiping out what sign of wagon tracks I could. Untied my horse to let him graze, then went back to my tree.

I was near spent, felt sick in my belly. Hoped Company A wouldn't show up for a while so I could rest a spell. I was tired of this whole affair. Felt bad about how I'd treated Sam and Artemus. I was fed up with trying to explain to folks why I was wearing this Yankee uniform, sick of worrying about everbody and everthing. Just wanted to be shed of the whole dern ruckus.

Well, they could all go hang theirselves, Rebs and Yanks alike, and their tomfool war. I'd had a craw full. Felt like finding Jeff and the two of us hightailing it for the swamps. Figured we could make out just fine till the Yankees give us up for lost and left.

Near had our escape all planned out when the clomping and rattling of men on the march shook me out of my daydreaming. Down the road a thin cloud of dust was rising above the treetops. I grabbed the reins and led my horse down the trace near the creek and hid in the shadows. Two-three minutes later the first colored troops come into view, marching in a column of fours.

I kept quiet, figured to wait till a officer or sergeant showed before I made myself known. I was worried them boys might be a touch trigger happy. More'n once I'd seen 'em shoot at shadows and such when we was back at Cedar Keys chasing them Rebels herding cattle. Weren't long till I seen a tall, lanky nigra marching alongside the column. He was sporting a beard and sergeant stripes. Knowed right off it was Sergeant Able. I kept hid in the shadows, called out, "Halloo, Sergeant Able!" Raised my hat high and chanced a step into the sunlight.

The good sergeant looked my way, then barked a order and the troops come to a stumbling halt. He turned and said something to one of his men, who broke ranks and trotted back down the column. While I led my horse up the trace I looked over what boys I could see, hoping to find Jeff. Weren't no sign of him. Walked on up to Able, pointed towards the creek.

"This here is Vickers Ford. Lieutenant Whitten told me to wait here and report to Captain Tracy."

Sergeant Able turned his head and spit a big stream of tobacco juice. "Done sent a runner to let him know we's here. They 'bout halfway down the column, you want'n to go ahead."

I fished my pocket for the last half-plug of tobacco I had. "Say, Sergeant, is Jefferson with you? I'd be obliged if I could see him a minute." Handed him the plug.

Able slipped the tobacco in his pocket. Pointed down the road, said, "His squad with the wagons, back of the column," then he turned and give the order for his men to spread out along both sides of the trace.

I swung up into the saddle, said, "Much obliged," and kneed my horse to a trot. I made maybe a quarter mile when Captain Tracy and two aides come riding around a bend in the road. I pulled up and saluted.

Didn't get a word out before the captain returned my salute, said, "Lead on to the ford, Private."

Turned my horse and trotted him back up the blue column towards the trace. It was late afternoon, the sun had already ducked below the tree line across the creek. Slowed my horse and walked him down the trace past where Able's troops was spread out.

Captain Tracy followed, then give the order to dismount. I let my horse wander on down to the creek to drink while the good captain took out his map and spread it on the ground. Him and two lieutenants I didn't know knelt down around it, so I done the same. The captain studied the map a spell, then looked towards the creek. "I assume Lieutenant Whitten has crossed with the scouting party?"

"Yes, sir, hour and a half, two hours ago. Said he was heading north up Williford Road."

"Very well." The captain traced a finger north along Econfina Road to where he'd drawed in the Marianna Cutoff I'd pointed out to him earlier. He went to tugging at his moustache, looked at me. "Is there time to reach this cutoff by nightfall?"

I weren't sure where this was headed but I didn't like the sound of it. I had figured the whole column would cross the ford and move north. Now it looked like they was heading for Porter's Mill after all. Made me feel a mite better about threatening old Sam and Artemus.

"Might be, Captain, but you'd have to hightail it to make it before dark. With all them clouds moving in, I wouldn't want to be strung out on the road in the pitch black."

Captain Tracy told me to go fetch my horse, then went to palavering with his lieutenants. When I got back he was folding up his map. The lieutenants weren't nowheres to be seen. "You will lead Lieutenant Miles and his platoon to the cutoff," he said. "Lieutenant Miles will secure the area and wait for wagons to arrive in the morning."

"Do tell? We best get moving then."

Captain Tracy put the folded map inside his coat pocket. "Stay with his command until further orders. Is that clear?"

I saluted and told him it was, then mounted my horse and headed up the trace. Just before I made the road the good captain called out, "Be sure and get there before dark, Private."

I didn't much cotton to the way he said it, like he didn't trust me or some such. I turned in the saddle but held my tongue. Grinned at the good captain like a egg-sucking possum. Give another quick salute and rode on.

FORTY ★ NINE

WE SET OUT AT QUICK time for the cutoff with near half of Company A in tow. I rode out ahead of the column to scout while Lieutenant Miles kept them colored troops moving. Just me, the lieutenant and his aide, a colored sergeant I ain't seen before, was mounted. The rest was hoofing it.

It had clouded up and thunder was rumbling. I turned my horse around and trotted back to the lieutenant. "You aim to beat this storm, we best hurry, Lieutenant. Got near three miles to make and it ain't getting no lighter."

Lieutenant Miles kept his eyes straight ahead. "Is there suitable ground for a bivouac at this cutoff?"

"It's mostly low ground thereabouts, but there's a oak hammock some fifty yards off the west side of the road. Ain't no other high ground around, 'cept the road itself."

The good lieutenant turned to his aide, said, "Sergeant, pass the word to the squad leaders to double-time on my command."

The sergeant give a smart salute and took off down the column to pass the word.

Lieutenant Miles turned to me, said, "Ride on to the cutoff and wait for us. Stay out of sight. If you see anything suspicious, report back to me, but don't let yourself be seen."

I saluted and hightailed it up the road at a gallop. My horse got a mite skittish ever time the sky flared and thunder boomed, but I managed to keep him under rein. The cypress swamp come into view so I slowed to a trot, then a walk. When I seen the cutoff, I dismounted and led my horse into the woods and tied him to a stout bush. Found a suitable hiding place near the road behind some bushes where I had a good view up Econfina Road and the cutoff itself. Moved some dead branches out of my way and sat down to wait.

Thunder was raising Cain, and it weren't long till I felt a few cold raindrops. I hurried to my horse and grabbed my slicker. I just took up the watch again when of a sudden lightning flashed and something caught my eye a piece up Econfina Road. My heart went to thumping. I hoped my eyes was playing tricks on me, but the next flash told me that weren't so. Riders, five-six, maybe more, looked to be wearing Confederate garb, but I weren't sure. I snuck closer to the road and waited for the next bolt. The sky lit up like day. It was Rebels all right. Counted seven in all, moving slow like they was looking for something.

Well, sonny, this was another deep ditch I'd stumbled into. They was only fifty yards away, so weren't time to get to my horse and back down the road without them seeing me. The Yankee column was coming at double-quick and couldn't be too far down the road by now. If them riders kept going they'd run slap into Lieutenant Miles and then things would likely go all to hell. Knowed I had to do something, and right quick. I made for my horse and led him north through the hammock till I figured I was on the backside of the riders. Then I mounted up and walked out into the road.

The Rebs had stopped in the road by the cutoff, forty-fifty yards away. Looked to be jawing over which way to go or what to do, so I figured I'd help 'em make up their minds. Pulled one of the Remingtons out of my belt. Cocked and fired two quick shots over their heads, then wheeled my horse and hightailed it north.

When the sky lit up good I chanced a quick look back. They was coming, sonny, hard and fast. Heard the crack of pistols and balls whizzing by. I leaned low over my horse's neck and dug my heels in his flanks till we was dern near flying. Looked back again and seen we was putting more road between us and the Rebs, enough that they had quit wasting cartridges on me. Kept my horse at a full gallop for near ten minutes, then eased him back a mite.

The Marianna Road was maybe a half-mile ahead, my own farm another two miles from there. A little farther on I slowed to a walk. Looked back when the sky turned to day and seen the Rebs a good hundred yards behind. Waited for the flash to die, then turned west off the road into the woods.

None of them boys had struck me as familiar, so I figured they weren't local. I took 'em to be a calvary patrol from up around Marianna or maybe over Calhoun County way. Hoped they would keep tracking north towards the Econfina-Marianna junction, but I weren't waiting around to find out. Even if they'd seen me leave the road, it weren't likely they'd find me where I was headed.

I dismounted and led my horse roughly northwest through the woods till I come out on a overgrown pig trail that run west towards Econfina Creek. Mounted up and followed it for a mile or so where twin giant live oaks stood on either side of the trail. A short piece past the oaks the trail played out at Bennet's Spring.

Me and brother Daniel and our pals had spent many a high time at Bennet's Spring in years past. Me and Hamp had built ourselfs a fort inside a small cave in the limestone bank on one side of the spring. Many a night we camped there, playing Indians and scaring each other silly with ghost stories.

The spring itself was a crystal-clear pool some thirty yards across and eight-foot deep. Sweetest water you ever tasted, that's a fact. The water come boiling out of a vent at the bottom of the limestone wall near the mouth of the cave. The spring fed a runoff that flowed through a stand of cypress trees on into Econfina Creek. Most local folks knowed about the place, but since the war, it had been little used. It would make a right dandy hideout.

Unsaddled my horse and staked him near the runoff where he was hid from view. I give him enough rope so he could drink from the shallow runoff and find shelter under nearby trees. Carried the saddle and tack and my blanket roll to the cave and crawled in. Used the blanket for a pallet and leaned back agin the saddle to rest a spell. Kept my pistols handy and my ears open. Didn't figure on having company, but I aimed to keep my eyes peeled till I was sure them Rebs weren't on my trail.

I was near whipped and it was a tussle to keep awake. Went to thinking how close I was to family and home, how my sweet Annie was only a few miles north at the Gainer plantation. I recollected our kiss, the queer way I had felt in my belly and groin. I missed her something fierce. If only this dern war and all its tomfoolery was over; if only things could be back the way they was before all this craziness come upon us.

But I knowed I was pissing in the wind. What's done is done, and feeling sorry for myself weren't no help at all. Hamp was dead and I would never lay eyes on him again. Yerby was crippled, in mind and body. And Annie was betrothed to my brother. She'd be marrying him soon as the war was over and he come home.

I stared out into the dark and listened to the bubbling spring and croaking frogs. A owl called out, *"Who cooks for you, who cooks for you all?"* Then the wind picked up and the rain come pounding down. I grabbed my slicker and covered up. Next thing I knowed, it was morning.

FIFTY

AT FIRST LIGHT I CRAWLED out of the cave and done my business. Fetched my canteens and dumped what water was left, then filled 'em from the spring. Fetched the last of the salt ham and hardtack from my saddlebags and sat on a rock by the spring to eat. It was a mite rancid, but I ate it anyhow and was glad for it.

Sun hadn't quite topped the trees, but the sky was clear and already turning deep blue the way it does after a good rain. Birds was flitting in the trees around the spring, singing purty as a church choir. It promised to be a fine day. Felt peaceful being in such familiar surroundings. Then I recollected how I come to be there, and the feeling passed.

I had some deciding to do, sonny, and it weren't going to be easy. First off, I sorely missed my family and wanted to go to them. But I figured they had already been warned by Yerb or Mister Watts. If I was to show up there it might only cause more of a fuss, and what would I say to Jeff's folks?

Ol' Sam had surely told the Porters about meeting me on the road to Ard's Ferry and getting turned back at gunpoint. And word would've reached the Gainer plantation, Mister Watts would've seen to that. Fact is, by now the whole of Econfina Valley most likely knowed there was a raid coming.

I sat there for a spell, squabbling with my thoughts. Figured I could stay right where I was till the Yankees left, and live high on the hog doing so. The woods was full of game, fine fishing to be had in the creek, crops aplenty at farms nearby. If I moved at night, nobody would ever know I was there. I could visit the family after dark, help out with chores and whatnot. And Annie. I could see my sweet Annie.

Chance was the Yankees would forget all about me after a spell, if they even bothered to look for me at all. Anyways, it weren't like I had up and volunteered myself to be in their dern army. It was them scoundrels that went and shanghaied me and Jefferson.

Jeff! Well, sonny, that's when it hit me like a mule done kicked me upside the head. All my highfalutin plans disappeared like the last of the mist rising over the spring. If we was both here right now we could desert easy enough, but we weren't, and there weren't no way I could leave Jeff to fend for hisself. I had got him in this fix and it was my duty to look out for him best I could.

Knowed then I had to go back. The war couldn't last forever. I saddled my horse and made ready to leave, but there was one more thing I needed to do before I set out. I crawled inside the cave, got to my feet and walked stooped over to the back where sunlight shined in through a big crack in the limestone overhead.

I squatted and found where the three of us had scrawled our names on the cave wall with a jacknife:

Hamp W.
Annie G.
Eli M.
Friends forever. June 14, 1860

I run my fingers over Hamp and Annie's names and my throat tightened up till I near choked. Weren't no way I could stop the tears.

FIFTY ★ ONE

A HALF-MILE FROM THE cutoff, I buttoned my Yankee-blue jacket up to the neck. Figured I'd be running into pickets anytime now, and didn't want them boys taking me for a Reb and shooting me off my horse if they seen me first. Weren't more'n a hundred yards later I come around a bend and seen some colored troops sitting around a fire they had built in the middle of the road. Them boys could be right smart soldiers whenever a white officer was around, but they sometimes proved a mite undisciplined when left to theirself.

I grabbed my hat and waved it high, hollered "Halloo, boys!" and walked my horse towards 'em. They went to scrambling for rifles and such, then spread out across the road in kneeling position, rifles at the ready. I pulled up, waved my hat again. "I'm Private Eli Malburn, Major Weeks' command."

A soldier with two stripes on his sleeve stood up. He said something to the others. They lowered their rifles and got to their feet. Then the corporal waved for me to come on. When I got closer I recognized them as part of Sergeant Able's platoon. Didn't know none of their names, but they knowed who I was and that put me at ease. A pan of fatback was frying, and steam was rising out of a coffeepot.

I dismounted. "That coffee smells mighty good. You fellers got any to spare?"

One of the boys dumped what was left of his cup, grabbed the pot off the fire and poured me a cupful. I thanked him, took a sip that near burned my mouth. The corporal walked over, said, "Lieutenant, he tell us be lookin fo' you. Say you might be gone over to the Rebels."

Near fell over when I heard that. I looked hard at the corporal. "That so? And did the good lieutenant say why?"

The corporal seemed a mite uneasy, kept looking up the road like he was expecting more company. Kept both hands on his Springfield. "This mawnin Lieutenant tell the Cap'n you ain't where you s'pose to be, say you might done deserted, gone to warn folks we comin'."

"Do tell." Well, sonny, this was a fine howdy-do. Here I had went and risked life and limb leading them Rebs away from Lieutenant Miles' troops, and he ups and calls me a deserter. I'd dern near had a craw full of this army life and I aimed to give both them highfalutin Yankee dandies a earful.

I took another sip of coffee, dumped the rest and tossed the cup back to the nigra who had give it to me. "Well now, it looks like I got some explaining to do, so I best get to it." Then I swung into the saddle and started down the road.

"Halt!" the corporal called out, sounding all official-like. I stopped, turned in the saddle and seen him pointing his rifle at me. "Lieutenant say if'n you show up, we's to take yo' guns, bring you in under guard."

Well, sonny, I was some riled, that's a fact. "Look here," I said, "you boys want to follow me in then you come right along. But ain't nobody taking my weapons. I seen Rebel cavalry on this road last night, and I don't aim to get caught empty-handed if I come across 'em again." Then I turned my horse and kneed him to a trot. I half-expected them to shoot me in the back right then and there, but I was so dern mad I didn't much care. Made a hundred yards and looked back. They was tending to their fire and breakfast, so I put the heels to my horse.

Made the cutoff in another ten-fifteen minutes. A passel of colored troops was scurrying about. Some was unloading supplies from a line of wagons that stood in the middle of the road. Others was off in the woods, chopping down trees for a barricade of sorts they had started building across Econfina Road. I rode around the log barricade and walked my horse past the wagons, looking for Lieutenant Miles. He weren't nowhere to be found, but I seen Captain Tracy down past the cutoff a piece, palavering with some other fellers.

I rode on up near where the captain was having his powwow and dismounted. Figured I'd let 'em finish their business before reporting in. Reckon the good captain seen me coming. I no sooner cleared the saddle when two men left the group and come my way. One was the other lieutenant the captain had been jawing with at the ford yesterday evening. Other feller was a stout redheaded sergeant with more freckles than there is stars on a moonless night.

I shifted the reins to my left hand when they got close, come to attention and saluted. Said, "Private Malburn, reporting in to Captain Tracy, sir."

The lieutenant returned the salute. He locked eyes on me, his bushy eyebrows coming together like a big hairy black caterpillar. Kept his beady eyes fixed on mine, said, "Sergeant, disarm the private and place him under arrest."

FIFTY ★ TWO

WELL, SONNY, THEM WORDS JOLTED me like a bolt of lightning. I was dumbstruck, my knees got so weak felt like I had the palsy. Just stood there like a hog on butchering day and let that sergeant take them pistols out of my belt. Some colored soldier come and took my horse, then Lieutenant Caterpillar and Sergeant Freckles marched me off the road and through the woods towards the oak hammock.

Must've been twenty-thirty tents set up amongst them oaks, but only a handful of troops was stirring about. We halted. The lieutenant had a few words with the sergeant, then took off back towards the road. The sergeant led me over to where Captain Tracy's headquarters tent was pitched in the shade of a big live oak and told me to have a seat up agin the tree. Then he called over two colored privates armed with Springfield Rifles and give them the order to watch me like a hawk.

After the good sergeant left, I took a few minutes to settle down and fetch what wits I had left. Went to thinking what I would tell Captain Tracy when he asked about my whereabouts last night, how come I had disobeyed Lieutenant Miles' order to stay put at the cutoff. I knowed I hadn't done wrong. I'd risked my own neck leading them Rebels away from the column. Couldn't of made it back to the cutoff last night. Too chancy with that patrol on the road. Sounded right convincing to me. Figured Captain Tracy would see it that way too, once he heard me out.

Weren't long before the captain and lieutenant and the redheaded sergeant showed up and went inside the tent without giving me so much as a sideways look. Few minutes later the sergeant come out to fetch me. I stood tall in front of Captain Tracy's table and saluted. For a spell things was quiet as a church mouse on Sunday. Then Captain Tracy showed me a sheet of paper with fancy handwriting on it. Looked hard at me, then said all official-like, "Private Elijah Malburn, on Lieutenant Miles' recommendation you are being charged with deserting your post and collaborating with the enemy. Do you have anything to say in your defense?"

Well, sonny, I had a heap to say and I went to doing just that. Told him how I'd spotted that Reb patrol coming down Econfina Road, how I snuck behind 'em and fired two shots to get 'em to chase me so they wouldn't run into Lieutenant Miles and his men.

"Check the loads in my pistols," I said. "That'll prove it."

Sergeant Freckles took my Remingtons out of his belt, opened both cylinders, said, "Two spent loads in this weapon, sir. The other is full."

Captain Tracy stroked his fancy moustache two-three times and picked up that sheet of paper again. "That proves nothing. Lieutenant Miles mentioned no gunshots in his report."

I was some hot, that's a fact. Had a mind to grab that Yankee dandy and give him a good thrashing, but figured that would only put me in hotter water. The kettle was near boiling already. I looked the good captain straight in the eye. "I don't much cotton to being called a liar, Captain. Everthing I told you is the truth." Which it was.

Well, sonny, turned out the good captain would've sooner believed me if I'd told him the sun rose in the west. None of his patrols had seen any sign of Rebels, he told me, but reports was coming in from patrols all over that near ever farm or cabin they raided seemed to know they was coming. Captain Tracy give me another hard look. "Some of these farms are far too prosperous to be so lacking in provisions. Can you explain why we're finding such meager spoils among these people?"

Them words of his plumb tickled my ears, that's a fact. Course, I didn't let on to the good captain how much it pleased me hearing that. Instead I shook my head, put on my best solemn face. "Folks in these parts ain't rich, sir. This war has been hard on most everbody."

Captain Tracy come off that stool like he'd done sat on a tack. Slapped the table hard, shook his finger in my face. "Nonsense! These people have been alerted, and it is more than likely that *you* did it!"

By then my craw was plumb full of the captain's hogwash. "Look here," I said, forgetting my military manners, "I ain't done no such a thing, and you ain't got no proof! Nobody heard me shooting because it was thundering like hell. And there ain't no sign of tracks them Rebs put down because it rained a gullywasher last night."

You could dern near see smoke coming out of Captain Tracy's ears, that's a fact. He turned red and his jaw went to twitching. He come around that table and walked up to me, his eyes burning mad. "I'll not tolerate insubordination, Private Malburn."

Then he said, "Secure the prisoner, Sergeant, and if he so much as opens his mouth again, gag him," and stomped out of the tent.

Sergeant Freckles told me to stand fast, then he took off, leaving me with Lieutenant Caterpillar. I stood quiet for a minute, then figured I didn't have nothing to lose by chancing some words. "Lieutenant, I want to see Major Weeks. Seems I got that right, sir, being under arrest and all."

The lieutenant fished a skinny cigar out of his coat pocket and lit it. Took a puff and blowed smoke towards the tent top. "Word has been sent to Major Weeks," he said. "You'll have your say at the proper time. Now I advise you to remain silent as the captain instructed."

Weren't long till the sergeant returned with them same two guards and some rope. They marched me over to the big oak. The good sergeant took a length of rope and tied my hands behind my back, then used another piece to hobble my ankles.

Spent the next two-three hours sitting agin that tree with them nigras watching over me like I was some big outlaw or such. Tried to jaw with 'em a time or two, but they told me to hush up or they'd report me to the sergeant.

Come midafternoon, Sergeant Freckles showed. Said they was moving me by wagon back to Ard's Ferry, which was being used as headquarters for this whole affair. But first, I had business to see to. The good sergeant untied my hands so I could unbutton my own breeches. Left me hobbled so I couldn't run off if I had a mind to. When I was done he retied my hands—in front this time—and we set out for the road. Marched through the woods with me shuffling along best I could till we come out onto the road. Went a piece farther to three wagons that was loaded with what I took to be more of the major's spoils of war. The two guards helped me up onto the bed of one of the wagons where I took a seat on some grain sacks.

Waited there a spell longer till two colored privates carrying their brogans slung around their necks, come hobbling up to the wagon. When the guards helped 'em climb up I seen both them fellers had bloody bandages tied around their feet. A minute later a squad of colored infantry led by a white first sergeant come marching out of the woods, maybe twelve-fourteen in all. They split up into two columns, one on each side of the wagons, and we took off south down Econfina Road.

It was a good two hours to the ferry, so I figured I best get comfortable. Moved a couple of grain sacks so I could lean back agin 'em, and settled down for the ride. Ever now and then I heard a scattering of gunfire. Seen smoke rising here and yonder on both sides of Econfina Creek. Seems the Yanks was hard at doing what they done best.

To get my mind off the pillaging and such I went to jawing with them footsore nigras a spell. They had been conscripted into the army just a few weeks back. Turns out both was so big of foot, the quartermaster couldn't find shoes to fit proper, and now their feet was a passel of raw blisters.

Come to find out they knowed Jeff and Nebo. Jeff's squad had been reassigned to wagon duty and had crossed the Econfina at Vickers Ford with the main column last night before the heavy rains come. I was glad to hear Jeff was driving a wagon, figured it might keep him out of trouble, but I still worried a mite. Weren't no way to look out for him with me being a prisoner. I hoped he would recollect and mind what I'd told him about obeying orders and such.

We made Bear Creek at dusk. The ferry was waiting and took us right across. Mister Ard's place didn't look much like a army headquarters. There was tents scattered here and there in the clearings. Only a few cook fires was burning, but the brown smell of fresh boiling coffee and frying pork set my belly to grumbling.

We come to a halt near one of the bigger tents not far from Ard's house. The first sergeant ordered his men into two columns facing the wagons, then walked over to the tent and went inside. Few minutes later he come back out with two other fellers. It was near dark by then, but I seen right off one of 'em was that scoundrel Sergeant Bullard!

FIFTY ★ THREE

I HEARD BULLARD SNORTING BEFORE they got halfway to our wagon. They walked on over and stopped beside me and the two crippled boys. Sergeant Bullard put his hands on his hips, said, "Well, well . . . what have we got here?"

He looked at me with a ugly sneer spread across his bulldog face. Turned to the soldier who was with him and the first sergeant, said, "Private, show these two men to the colored aid station."

The two nigras climbed down off the wagon and limped along behind the private towards a big tent over by the piney woods back of the Ard house. All the while Bullard kept his eyes stuck fast on me. After a spell he hawked up a wad and spit. "First Sergeant tells me you got yourself in some trouble, Malburn. Now why is it that don't surprise me none?"

Well, sonny, seeing as I was already in the sinks, figured there weren't much use putting on airs for the good sergeant no more. I give a cantankerous grin. "Why Sergeant Bullard, fancy finding you here. I figured you to be off plundering and burning out some poor widow woman."

If looks could kill I was a goner for sure, that's a fact. Before

I knowed what was happening, Bullard slugged me hard upside the head, grabbed my jacket by the collar with both hands and flung me out of the wagon. I landed hard and it knocked the breath plumb out of me. Bullard went to kicking me in the ribs before I could catch my wind. I curled up best I could, still couldn't breathe. Heard the good sergeant yelling "traitor" and "deserter" along with a passel of other fine words till I was near to passing out. Reckon the first sergeant pulled the bulldog off me because the beating finally stopped.

Took a spell to clear my head, it was spinning so. My ribs ached something fierce. Felt like a mule had kicked me in the jaw. I coughed hard, spit out blood and a tooth. Next thing I knowed somebody was pulling me to my feet and some colored soldiers was marching me towards one of the cabins Mister Ard rent out to travelers.

I more stumbled than marched, being I was still tied hand and foot and had just got beat halfway to Hades. When we got to the cabin one of the guards held open the door, another helped me up the steps and over to one of the bunks. The door slammed shut and I heard the clink of a padlock snapped fast. Then a voice come through the door.

"Damn shame, you falling off that wagon so hard, you secesh son of a bitch!"

Of a sudden there weren't no pain, just the fiercest anger I ever felt for man or beast. I jumped up and hollered, "Open this door and untie me and we'll see who's a son of a bitch, you coward bastard!" Meant it too, sonny. I was ready to kill the dirty scoundrel right then and there, and there weren't no doubt in my mind I would've done just that if he'd took me up on it.

But Bullard weren't have none of it. He just laughed and walked off, leaving me to the dark and pain, which soon come back fierce as ever.

FIFTY ★ FOUR

WOKE UP AT FIRST LIGHT to a mockingbird singing. The sun was slipping through the slats nailed over the windows. I seen a pail under the other bunk which I took to be a chamber pot of sorts. Pain jolted me when I got up to do my business, but I managed.

A hour or so later colored guards come and unlocked the door. One feller come inside with a canteen and my breakfast on a tin plate. Two others stood by outside, muskets at the ready. When their duty was done them boys locked the door on me and took off to whatever other soldierly duties was waiting 'em.

Breakfast was fatback near burned and cornbread with a goodly share of husk mixed in with the meal. It was a tussle to eat, my jaw ached so, but I managed to get enough down to quiet my belly. Uncorked the canteen hoping for coffee, but it was water, near foul at that. Thought about them canteens I had filled with good spring water just yesterday, but it didn't make what I had go down no easier.

Long about midday it growed so hot inside that boarded up cabin I dern near couldn't bear it. Pulled off my boots and socks. Then I leaned over, reached behind my head and tugged at my coat and shirt till I got 'em off my body and hanging on the rope between my hands. Spent the rest of the day on the floor where a draft rising through the boards made things a mite more tolerable.

Come dusk them same guards showed again with my supper and a fresh canteen. The one toting my plate went to staring at me standing there in my breeches, the coat and shirt hanging off my hands. So I told him it was dern near suffocating in here, and would he kindly untie my hands long enough to slip the sleeves off the rope.

He looked me over a spell, then set the plate and canteen on the bunk. Untied the rope binding one of my wrists and pulled the coat and shirt off. Then he retied me, not near so tight.

"Much obliged. Reckon I might could have some coffee in the morning?"

He shrugged, said, "Ain't my say," then turned and walked out. The lock snapped shut and the dark set in.

———•———

Well, sonny, that there is the way it went the next three-four days. Only left that cabin when the guards let me dump my pail a time or two, and even then I was hobbled. I ate what they give me twice a day. The food was tolerable, even got used to the water after a spell. Never did get no coffee.

Rain set in for a couple of days, then one morning the sun come up and that mockingbird went to singing its morning song again. A hour or so after breakfast, a white corporal showed up with some different colored guards. He untied my hands and feet and told me to get dressed. When I was done they marched me towards the Ard house. My jaw still ached some and ever breath I took hurt my ribs, but stretching my legs felt mighty good. I pulled my hat low over my eyes, but the sun still near blinded me after being shut in the dark for so long. Kept my eyes squinted till we got up the steps and onto the covered porch. Waited there with the colored guards while the corporal went inside.

Short spell later the corporal come and fetched me inside to the parlor that Major Weeks had turned into his headquarters. My eyes was getting used to the light by then. The good major was sitting behind a desk. I near fell over when I seen Lieutenant Miles standing to the major's right, next to the fireplace. Wondered what I was in for now.

I was plumb out of military manners, sonny, so I just stood there in front of the major waiting for him to have his say. He stared at me a spell, looked over at Lieutenant Miles. Opened his mouth like he was fixing to say something, then stood up and looked back at me.

"Who did this to you, Malburn?"

Done my best to work up a grin. "Why, Major, reckon I was a mite clumsy getting off the wagon that brung me here. Fell slap off it."

Major Weeks went to pulling on his goatee. "I see. And did you happen to have help *falling* off this wagon, Private?"

I shed the grin and locked eyeballs with him. "Best I recollect I done it all by myself. Least, that's what Sergeant Bullard told me."

The major sat down again, shuffled some papers on the desk, then turned to the lieutenant. "Lieutenant Miles, I believe you have something to report?"

"Yes, sir," the good lieutenant said. He looked a mite fidgety as he walked over and stood beside the desk with his hands behind his back. Kept clearing his throat like he had a frog stuck in it. Finally managed to spit it out.

"Private Malburn . . . while patrolling the Marianna Cutoff late yesterday afternoon, my men surprised a small party of Confederate cavalry. A brief skirmish ensued, during which one enemy soldier was wounded and taken prisoner."

The lieutenant stopped talking. He looked fretful, like he had chiggers in his breeches or such. Major Weeks looked up at him, said, "Lieutenant?"

At that the good lieutenant found his tongue again. "While interrogating the prisoner I learned his patrol had come under fire a few evenings ago near the junction of Econfina Road and the cutoff. He said they gave chase for a couple of miles but lost the attackers in the dark."

Lieutenant Miles went silent again. He reached over and picked up a piece of paper from the major's desk, said all official-like, "This is my original report stating your absence from your assigned post, and my recommendation that you be charged with collaborating with the enemy." He held it up for a spell, then made a big show of tearing it in half. "Private Malburn, I have withdrawn all charges, and I offer you my sincerest apology for the misfortune you've endured these past days."

I didn't rightly know what to say. Just stood there thinking how I'd been called a liar and branded a traitor by more'n one highfalutin Yankee officer of late. How I'd been beat like a cur dog while tied hand and foot, then throwed inside a hothouse to slow cook like a curing ham. Reckon I was more'n a mite bitter, that's a fact.

It tickled me some to see Major Weeks and the lieutenant squirming like they was struck with the trots during Sunday sermon. Neither one said a word for what seemed a good minute or so. Then the major stood up behind his desk and went to rocking back and forth on his heels. Tugged on his goatee a time or two, said, "The corporal will see you to the aid station. When you are declared fit you'll be returned to full duty as scout and courier under my direct command. Until then, is there anything I can do for you, *Corporal* Malburn?"

Well, sonny, seems the good major had seen fit to swap corporal stripes for the black and blue ones Sergeant Bullard had give me. Can't say I weren't tickled at that, but right then and there I'd've give 'em back for my missing tooth and other ailments. But being the major had asked, I figured there weren't no sense letting a kindness go to naught.

"Why, yes sir, Major. I ain't ate all that well lately. I'd be much obliged for some good flour biscuits and bacon, maybe some fried eggs from Mister Ard's henhouse.

"And I sure could cotton to some fresh coffee."

———•———

Spent the next three-four days lazing around the hospital tent and headquarters, mending and eating high on the hog. The ferry run morning to dark as raiding parties made it back to camp. When all the patrols was in and the commanders had give their reports to Major Weeks, we struck camp and took up the march south for Bayhead.

Having big ears and being more'n a mite curious, I had managed to listen in on some of the officers' reports on the raid. The Union Army had done a heap of damage to the Econfina Valley and the Confederate cause, that's a fact. All told, the different patrols rounded up over a hundred and fifty contrabands. Them nigras of soldiering age would be swore into the army back at Cedar Keys. The rest would live near camp and work as servants or laborers or whatnot.

Near four hundred head of cattle, horses and mules was rounded up from farms all over the area, along with two dozen or so wagons piled high with provisions. What them scoundrels didn't want or take, they destroyed. They seen to it them poor folks was left with nothing but the clothes on their backs and what they had managed to hide. Crops was ruint, feed and seed and salt trampled underfoot, smokehouses and pantries plundered. If spoils of war was what the good major had figured on, he had ever cause to crow like a barnyard rooster.

Mister Porter's gristmill was destroyed, along with the silos and supply sheds. The raiders did spare the Porters' house, but they dynamited the dam, burnt the bridge over Mocassin Creek and another bridge on towards Marianna before turning back.

Weren't no word on how my own farm and family had fared. Found that a mite worrisome, and then recollected how Aunt Nettie used to say, "No news be good news," and let it be.

Folks on the west side of Econfina Creek suffered hard too. A raiding party burnt the Williford Road bridge south of the Gainer place. The Gainer plantation was hit hard. Near ever outbuilding was burnt, even the slave cabins. The main house was plundered, but it was spared the torch. Raiders took over a hundred slaves off the place, left behind only the women and them too old or young or crippled to be of use to the Union cause. Found out later Mister Gainer had sent his family north to Alabama to stay with relatives till the danger passed. I was some relieved to hear Annie was safe, that's a fact.

Worse of all, Yerby Watts made good on his threat, of a sort. The Yankees come under fire from the woods around the Watts farm and a right hot skirmish went on for ten minutes or so. Weren't nobody hurt, and Yerb and them with him escaped. But the Union Army figured to make a example to show folks they meant business and weren't going to tolerate no resistance. So they burnt the place to the ground. Not even the privy was spared. For near twenty-five years Coleman Watts had poured his sweat and blood into that land. Now it was all done in.

Later, I learnt poor Jeff had seen it happen with his own eyes.

———•———

Back at Cedar Keys Major Weeks give me the run of camp for near two weeks while I finished healing. Turns out the beating Bullard give me had cracked my jaw and broke some ribs. The good major had me report in to him mornings after breakfast, and evenings before supper. Otherwise, the days was mine to spend as I seen fit.

One good thing come of the beating I took. For his troubles Sergeant Bullard got busted to corporal and earned hisself a transfer to the Union outpost at Dry Tortugas, a island way out in the Gulf, off Key West. Way I figured, it couldn't of happened to a more deserving feller.

After three-fours days I felt near fit as a fiddle, but I didn't let on to the major. Figured I'd milk his cow long as I could. I was chomping at the bit to find out how Jefferson had fared during the raid, so on Sunday I saddled my horse and rode over to the colored camp.

Found Jefferson and Nebo at their tent. They'd just got back from church services. Nebo had took over the regular preaching duties a while back, and Jeff helped him with the singing. I was right proud of them boys, that's a fact. We jawed a spell about church, them new corporal stripes on my sleeves and other whatnot. Then I told Jeff I needed to stretch my legs and would he take a walk with me. We headed towards a rise covered with wind-bent scrub oaks that give a fine view of the Gulf.

"Jeff," I said, "do you know what happened at Mister Watts' place? Heard they got burnt out."

Jeff didn't say nothing, just frowned, took off his kepi and stared at the ground.

I waited a minute, said, "I met some fellers that knowed you and Nebo. They said you was with the wagons that crossed the Econfina that night before the big rain."

Jeff give a little nod but didn't look up. "Sergeant Able say they need drivers fo' the wagons. Me and Nebo, we say we can handle a team right fine."

I knowed by the way he was acting that Jeff was holding back on me. We got to the top of the rise and took a seat in the shade of the oaks. A cool breeze was blowing and there weren't a cloud to be seen. Sunlight was dancing on the blue-green Gulf waters.

"The ocean sure is purty, ain't it?" I said.

Jeff was sitting with his arms wrapped around his knees, staring at his feet. He looked up, mumbled, "Uh-huh," and looked back down.

"Look here, Jeff, I know you was with the main column that raided the west side of the valley, so I figure you was at the Watts farm. Now, I know whatever happened weren't none of your fault, but I need to know just what you seen."

It took a spell but Jefferson finally let it spill out. When him and Nebo drove their wagon up to the Watts place, soldiers was spread out in a line of battle firing volley after volley into the woods behind the main barn towards the creek. Jeff and Nebo jumped down off the wagon and took cover behind it till the gunfire stopped. Then Captain Tracy come riding up and give orders to take everthing that weren't nailed down and burn the place. Some sergeant ordered Jeff and the other drivers to empty the barns and sheds and load up their wagons. Next thing Jeff knowed the whole place was afire, even the woods along the creek where the bushwhackers had been.

Jeff was getting ready to drive his wagon away when he seen Coleman Watts being drug out of the house with hands tied behind his back. For a second their eyes had met, and Jeff swore Mister Watts knowed it was him. Then Captain Tracy ordered two soldiers to force Mister Watts to his knees and made him watch while his house burnt to the ground.

Tears was dripping down Jeff's face when he was finished with the story. "Why they done it, Eli? Mister Watts, he a good man. I's wantin' to he'p him, I surely was, but they say I got to stay wid my wagon. Why they done it?"

What could I say to that? I told Jeff again that it weren't none of his doing, and that he had done right by obeying orders like I'd told him. It was war, I said, and war makes people do bad things.

That seemed to comfort Jeff some. Made me feel a mite better too, but deep down I knowed no good could come from this whole sad affair.

And I weren't wrong, sonny, that's a fact. But there weren't no way of knowing then just how bad things would turn out.

Calvin Hogue
September 1927

FIFTY ★ FIVE

WHEN UNCLE HAWLEY CALLED ME into his office early Monday morning, a sense of dread swept through me like a cold chill. I had no idea why. Our readers' overall response to the weekly installments of the Malburn brothers' story was going better than I'd ever imagined, and the *Pilot's* advertising revenues continued to grow. I was also meeting the deadlines for my other assignments. Still, the sense that something was wrong followed me through the door.

Uncle Hawley was sitting at his cluttered desk, an unlit cigar clamped in the corner of his mouth as usual. He balanced the chewed cigar on the rim of an ashtray. "Have a seat, boy," he said, motioning to the chair in front of the desk. The tone of his voice did little to appease my uneasiness. It was missing its usual gruffness, and his face looked drawn.

I pulled the chair back a couple of feet and sat down. I held up the stack of paper in my hand. "The latest installments are ready, sir, in triplicate."

Uncle Hawley sighed, reached across the desk and took the pages Jenny had carefully proofed and typed for me. "I'm afraid I've got some bad news, Calvin," he said, placing my work under a paperweight and picking up a yellow sheet of paper.

It felt like ice water was coursing through my veins when I recognized it as a telegram. My first thought was that something had happened to Daniel or Elijah, and Alma had wired the bad news to me in care of the newspaper. But Alma had a telephone, and if for whatever reason she'd decided to send a wire, then why hadn't she sent it directly to me at the boardinghouse?

"I'm afraid your daddy has passed away, son."

The words seemed muffled, as though they'd passed through several walls. I didn't want to believe what I'd heard. My father was only forty-eight years old and had always enjoyed excellent health. I couldn't recall him having so much as a common cold. I must have misunderstood; surely Uncle Hawley couldn't mean that Father—

"He fell ill Friday evening," Uncle Hawley continued in that strange, faraway voice. "They rushed him to the hospital and did everything they could, but he passed early Saturday morning."

I don't remember my uncle handing me the telegram, but there I was, reading the dreaded words pasted onto the yellow sheet, each brief sentence punctuated with a cold, heartless *Stop.* According to the doctors it was a heart attack, Mother had written. During dinner Father had suddenly clutched his chest and slumped forward onto the table. Everything that could be done was tried, to no avail. Funeral arrangements were pending my arrival home.

The decent man that Uncle Hawley was deep down inside, he had already purchased my railway tickets and obtained a copy of my schedule. Early Wednesday morning I would drive to Chipley, about forty-five miles north of Harrison. There, I would board a train that would take me through Atlanta and on to points north. This would allow me the time needed to put my affairs here in order without being unduly rushed and still get home to Carlisle in time for the funeral. Uncle Hawley, with my mother's permission and heartfelt gratitude, had made the arrangements via telephone.

Later, I would learn Uncle Hawley had also covered all expenses for the funeral, including a grand headstone noting Father's membership in the Sons of Union Veterans of the Civil War, a fraternal organization in which my father was proudly and actively involved.

Tucked inside the envelope with the tickets and schedule was two hundred dollars in cash. Before I could ask the question, Uncle Hawley said, "Consider it a bonus for a job well done, boy." And then he walked around the desk, wrapped his beefy arms around my shoulders and gave me a warm hug. "Don't forget that it's okay to cry." He patted me on the back, adding, "You've got the makings of a fine newsman, son. I hope you'll be back, but that's your decision now that you're the man of the house."

———•———

When I returned to the boardinghouse to begin packing, I first sought out Mrs. Presnell. After explaining what had happened, she nearly came to tears expressing her condolences and readily granted permission for me to use the house phone as needed.

I dialed the operator and she placed a call to Alma, who promptly broke into tears at my sad news. "I'll make sure my daddy and Uncle Dan are here in the morning, sugar. You can count on it."

I then packed my travel bag with everything I thought I'd need for the next couple of weeks. Should I decide that Mother and my sisters needed me home to stay, I would make arrangements with Mrs. Presnell to pack the remainder of my belongings in my trunk and have them shipped to Carlisle.

That evening I called Jenny and arranged to meet her at her house after she and the family finished supper. I managed to keep a stiff upper lip as Mister and Mrs. Cotton greeted me at the door. They invited me inside and we chatted amiably in the parlor until Jenny appeared. She was dressed in a pretty yellow summer skirt and white blouse. I complimented Jenny, and then asked her parents' permission if I might escort their daughter for a walk in the fresh air of the mild late-summer evening.

Crickets chimed a serenade and a pleasant breeze cooled us as we strolled hand in hand along the sidewalk. "I have some news," I said, motioning to a bench just inside the entrance to McKenzie Park near the town square.

Jenny flashed her sweet smile as we sat together. "Good

news, I hope," she said cheerily.

"Well, good and bad," I said, turning to face her. "Which would you like first?"

"Oh my, the bad I suppose," Jenny said, a hint of a smile still lingering on her lips, obviously not expecting what was coming.

I gripped her hand more tightly and took a breath to steel myself. "I just learned my father died Saturday."

Jenny's free hand flew to her mouth, smothering her gasp. Her eyes welled with tears as she choked back a sob. "Oh, Cal, no!"

Moving closer, I wrapped an arm around Jenny and hugged her to me. "I'm afraid so. I'll be leaving by rail early Wednesday."

Jenny leaned her head against my shoulder and I could feel her shuddering. "Then I'll go with you."

I hugged her tighter. "Thank you, but that wouldn't be appropriate. I'll be gone at least two or three weeks, and you have your job to consider. Plus, I expect things will be in a quandary for quite a while at home." I didn't have the heart to tell her I might be moving back to Pennsylvania to stay.

"Then I'll quit my job," Jenny said, sniffling and burying her face against my chest.

Gently, I pushed Jenny away to arms' length and forced a smile as I gazed into her beautiful brown eyes that were still awash with tears. "That's a crazy idea, my crazy girl," I said, pulling her to me again and hugging her tightly. The feel of Jenny's breasts pressed against my chest filled me with desire, so much so that my father's death had somehow taken a back seat to the moment. Guilt swept over me then, and I managed to force myself away from Jenny's delightful embrace.

"There is one thing you can do," I said.

Jenny sniffled and dabbed at her tears with fingertips. "What's that?"

"What I hope you'll take as the good news." Reaching into my coat pocket, I pulled out a small blue velvet box, opened it and held it out to Jenny. "Will you marry me?"

The gold ring with its pear-shaped diamond sparkled in the glow of a nearby night lamp. Jenny covered her mouth with both hands and sobbed. Just when I thought I'd struck out, she blurted, "Dear God, Cal, yes, yes I'll marry you!"

When I arrived at Alma's home Tuesday morning, Daniel and Elijah greeted me with heartfelt hugs and comforting words. It dawned on me then that this was the first instance I'd been in the presence of both brothers at the same time.

"Losing folks ain't ever a easy thing, Calvin, but the good Lord will see you through it," were the first words out of Daniel's mouth.

True to his nature, Elijah was a little more blunt and straightforward. "I remember back in the winter of 'fifty-nine when our own daddy fell off the barn roof and broke his neck. Thought I'd never get shed of that pain, sonny, but I did. Time's got its own way of scabbing things over, you'll see."

Poor Alma bawled like a baby and nearly smothered me with motherly concern. "You'll get through this, sugar, I know you will. We'll all be praying up a storm for you, you can count on it."

After the condolences and crying, we made ourselves comfortable in the parlor. Things were silent for a moment while Alma poured coffee. Finally, Daniel took the lead. "I reckon you'll be coming back soon enough?"

I hesitated while I stirred in a spoonful of sugar. "I'm not sure, sir. I guess it will depend on how things are back home. My mother and sisters might need me to stay and take care of family affairs, at least for a while."

Daniel's thin lips tightened and he muttered, "Hmm."

Elijah set his cup on the table in front of the sofa where he sat beside his brother. He took off his wire-rimmed spectacles and made a show of cleaning them on his shirtsleeve. "What you saying is, you might not be coming back at all, ain't that so, sonny?"

I felt my face flush and was almost at a loss for words. "No, sir, well, not exactly."

"Now, Daddy, that's no way to be talking to Calvin, not after the loss he just suffered," Alma said. "Lord knows, he's got the world weighing on his shoulders right now."

"Never said he didn't," Elijah said. "Just seems to me a feller's word ought to be his bond, is all." He looked at Daniel.

"Cat got your tongue, brother?"

Daniel reached inside his shirt pocket and took out his pipe. After staring at it longingly for a moment, he slipped it back in the pocket. He glanced my way and then fixed his good eyes on something behind me. "Well, sir, first time I met you I recollect you pestering me to tell you my story. Told you then that if you was willing to sit still and listen, I reckon it was time I talked it out."

Daniel scratched idly at the scar above his ear, and then stared me straight in the eye. "I'd be much obliged if we was to finish what we started, but I ain't aholding you to it. You got to look inside yourself and make up your own mind."

———•———

Far into the night the train rumbled onward. Now and again it gently swayed as the cars navigated around some obstacle man or Mother Nature placed in its path that engineers had decided not to tear down or blast through. My best guess was that we were currently passing through the countryside of Maryland. By midmorning the train would pull into the High Street Train Station in Carlisle. From there a short cab ride would deliver me to the family home on North Hanover Street.

I lay awake tucked inside my berth in the Pullman car. The gentleman above me snored incessantly, but that wasn't the real reason I was unable to sleep. My thoughts were plagued by the decision awaiting me, a decision that might affect the rest of my life, personally and professionally.

My mother was a strong woman who, with my father's blessing, had taught English at Carlisle High School for the past fifteen years. Father's salary from his managerial position at Masland Carpets would be missed, but there was no mortgage owed on the family home and I knew my father had provided for Mother with a large insurance policy. My sisters, Alice and Rebecca, were students at Carlisle High and both would be graduating within the next three years. So, my family wasn't destitute or in need of shepherding by any means.

Jenny had lifted a lot of the burden from me when she said she would be willing to quit her stenographer's job and move wherever I chose to live after our wedding, which was planned for January. But I also knew she had studied and worked hard to obtain her current position at the courthouse. Would it be selfish of me to uproot Jenny from her close-knit family and career?

And then there was the conundrum of the Malburn brothers. I was the one who had sought them out and convinced them to tell their saga. Was it fair to Daniel and Elijah, or the *Pilot's* readers, to simply end things as they were? Surely my father's unexpected death was a legitimate reason; people would understand if I had to move back North to care for my widowed mother and younger sisters, wouldn't they? Daniel himself had said it was my decision to make, and that whatever I decided, he wouldn't hold it against me.

Two annoying and persistent inner voices kept whispering opposing advice. I turned on my side and covered my head with the pillow to try and shut them out.

———•———

Somehow, I finally managed to drift off and sleep for a few hours. The next morning I was sitting in the dining car finishing breakfast when the car attendant walked through and announced that we were approaching the station in Carlisle, almost an hour ahead of schedule. I hurried back to the Pullman and quickly finished packing my travel bag.

Ten minutes later the train slowed to a stop and the doors opened. I followed the line of passengers as they began to disembark from the car. I walked down the steps onto the platform and was greeted by bright sunshine and the brisk Pennsylvania air. Suddenly Daniel Malburn's words came flooding back: "If you willing to sit still and listen, I reckon it's time I talked it out."

That's when I knew for certain that the rails ran in both directions.

{To Be Continued}

NOTE FROM THE PUBLISHER

The sequel to *Of Blood and Brothers* will be released in March of 2014. The story of the Malburn brothers, Daniel and Elijah, picks up where Book One in the series ends. Below is an excerpt from the first chapter.

Calvin Hogue
October 1927

ONE

THE DOOR TO DANIEL MALBURN'S cabin swung open and there stood the Confederate veteran "grinning like a suckling shoat," to borrow a phrase from the venerable old gent's own repertoire.

"Welcome back, Calvin," he said, stepping aside and motioning me inside. "Thought I might never lay eyes on you again in this here life. Here, let me get shed of that hat and coat for you. Pull that chair yonder over to the stove and I'll go pour us a little snort to limber up your writing hand, heh-heh," Daniel said with a wink of his good eye, the other being clouded by a cataract. "It's right nippy today, ain't it? Yes, sir, nothing like a good wood fire and a sip of corn squeezings to warm up the old bones."

I agreed and moved the straight-backed chair near the potbelly stove. I waited while Daniel ambled to the kitchen to pour the "little snort" that I knew would be a hefty glassful of moonshine. One of his nephews made the fiery concoction, reputed to be the best corn whiskey available in three counties. Five-thirty on a Friday afternoon was a little early in the day for me to imbibe, but I didn't want to chance offending the Malburn family patriarch.

It had been more than three weeks since I'd traveled by train to my hometown of Carlisle, Pennsylvania, to bury my father, who had passed away suddenly and unexpectedly at age forty-eight. Two days ago I'd returned to the Florida Panhandle town of Harrison and my job as a reporter for my uncle Hawley Wells's newspaper, the *St. Andrew Pilot*.

When I met Uncle Hawley in his office upon my return, he'd handed me a stack of letters. "All these arrived from our readers since you've been gone, boy. Nearly every one of them is complaining about how much they miss your story on the Malburns, and wondering when it's going to continue. You'd best get to it. Disappointing our readership is the last thing we need."

"Right away, sir," I said, itching to get back to work.

Daniel returned carrying two glasses filled to the brim with clear liquid. I could almost feel my tastebuds and sinuses cringe as he handed one to me. Daniel eased himself into his padded rocker opposite my chair and held his glass aloft. "Here's to what ails you, heh-heh," he said and downed a hefty swallow. He looked admiringly at the glass. "Ah, even better'n it was this morning."

I lifted my glass in return and took a sip, trying my best not to squint as the liquid fire trickled down my throat. "Thank you, sir," I managed after catching my breath. "That is mighty fine whiskey."

Daniel leaned back in the chair and rocked slowly. "Now, where was we when we left off?"

I found the marker in my notebook and scanned down the page. "You were home on furlough and had just given Annie the ring while the two of you were sitting by the big spring," I said, reading from my notes. "Annie had said she couldn't marry you until the war was over, but that she would wear the ring for the rest of her days."

Daniel's face seemed to light up at the remembrance. He took another hearty sip of whiskey. "Yes, sir, that was a mighty fine time, all right. Didn't have a clue then that things was fixing to turn upside down for me."